GW00758867

SAXON
PEPPERDINE

BROKEN
LEG

BESTSELLER

This edition published by Burning Eye Books 2016

www.burningeye.co.uk
@burningeyebooks

Burning Eye Books
15 West Hill, Portishead, BS20 6LG

ISBN 978 1 90913 675 5

SAXON
PEPPERDINE

BROKEN
LEG
BESTSELLER

A SHORT
LIFE CHANGING NOVEL

A MULTIPLICITY
OF
LIMINALS

PART 1: PLEASED TO MEET YOU

(sussex)

1

The motor of life is desire (I think).

Hot innocent bloody *bangbang* vital (I write).

This could be a very short story. Perhaps it *should* be. Maybe it *is*.

It may also be about average in length, but it's all a matter of PERSPECTIVE & PERCEPTION, which is a goodGod thing because they're both always *free*. So grab some... and for Chrissakes hold on.

I've written a novel. It's not too long. *LEISURELY MOVING WITHOUT HASTE*. It's a best-seller. A bestseller. A BEST SELLER. Don't know about the *New York Times* or the *Sydney Herald*, but the *Sunday Times Culture* know their lists, know their numbers, and sometimes even know their words, and they swear it'll be up there where it belongs: BEST (how can there be so many BESTS?) – beasts, the lot of them, but best I get back to this story (bless).

(A sweet, dreamy, honest piece of previous deliciousness by a novelist I reckon I've never heard of (*The Restlessness of Virtue (Light & Dark)*) has opened all my creative valves and pulsed this work free... I am quite serious... believe me you must... now if only I could be so SO damn original like that... is that distinctly in any way possible? Is the novel I have produced as LUCID and penetrating and truthfully as hearty as that?)

My novel's on a memory stick. A USB fob, whatever the jinx and kings of Jobs it's called. And I've bust my leg. Left. Definitely not right. I sit here, sun pouring down onto me and this garden, the old barbecue warming up on the side-lines, stretching off, getting ready for another season, gulls on the caw, cows on the low, chimney stacks on the cool scarlet holler, all that business.

The last vestiges of spring, the threat of summer, and T-shirt and shorts and oh yeah, a nasty great big plaster cast and crutches for help swinging about. How'd I do it? *I* didn't. That dance-floor did. And the Saturday-night bouncers all trying to impress the birds dragging me out, my ankle hanging off, real classless doormen, an army of them, pointing up at the top-tier dance platform giving it, "This bastard just jumped from up there," and gawping onlookers saying, "We know."

Double fracture and my hip's as black as night, all the way down to the top of the pot. Ah well, it'll give me time to polish and preen and prime this memory stick novel that's sitting here on the garden table, warming its own un-busted bone, getting some fresh air with me. No, wait... it's perfect already: 18 rejections. 14 redrafts. 3 complete restarts. 1 replete mental breakdown.

But now, oh yes now, Dan Kemp, yes *Dan Kemp*, a *Sunday Times Culture* friend of mine says: Best Seller and I say: I will.

(Please note quickly and unobtrusively if you wouldn't mind: it is very hard to express the feeling I have right now, having actually successfully completed this best-seller. It is an extreme relief/release/abject elation. A true beautiful high. A high of resignation I suppose, of surrender, but one which had to be done, and now I've done it – I've got it made.)

As you can tell, this could be The End, and in some ways, it is. Because this right here is where the novel concept and all elation suddenly obliterate into thin air and unprecedented truth-undoctored takes over because insanity descends...

2

One of these gulls out here, a huge big ugly proud thing, all sinister and sass, looms into my space like a bad film and, thinking it's a barbecue boon or an idle bug or something else to wolf down sharpish, *beaks* up the USB fob best-seller off the garden table *SNAP!* and in a blur is gone, sweeping back up to the chimney pot, a majestic cocksure Immelmann.

You hideous bastard.

My novel. My *fucking* novel.

You bastard seagull BASTARD. Wait, you're a herring gull, not even a SEA, you're a HERRING, you bastard. And I spring up onto my one good leg, wince at the effort, squint up, wince more, wobble hand on table, clatter go crutches, that herring gull bastard chewing and nodding and gulping, GONE down his bastard neck, my memory stick BEST-SELLER and it slips down into his gut GONE and he's just staring at me now (he had a cartoon moment with the plug-in fob thing going down his neck, the shape jutting out the sides and I thought *Choke, you bastard, choke*).

Now here's where I need a breather because if I just rattle on to what played out hot and fast, reactionary booming and all that, then reader whizzwallop nausea would surely comic-lure you off into sputtering frenzy and put-downable slap (not good for bestseller status... but wait, the bestseller has gone... Christ, I'm in a spin). So here's this:

Why'd you want to write a bestseller anyway?

To make my own brass, of course, and plenty of it.

11

But what about ART and integrity and the respectable *Middle* festival shortlists?

I need the feeling of power, the ability to earn, money is respect.

Ah, OK.

But, yeah, then, novel two would all be about ART and being true, writing from the heart, you see? Everything thereafter. Of course.

Ah, mmm, OK. And how does *Dan Kemp* know this one will be a best-seller, the first one?

He knows, he just *knows*.

How?

He works for the *Sunday Times*.

What, the *actual Sunday Times*?

Yes.

Ah, OK.

He played first-class cricket for the Netherlands, too.

Right(?), OK.

So this is the breather then?

Yes, indeed it is. I must congratulate myself on this notion actually as, looking back now, I didn't realise I was such a thoughtful fellow back back, back then, you know, way back then before I'd even sold a *word*, let alone a *book*. Thoughtful, yes, ah bless me.

I suck in a deepdeep lungful and then a deeper bit more, allow all my senses to fill sweet and true, I'm a SENSUALIST, yesyes, a connoisseur of the hari-rama here & now, and balls to the anything else, the no-matters happenstance and leaps and dives of fate – FATE, pah! I demand the TRUTH.

Every last mortal thrum passes over me easy as a breath, breathing, existing. And BANG! it's back to that bastard gull looking down at me, imperious, connivery, like the moon, its brother the sun, ah yes, sashay you godless blaze, fill the sky... least I got that warmth, but what about my toiled-out novel?

You have copies elsewhere, you must.
    <PAUSE>
No. I simply do *not*. Wait. I must have e'd one to Dan Kemp of the *Sunday Times Culture*, yesyes I did. (Everything must pass, go easy, breathe...) & my cast ankle hums its tuneless doleful vice, crutches asplay aground; a CROSS, no help, so I gather some calmness and sit back down and gull still staring down mockery, I can just tell.

Now let me think this over peacefully... a bird has stolen my novel. And eaten it. Damn sky pigs, they eat anything. One more notch, I suppose, on this belting crease my life has become... a buckle fuckle Huckleberry chuckle life, holding up nothing, not even two-storey dance-floor flights of fancy and *snapsnap*.

Unbelievable, I realise, but it's the hideous truth, blind eyes and deaf tongues suck-sucking snap-snapping ah whoom ah whee and I actually ease on out a rolling giggle, even though my fume pin is still on the grenade pull, about to give, and my viscerals pump and it's MY DAMN NOVEL, right? and it's sudden giggle cease and I hobble fast and go get my gun.

Never been a fan of gulls. Any sort. Now, even less so. Jackdaws and tits and finches I quite like to admire, flickering keen and sparky, and smart. Nightingales and whippoorwills too, but I wouldn't know either one if it landed on my nose-end. They sound good though. But gulls – o bully – and just oozing that smarm. I realise they're just doing what comes natural to them, but my ding-a-ling, they're a grimy blot on seascapes and skylines and coastal cottage chimney pots for sure. And what about their riding endless goodGod-awful din?

He's now in my .22 sights, .22 bullet, no gutshot, I got the skills package, worry not, neck & head, neck & head, there it is, keep still, one-shot, that's what it's about, and no-breathe, relax mind and finger and... wait, what the...? – and I de-trigger and feel at my top lip and a fucking nosebleed, a real gusher.

I lower the rifle.

The gull smirks and sneers his playground eyes at me.

My *Sunday Times* on this table under my nose is vermillion mulch now, my pot bones boom and hoom in their tib-fib ridiculousness and I reckon the whole garden and back fence and one dying elm are all watching on, taking the piss now.

Performed a fast three-sigh meditation. Felt immediately much improved. Scratched out a little poem called 'The Trenchant Hector' (*fly away, flee*) and only then realised that the *Sunday Times Culture* page I'd subconsciously chosen to ink and bleed all over was the one particularly set aside for *Dan Kemp*'s weekly insights, bloody downright wordy assassinations and poesy gutshot. Some writer and understander and interloper that poser Dan Kemp, and that's what comforts any of my BEST-SELLER doubts I may have. He's the man, that *Dan Kemp*.

The gull up there still by the smokeless stack, now on one leg, with the parody-other tucked up into his puffed-up body, of course he even lets out a victory cry, long and sharp into the air: *Chin up, Buster!*

"You thieving bastard beak," is all I can human-muster.

All things must pass.

3

Here's a few headlines from the rest of the *Sunday Times* (best-seller lists are always littered with books which ooze historical non-fiction mentionings giving a date feel and real charm. But hang on, this isn't the bestseller, is it? ...hasn't that been eaten?):

Civil war in Russia-Ukraine-Crimea over who has the fanciest maps and most unsightly local authority buildings.

Malaysian Airlines flight MH370, a Boeing 777 rammed to the pax bulkheads, has gone missing in a celestial panic wet weird vortex.

Shameless MPs bicker.

Legless runner kills his beautiful lover and does not run away.

NHS sells a billion patient records – now that *is* bestselling, I'll tell Dan Kemp. Actually, I better had e him or phone him about my novel. Or what about *Sent Mail* history? yesyes, a way out of this mess...

FUEGO blam! I fired one down.

FUEGO blam! and another.

Two shots of Bulleit Bourbon and it's way gone noon.

Shit, my *Sent Mail* folder is set to delete. Now why the hell would I do that?

I live alone. Yep, I know. Even the dog up and left last week. The cottage walls are sick of the sight of me. These crutches piss me off. Dried blood tugs at my facial hair. I find an old pack of wet wipes under the sink but they're dry as a vicar's wit and ergo useless. (Ergo, aarrgh, why? I ain't no best-selling author *yet*. This ain't even the damn best-seller.)

FUEGO, FUEGO, two more quickfires and this thick mauve curtain all velveteen lonely gruesome hopper fabric is lastly manag(e)able what judg(e)ment e-less or not ah whoom ah whee quarter to three supine unshowered taking stock Bulleit's all gone what a story.

CHINGAO CHINGAO... what do you do to me? Why?

Oh that's right – *verdad, my dad, Papa, verdad* – it's my own self-assembly, my own making – finally finish the truly great literary ladder hot-stepper money and reputation and legend-maker after all the resentment detachment ridicule torment and only have the ONE copy on the bird fob GONE and why no answer from that FUCK *Kemp*?

Gotta reload but I've no Bulleits left, simply not right, and it's on the phone to over-the-road Rob for more ammunition, he's the super-duper convenience store for more war, civil perhaps, lusty yes – curdle-cut, hopeful, wanton, wanting something and YES it's here already after just a couple cod(e)ines couple Solp(a)deines and agua friZZANT(E).

The bloodblack seal *cracks* and the honey snakes get slithering out and it's more FUEGOFUEGO! and that bastard gull, he's probably still up there, past the fireplace, up the breast, the beast, that BEST-SELLER slug, will you die? hyphen-or-not... will it kill you? and over-the-road Rob says, "You got a nosebleed or something," and I reckon it'll be the death of me now I'm rid of the novel, now it's out there, it's *not OUT THERE*! it's just *gone*.

Ah, the horrendousness, the cognitive dissonance, the fox, the wine, the Bulleits, my love, my blood, and over-the-road Rob humbles his tumble-up-down pills and more drinks and disappears off again into the pleasant Laurie Lee-ether out there, one more gull herring squawk and it's curtains for me. Desire, desire, my motor's all a-cough.

I climb endless stairs to bed-join me hopping dragging hophop shuffle curse CURSE-PersPecTive and foolishness I like and live and love alone but for the lot of you in my head. Average, way better than average, the length maybe not so, and I wonder about *Dan* bastard *Kemp* that glorious fence and that damn bird (unbless).

It's HYPNO-snooze time...

Bells peal flora and fauna
Agency deal PUBLISHER
Slush pile template response
Thank you sincerely for the opportunity
To read your SLUSH
Do you have piles?
It's just not right for us
At this time
Good bye Good luck
Good fuck Forever

Ring them bells
Peel the fruit
The true sincere mirth of
Chase-yer-tail make-it-as-a-writer
ding-a-ling
Yours etc.
LONDON

P.S.

Have you ever thought about

Self-public-flagellation?

& before all that tragic communicatory STAB-STAB is the actual work itself. The graft of the craft. Years of nurture and expectation... art? real? will it sell? you don't know the market, you don't know a thing, you're an UNKNOWN, just WHO ARE YOU?

& repeat until you whimper and crinkle and get a real job, man <ticker going batso and head's a mess getting worse by the *ticktock*>.

OK, well, that's it. This is it, and this is THIS. From here on in, it has to be

whooming caprice

rewriteless

spontaneous enlightenment

don't look back hook-back grab-ass, no, none o' that

(Culpable Gull still up on this cottage top

plucking and preening and polishing

& digesting) and my bust left leg has its final bonal-lunge vhoom of the day deep in there and I'm gone mattressly sound thinking:

What shall I say at Hay-on-Wye?

Two more pills and that's me.

PUT ME DOWN. Please.

{{(Based on the Bestselling Novel by Saxon Pepperdine

a novel

by Saxon Pepperdine)

(suppose it should be called *The Broken Leg Bestseller* this short tome I've written to me and to the WORLD but I'd like the front of the book to be like that above or something of that ill ilk. Now did that genius ex-journo who pulsed out (*Light & Dark*)... er Luca he's called, yeah Luca I reckon... well did he go through this ceremony of title-thought or did he just whip it out and done?)}}

No fear. No envy. No meanness. Decent early sattva voice.

But you MUST write something which is COMMERCIALLY VIABLE, has a plot, preferably a circular story with some love and sadness and a few quirks thisaway and that, speckled with that lovestory don't forget, yet must be UNIQUE, just like all the other bestsellers, see?

Well I finally did all that, much to my own personal cha-cha-chagrin, and the wowness of inner wrench pride sell-out biliousness overwhelmed me throughout, yet my perseverance switch clicked and cluttered it all OUT and I got right in line at the till and carved out a Middle of the Avenue special with a kiss.

Now it's gone. And all these sick salacious dreams with a twist serve me right. Not much left. & I hobble up out of bed for another day of Paradiso clawing at my ribcage dying to get out and ball across the skies hollering silliness about decent karma but right this now, this sumptuous hereNOW, right as I write here, well I'm telling you... just some sweet strong coffee will do for me.

So where is this? and what am I? Just who, who am I?

4

FM radio chimes out the daily by the hour loop-the-loop
kookNEWS: that 777's still lost, some Englander scooped a billion
on the lottery, swears he's gonna spend it on engine parts for his
Citroën Saxo. Death is everywhere and the pandering fawns who
run the whole machine are fast running out of Rhetors' Oil, yet the
public and Middle England who hold sway in the election booths
and selfish-service check-outs are all far too busy posting pictures
online of their children and their holidays to even care a jot about
what's actually happening in the (un-de)Real World, so it all
trickles on by like a savage stream of unconsciousness and *must
have more receipts.*

fish skin deflectory
mud bank rocks
bald branch canopy (even in a healthy spring)
everything moves not a thing stops

It's sunny again and the coffee is big and meaningful. In it there's a
plot and it all goes down accordingly. A dozen or more gulls out
here on the wing cackling and lazing about the garden eyeing up
everyone and everything. Plot plot plot. Which one of you
bastards is it? who devoured my novel? come on now, how does it
feel?

These crutches creak and groan at me, each swing-lean on
them is a real surge of strain and pressure. Man, muscle, bone,
plastic, energy, heal, process the break, process time, repeat repeat.
The all-weather barbecue is rusting away quietly. I suck in the
world and attempt a little *Understanding Totale.*

Oh, Jesse James, there's my gull. Oh yesyes, it's him alright. And we have a little stare down, man & bird like this and the situation makes me feel both oddly *and* sweetly soporific and full of inner calm, staring-down contest like this, where nothing else exists, just me & bird and the absurdity is tweaking me high, & slowly corrupting the peripheral Zen clouds into gentle alphabetti mauve confusion.

Hang on a sec.

Over-the-road Rob knows about computers and what-knot, I'll get him to undo the troubles and twists and undelete *Sent Mail* and retrace the novel somewhere on the soft-drive hard-fi motherboard and all will be A-OK, OK? *I'm just a patsy*, all will out in the clean-up operation.

Forget it, bird.

Bobby Ford, how did they ever manage in the typewriter days, the parchment era? Those good heady days punching out lines of verse and lucid prose and sending it to London village, just the ONE copy, right? And here I am now with all the technology God and Jobs and Atari can throw at me, yet still I manage to fuck it up.

What does Martin Amis do? Cecilia Ahern? Will himSelf? They'd all look at my woeful workings and howl in contempt and shrug at the ludicrous Dilly Tanty success: "Lost his ONE copy?! Ahhaaahahaaaa! What a TOOL."

Isn't ALL success the same anyway? Christ, where's my Bulleit? where's my Cross, my wooden watchtower in the sun?

FUEGO blam!

FUEGO blam! and I'm back on the ground, level headed, breathing deep from sole to frontal lobe like gushing authority taking over without words, without anything but

vital humming power *mmmmgh mmmgh mmmaahh, mmmgh mmmgh mmmaahh*

like delicious SURF bluesky whitecaps the folding ceaseless planet keeps on keeping on rolling and spinning until the crisis bastards take over again, then the chaos will repeat loom again, and... ahhhh

...thank Bulleits it's over-the-road Rob and I set about telling him the novel recovery mission details and hand him the Toshiba and he says, "Good system... can be a *Thomas* though..." I think he means a *pain* or something of that order so I ask him to do his best and he leaves a mittful of pills on the dining table and taps at my plaster-cast leg prison, "Take it easy," and is gone with a grin and I salute his geniusness at producing these little keys to the mind in all their mental variants and wait, what's this, a PINK one? and FUEGO it's gone.

I hop about a bit and finally settle in front of more omnipotent death and disease-news (why?), where illness continues to spew forth in smashing hyperbole like Americana is taking over this whole limping coughing rolling in the Hay-on-Wye planet. Fantastical trauma and unprecedented repetitious dripdrip mechanical oil-spill of high-torque overuse and useless verbiage applied to cleanse but all it ever does is S-M-U-D-G-E.

WAIT WAit wait...

the pink's gotten me and I'm finally alright, lefties...

Garden sounds swill in; high up there love nest squabbles, jet planes, a van puttering up a hill-climb somewhere, up & UP, spring rustle, and yes, that one fed-up gull, the fob repeating repeating on him and he wishes he'd chosen something easier to repeating digest. Oh fly away, fuck off flee, Trenchant Hector, flee! and my laughter peals out scornful, thornful now and oozing dark promise. Just like them bells. Damn or damned freak-out bells heard the world over riding Pacific crests and skimming over lost Malaysian fuselage and wing bits.

A longing sudden and bursting to have ripe fruit and a girl with canned mandarin eyes serves it up juicy as the squeezed-out sun and tasty as sin itself. Down it all goes, probably someone else's one-copy bestseller and eye & Trenchant Hector are quickly morphed into one-copy man beast. I am a sky pig, lusting and leching even more frivolously than the true pigs, and me and my pot leg go soaring *ah whoom ah whee* the rhapsodies of me-goof, look at me, the world in its death & rebirth at my UnderCarriage PersPecTive de-blinkered & all-seeing thrumming and sprawling vast.

Look! Ecco Ramones! Go-vinda India, the plumes of life, nothing is AVERAGE, everything LIVES, but only few things TRULY DIE.

Christ, there's Raymond Briggs and Lennon in a vest curlicue heaven, dummies all crashed, IT'S A TEST

Fruit and juice go down swinging, these crutches now, that legless runner on a murder rap and that's me too. Death of a Bestseller Man *blamblamblam!* you must be Blake's winged shooter, Miller, *blamblamma blam...*

...*blamma* and the door nearly caves in and it's Dan fucking Kemp in all his polo-collar kula-shakery and it seems he was just passing (175-mile round trip out of his way) and, "Oh, have you been phoning? I've been overseas," and my one copy one thieving ravenous gull regale tale seems to humour him to such a degree, he needs cool beering down before he chokes and croaks it.

"You bastard, I'm serious," I try but his laughter soars high above the cottage, tickling at the carving swifts cartwheeling through the bull-gullery, on and on.

I look at Dan Kemp and I see perhaps me, a different life me, a different time. But ALL lives in one single speck of time are the same life and for that instant I can taste what he tastes, laugh with him, feel his insides and malady valves and deepdown thinkers.

A writer. A get-in-line writer educated to formula, earning a decent weekly wage, people reading his words regular as *cock*work, a wife, a semi, a LONDON semi, probably two cars and two holidays, Rufus and Henry at Harrow and 12-bit pension in 20 years' time.

Is that me?

For a two-second speck, yes, then I'm back real me.

"So let me get this right," he says. "Your bestseller, which *I* have discovered... wait! who else has read it?"

"Not a soul," I confirm.

"OK, good. Now, it's sitting on a memory stick," takes a swig breezily, "out in the garden. And you're sitting there too, bust leg and all from a *disco leap* – a fucking DISCO LEAP? See something you fancied, did yer? – and down swoops a seagull and takes the memory stick away?"

"Herring gull."

"What?"

"It was a herring, not a sea."

"Right, OK, sorry..." swigs beer to a can finish and fills the cottage again with a suppressed guttural laughter, kid-in-class type, mad, endearing, kind-of.

"Why is it so funny, Kemp? It's gone. GONE. You understand...? *Intendiende? – Poota Mata Kee Asees.*"

"It *has* to be somewhere, man, the technical ether nowadays is permanent," and the amusement for this particular bastard continues, not so endearing now, kind-of.

He starts at the, "...don't you see the connotations here...?" and all that education accepted dissection rattle drawing comparisons with me and the gull, falling, swooping, breaking *beak*ing, maladjustedness inner turmoil, man is beast and trained to survive, go after what he wants, what he *needs*, feed, rattle, and loom that gets these beastly people secure writing jobs all over the damned animal planet.

"Now let me see your laptop, where is it? who the hell is over-the-road Rob? I'll give my office a call... and for Chrissakes, stop worrying all the damn time..." and confirmations I'll be on his employer's bestseller lists by Christmas and getting in-store handjobs till next spring and, "I'll be your agent as well... worry not... I was just passing, needed something in Brighton (bullshit) ... like my new car? where's your dog? and how the devil are you?"

It all makes me feel truly sick.

Here's where I use words like *like* and *risible* and proper *dilettante* and *hideousness* and *like* and *you know* because I just can't help it.

Dan fucking Kemp. He's the man.

Thankfully the radio purges some sweet little old melody and it gets me all a-tap, and realisation that all novels are really just cover versions anyway. It's the manifold PR nu-media *BBC Breakfast* middle-England promo that makes them bestsellers. "Yeah, of course it is," and he's off, gone, in a shiny foreign convertible back to the city with that grin and that *click*-wink thing he does.

Mendacious. Quidnunc. Tolerant. Tolerable.

Now dissect that lot, *Dan Kemp*, London village, graduate underlings earning your way to middle Avenue stripedom and sofas and ditsy springer spaniels and BOSE. (Christ, my *CENTRAL* hang-ups drive me to mad distraction, I know, OK, I promise.)

I crack myself a cold beer and hunt down a little pink friend because I immediately require me some me-time again, that conversing has me all rippling and churlish and simpering and I miss my dog terribly now, that gull is still up there somewhere, I just know it, and I'm not worried, I am, I'm not, we're all the same, just *like* the o'clocks.

FUEGO! blam and I feel myself again. My bust left leg is starting to itch front and centre the unscratchables. Heaven's crying out for me but there ain't no heaven, Jesse James, so it must just be thunder or winged sky parson gutsome rumbling. Or the radio, yep the radio. This sonic boomer dabbling in arousal today, this now, this right here now, where hobble sticks clatter

folk groan
ends meet
tied-up
endless
undo, unpeal
take it back
pelados
take it back

FUEGO! blam, my .22 rifle back in the shed bored stiff in the corner thinking, IF ONLY he weren't Robert Ford or maybe he should be, (meaning me) the cheeky shooter, what a wheeze, the sun-thunder on the make now round this ping-pong Earth, this nuzzling bulb awaiting its final blow, its ultimate SMASH.

Back beer, a little blue pal now as well, and it's all slow song wonderment: over-the-road Rob – any joy? – Dan bastard Kemp – capital! capital! – OmniGull – how's the belly? you need a good read? – and me: wall-eyed and pathetic as dust.

What was my fresh sattva voice again? ah, yes:
No envy – Kemp had the Dutch orange lion on his polo shirt from his globe-trotting sham cricketing past.
No fear – What if he can't find a copy somewhere? Over-the-road Rob, too? What then?
No meanness – Cunts.

Early teething problems, most notably in the startling key of C, but the good will out, I say... *the good will out.*
You see, from my point askew here on one leg, which is getting sick and tired of taking all the no-crutch strain, everything is a mile off. Every last little mortal thing: money, my own earned money. Respect, pah! Happiness? Don't even think about it, pelado, just who the hell is happy out there anyway? You make me laugh.
There must be a million other best-selling souls here on this silly cruel Earth who just haven't the means to prove it. Think third- and henceforth and fifth-world starving geniuses out there, weeping. So screw it, suck another one down, dustman, go ahead, the walls are getting closer by the tick-tock, the sky waves crimp and purl, Britain and her princesses curl and whimper thinking,

We could all break down any Buddha-given minute, where a minute is so minute, it is seconds split infinitely until we all gather In Memoriam and explain ALL our perspectives and perceptions as if our own sell-out PLOTS actually matter.

Say hello, *cielo*, say hello, and this day gulping me up now, all the way down to the guts of dusk. Out there, the two-legged homo-sapo-souls hopscotch about, even the families and kids taking the piss as well, the birds too, ALL of them now on the irascible smirk. They just *know*. And there's nada I can do but jiggle and crouch down. Finish the bottle. Slumber like a king. Ruler of this melting rumble-down cottage corner while the universe in a tiara whispers its plan.

Godman, whatever and wherever you are, put down your looking glass and finally finish me for good.

Oh, Jesse James, what have I been rattling on about? Man alive, I haven't the stomach nor the balls to look back over these words, these notes, this little ragtag notebook... but wait, yeah, it is an exercise in no revision and no correctedness, isn't it? yeah, remember, spontaneous revelatory penmind fire, yeah, penned in by the PEN DIN! whhhoooohhoooo yip-yippety yahhoooo

My raggedy trousers flap around the pot leg and the free leg and I reckon it's about time I try to shower. Been putting it off for days now. Shave maybe as well. Yes. In the average mean time, here's what I scrawled directly onto the wall in my hazed-out philanthropy before being lured off fully to the delicious world of fresh-clean spare room zedbed zedhead fooooolsszzzz:

Tracey EmiN (thiS iS the end of ART)
For the express purpose of making my own brass and wholly discarding what little artistic integrity I've ever

regarded, I wrote dot.dot.dot. & decided to write a bestseller.

Chopin played on & on hot like a hummingbird and I wrote...

van Beet played fleet as knives and I wrote...

the night kept crawling over and over us all drinking sucking swallowing every last little thing down making our still-lives PELT & SWOON and I wrote...

...till THE END.

Dedicated to THE END. Without you .dot. I wouldn't have made it and now the *Sunday Times Culture* at my door with iPhone and iPad and i'm still iN bed wiTh Tracey EmiN.

i'm aliVe and delicious and promiSes to the publiSher that thiS iS just the begiNniNg a triPtych so...

advance

ADVANCE

Advance

...on we go
brassed up
selling. .dot

Then it's back here cut shaving blood sink quit that limp hot stretch rest; gloopy yet rather happy.

The big reveal. The payoff. Flashbacks in time, years or so, back and forth, a death, some magic, quaint mystery, a detective, a ZOMBIE, yesyes! unexpectation, cherry-pick the plot, perfecto, JJ, now shoot the crows and disembowel the gulls, holler over the road, sit back on pots of gold. (Creepy Mailer would have *mewing* kittens if he heard about this.) SYMPATICO – be lik(e)able, with or without the e, the village idiots insist, Bobby Ford, do I even want a PAYOFF?

needwantneedwantneedwantneedwantdesire   desire   DESIRE vhoom

5

Now something just reached clean out the radio speakers, bust through me chest and ribs (spare +1) and wrenched to death any sinew of Paradiso I had in there: some justice secretary has banned prisoners from receiving books to read. & it sincerely makes me quietly weep. I wonder if I'm going to make it. I know I swear a lot and am fully glib and made up of strange plasmatic pushpush, but in me there is GOODNESS, somewhere. I swear it's there, a little, a lot, a jot, but it is good. So can I make it through the true bawdry ill with just an inkling of GOOD?

Answers, answers, too many damn questions, not enough sluicing time.

(WHAT would Dimbleby suggest? Or Radio 4 or Classic Archer & Agincourt?) so I revert back to what I know best, my safety rainbow soothers in their oval mystique and bottles going *clink* and this pot leg is such a selfish twist, it is inconceivable.

Gull, do me a favour. Gather all your brothers and sisters and maybe even the GOOD cousins too, and come pick me up, you owe me one for sure, all of you come PICK ME UP, fly me away, far-far-gone to somewhere far from here, Atlas Morocco, La Paz, Margaret's surf-sun River, and leave me there for good... & fuckslut!Christ, another gusher blashes out me dog-forsaken weak beak. I get busy with a towel.

30

Something is not right. More than this leg. Three blue toes and aching rattly chest. Now blood pissing everywhere again. More than all this.

La Tristesse Durera, sadness overtakes hope, slams on the brakes, and the double collision endures: two sudden SMASHERS plunder into now here reckoning:

1. Over-the-road Rob has utterly fucked the Toshiba.
2. Dan bastard Kemp and all his village cling-ons can NOT locate or retrieve or conjure up a copy of the novel.

Bestseller blues.
Bustleg blues.

Red nose, red lip, red towel vermillionaire fury, but silent fury, so animalistic I'll have cancer of the vacant rib by tea time.

I finally hop the shower with a plastic leg cover and I trytrytry to forget the world quickly and the hotwater feels good.

Some Drake tipples sweetly out the speakers now. A ripe real melody brutally soft, nearly guiltless, but not quite. Abject reality, objectively altruistic... here, have this for free:

ALL things are beautiful, every hum and bristle is ART. It just depends how closely your senses operate, yeah, how closely they work together and at what time of day and season it is, that's what determines beautiful capricious pieces of ART and life, if they're worthy or not or just way too much. Ask Nick. Jesse. Rob. Dogman Buddha. Mohancock Longpaw, the Native American Spirit of the Seventh Sense. What would Patterson & Brown & King do? Papa & JD & Jack? Hilary & Seb & Ian & Barbara? because they have the answers, JJ, and they exist, breathing, stepping out on every high street in every county of the OCCIDENTAL MENTALITY.

But who's really in charge? Who's at the helm, grinning?

The spineless bendies with all the money in the first damn place, that's who.

Now tell me, how are your piles now?

Dear London,

Fur queue. Get in line. Buy a pelt.

Yours etc.

– Kemp?

– Yeah, hey, how are you, man?

– Average, I suppose, like every prick else.

– Hup, yesyes! OK, what's up, man?

– What's up?

– Yeah...

– OK, Kemp, here's what's *up*... that bastard herring gull.

<Nothing, not a sound>

– Kemp?

– ...Yeah?

– You seriously don't have a copy of my novel anywhere?

– No. No, I don't. Do you? I mean, it is *yours*.

<Pause>

– Fur QUEUE.

– What?

– Buy a pelt. <I hang up and get back to my last rounds of Bulleit and remainder tic-tac-toes where three-in-line is a short heroic day>

ooo

xxx

ooo

6

Nameless cutlass-sharp morning looms up like a mighty spirit, slicing off its daybreak hymns and pops for all earthly LOWlife. Gulls all snoffing their beaks, the carving swifts and their travelling cartwheels, on & on, and the *whelp* of sun-up roofstacks and scarlet mantras. ALL I need is my reverse Immelmann to smash these bed chains and leg pot and cursive roja plight and grant me ONE MORE DAY, to have me believe in this handsome bloody stretch, this stint here in stinking sanguine LOWlife.

The best letter I ever received was

Today

Dear Me,
I'm Grace
Yours truly,
Anon.

& it reminded me of helping a blind feller across the road outside Bristol Temple Meads, ten, no, twelve years ago, and once safely ensconced the other side, he slapped me clean across the face and I thought, *Wow, helluva shot for a blind man.*

It was at that very moment in tempus fugit and carpe diem when I decided to become an ARTIST. More than a decade in, a seeping realisation has pored out blind all-me-over like a bad treehouse blanket in a shit storm – *wappity*SLAP! Skinny vicious city all-seeing trendsetters are at the helm, with fat and violent minds. And forever will be.

Ah whoom ah whee I'll never be free and over-the-road Rob now in his melancholy maniac garb has brought me a brand new unpeeled one-bite Apple laptop crystalline machine and, "Sorry about the Toshiba, have this, it's brand new, here's some more pinkies, a couple of blueys and violas too, and, hey, fancy some of these gammon steaks? I couldn't manage them."

It's all so crawdaddy FUNk town hilarious, we both end up contagion close to croak tears. Then he leaves and here I am again. Shall I start again? or just END? (DEDicated)

I wonder how long this story is. I consider PLOT. Payoff. All the while the radio pulses out cover versions of a thousand classics.

Oh Trenchant Hector, with rebel purity, have you passed it yet? did your tum get through it? what do you think? will it best sell or what?

ititit... dotdotdot I may forage through your waste

Perhaps this is a coming-of-age tale. A memoir of poverty and rape. Vampirical feed it to the kids, the *Funday Times*, see what sticks, what slides, what crawls to the floor and under the bed till the kids are fast asleep dreaming of growing up. Then slink away under the cover of adulthood, write another genre tick-box bestseller (maybe I will) for the middle-earner robots in semi-Britain, Cottage EU & Lakeside Americana, cleaning their rifles, pine plains on the retreat, and the sadsad Natives all in pure denial.

FOR YOUR CONSIDERATION

Bookshops are rotting away. Prisoners too (Grayling the imbecile). Is ALL the writing as well? The charm of the word? The magic of the eye-word-dance? Just what across the vast cerebral tundra is going on? MAT-ATARI, Jesse Ford, techno dream world is acting helmsman and we are ALL on the brink, worried to death. Or perhaps it's just me worried. Yeah, that's it. I'm the one. The seer who's reading the clues. (I once got tip-wet in a basement bookstore. It was then I decided to be an artist. I swear.)

This Broken Leg Bestseller notepad is quite assuredly filling up, here back in the garden, scene of the beak *SNAP!* and dogfight climb. Crutches resting here tableside and I pick one up and raise it to my shoulder like a rifle, get the arrogant sky-pig villain in my sights and *ppffftt!* a one-shot sniper takes him down and the memory stick lands bloodily in my lap. Hup, if only.

Think I'm actually starting to care very little about it all now. All this messy outplay of potty circumstance and bastardness. What do the spiders in the grass dancing with the worms and slugs reckon? Just a huge fat NOTHING, meaningless to the stars and the terrible firma and brinks and banks and river trout worthless in springs berserk.

I need a woman again.
A reality check ✓
Good trusty love, if that ever exists.
I need control, juvenile hope.
I need a pinky and a couple Bulleits.

Mendacious. Quidnunc. Tolerant. Tolerable. It's all one big race, a race to find out what it is we actually stand to lose. The podium's all polished, there's champagne on the *pop* and celebratory STABSTAB into review write-ups, sports pages, sponsored bikini briefs.

The Boeing's still missing, the Malaysian authorities still missing the point, that runner's legs are still missing, everything is stationary, pelting through time zones, selfish beyond

Understanding Totale & GodmanBuddha tries to hide the tears but can KNOT undo all the wrongs.

My religion is nil. And lessening by the *click*wink, and the village bell peal which signifies feeding time for my hungry ouching soul within earshot headshot gutshot is floating aimlessly on a breeze. Evergreens fade. Tulips flex and go. One solo iris hiccups at the bees (not their knees). I'm gardenly digesting all this where as a child I once poured milk to the ground and told my now dead parents, "Grow myself a moo-cow!" and they had laughed lovely and loud.

This could be The End. <Ded>. And in a way it is .dot. but the pink kindly gets a grip on me at last and off I spin to a gloopy kook elsewhere for a bit, instead of making all this clear clear seer sense.

There's a huge great crack in the dry ground and I try to make my folks laugh again with, "Whose FAULT is this?" but I'm met with shattering soundlessness peppering my skull like bugs so I swat at them with my crutch gun. They go.

Least I don't have to pay for this cottage. And my monthly stipend from the McIlhenny's TABASCO® hot sauce COMPANY takes care of bills and food and booze and fruit and any other receipts that dash through the door from over the road, from all over the damn planet, from Capri-cancer to Amundsen's teeth.

I make a mammoth fruit smoothie thing and my body squeaks with vit. C pleasure and thanks. While I'm at the chopchop blendblend station and on about it, my buds get a real continuation fizz-on, so I get to Bloody Mary considerations, and loose-arm juicing the Tabasco about a bit just sways the deciders and the blood and bulls of Mexico, of Spain, they start to lunge and thrash, the heart of MAN as beast and bird on the hop, on the prowl, legless caper flight and crested thinkers. *O hot chaos*!

P Coelho: "Stop being who you *were* and become who you *are*." I've scribed it straight onto the kitchen wall among all the other poems and thoughts and bulls hit that spews forth & fifth and six-cylinder ramped-up VhooOomMiNg: sound the trumpets, thrust the killer blow.

(What is the Perspective of these words? You know, how one reads them. How one writes them. The angle of interpretation, is that where genius exists? Or is that just the *ordinary*? Do you go for the catch... or let it drop? Howl at the moon... or finger-pick the harp? That inspiration has been directly and purposefully lifted straight from the deliciousness that is *The Restlessness of Virtue (Light & Dark)*, now have I mentioned that yet? My one true spice & brawl *SATORI* catalyst? Have I, have I...?)

O Jesse, sanguine hot Mary has me straightened up, seasoned to the gills naturally and I send gratitudinal winks out to Avery Island and to the jailhouse screws in my head and to over-the-road Rob for being a genius (remember this examinable statement if you wouldn't mind).

Now how can I 4see my days panning out? I can't.

Let It Bleed draughts out the radio, I check my vitals and my nose and face fluff and lip but I ain't bleeding no more, cariño, perhaps I've no blood left, right? Roo-cha-chagrin in all the bouncing honky-tonks in all the backwater bayous because needs must, and somehow I am now

FREE

blamblamblam

Yabberla Bood Yabberla Bood
One more time (Crush the Cruel)

37

Bet I'd have gallons of friends and family

    post bestseller

    post bloodshed

    post *Understanding Totale* (can I stop pretending to understand?)

"There's nothing wrong in being a dreamer... just don't *EVER* wake up." Think that's one of mine but I ain't sure, Gunnery Sgt, it may just be a cover version in my jailcell blanket cuff mind. Who knows? I don't even *want* to know. I'll ask Tracey EmiN, she's lying right next to me. Messsssed-up. Uni-formally. Stripes on arms.

And then in amongst this straight-forwardness time flow truth flow... my gone dog just APPEARS through the back door into this kitchen, ears back, tail down, happy sad face, half-cowering.

I loll back half-unbelieving and she figure-8s my pot leg and right leg, four that way, four the other, full smile passive now and I get her some cold fresh water and a big beef bone and she's back all pally in an instant. Curled up chewing ecstasy eyes and my body electric back surging and conducting this core ensemble peacefulness. Kemp calls and ruins it.

"Good news," he says with zero conviction, "the intern here, a right little slice, well, she ran a copy of your novel and took it away to read, what about that, *hay*?"

"Yeah, OK, and so what now?"

"What now, you ask, well here's what now... soon as she's back from France, we have a copy, moron, you understand, er, er, *comprenday*?"

"She's in France?"

"Yes, er, *mais... oui!*"

"Whereabouts?"

<PAUSE. I can hear a scratch-sigh.>

"Whereabouts? what the fuck does that matter? she's back on Monday."

"And what day is today?"

"Friday, man, all day long..."

I hang up. Get myself a drink.

So he writes for a damn newspaper and still gets an intern. Prick.

The dog & me lollop out to the garden and up there all-abouts, the cherubic brooding cloud is clearly planning stuff, maybe halcyon thunder or arty hail. I decide right now to be an artist. The dog likes the decision.

There's lawless heathenry out here. In offices the world over. At 7th Avenue kerb-side delis. Beyond Taiwan and their scuttle-bug ideology. Bent over and done, trembling, the lot of us, and in need of a hand, a steer, a pat on the black cap.

7

Today

Dear Trent and your brother Travis, somewhere in Louisiana Kentucky Ohio, I forgive you. A million other sons wouldn't, but I do.

Yours etc.

Lick, stamp, drop it in the mailbox sometime soon.

The dog agrees. She's got my back, and I'm glad she's back.

Ah, right, JJ, what's next?

Obviate. Misanthropy. Alienate. Disastrophy. Have a few pages of *Light & Dark* if you must, do it, be your true good self.

I've got five-day scratchy semi-growth but I'm so far from hipster, I'm shinbone, I'm toejam, I'm heelspur spinning, but

39

finally ALIVE. The dog scoots about the corners and shrubbery and the one fading elm, reacquainting herself politely.

I feel fine.

(I am rather glad I recycle my toothpaste tubes, you know, because with each pearly white smile I set free out here, there is one more flight pumping up and out of Gatwick and Heathrow and Bournemouth International. Offset strategy so we can all sleep sound as Rolls-Royce rivets. Ah, nightynight, sweet dreamers, the innatery of reason of misleading leaders who've already been misled and branded and popped.)

> Meryl's stooped on her knees
> at Dame Judi's trench
> Clooney's on the camera
> I gave up movies for lent (bent & spent, too expensive to
>   rent)

...another wall scratching that dates back years or more and I seriously can't remember writing half these idiot rhymes. If certain people were to read certain ones, I'd be sectioned under the MHA of a certain year under a certain BRIDGE under the INFLUENCE under the weather of a certain Jack the Hat mcNicholson.

> The ides of March
> The tides of spring
> What's preening on the skyline?
> Who'll ring your ding-a-ling?

...some of them are just... wait! Out in the middle of the garden, the dog is sitting, poised, calm, but poised ready for action or something and staring up at the apex chimney pot and YES, straight at my bastard herring gull. The gull stares back at the dog, a profound wild snapshot, a pitiful sketch that I begin reading UNDER the spell too much into, as usual.

They stare and stare unblinking. The dog's tail twitching mad now and the high bird is motionless, trancelike.

The cloud has suddenly amassed huge; a huddle of dubious grey.

Insanity is tickling under the chin of England.

I've had a mental breakdown before now, have I mentioned that already? Throughout my recovery, the dog remained right at my side, loyal beyond the call, yet just the other day she casually wandered off elsewhere out the garden, left and gone. I may break down again just thinking about that. No. No, I shan't.

I'm a realist (try! ...try!)

A sensualist (see?)

A here&now-ist, a pill-ist, a, a, a maudlin celebrationist

A wake-up artist (stop the snooze)

Matrices of realisation mix into this stormy ether out here; this ominous unruly blur of blue-grey loom and yep, here it is, a gale to join in, with sudden thrashing rain and I shelter this notebook as I write, the dog still here, resolute, the gull unflinching. This must be the moment, the speck in time I've been waiting for. *MUST* be.

But all I get is soaked through and fast chilled to the bone, snapped or not, hobble quick indoors, back to Bulleits BLAM! one more table-top pinky and lay down a drip-drip.

Breathe... way deep. Slow the machine, relax the malady valves and synaptic turbo. Breeeathe. Yabberla Bood Yabberla Bood... .dot.

Dog & bird... who won?

Reckon there's a fearsome old steam train somewhere being admired as it blasts on through some ancient mountains carrying the world on its back. And you know folk are taking pictures to show themselves in the foreground immediately proving they were here and there, and, face it, everywhere.

I've been humbled and rendered a fool by daft few days' happenstance.

About time I shaved (didn't I finish the job the other day?) and had a decent flush through, a deep deep cleanse, you know, all that.

It's then (now) when I have a serious look at myself in the mirror and it hurts. Sincerely hurts. Just who am I?

8

Not long soon after I'm freshened up in clean shorts and spray and talcum powder joy, even though I recall doing none of it. Somebody's tap-tapping at the front door, gentle as a mouse. It's not Kemp nor over-the-road, I can tell.

I hop-hobble down the stairs. I have butchered my bones like I butcher the classics, the bloody reams of covers, oh ART. Ah, the aloof virtue, untouchable you are, Tracey, now get up, come along, make coffee, hobble with me, there's somebody at the door with soft knuckles and decent intentions... a girl maybe...

SWISSSHHH open – IT IS! A lovely upright slender smiling blonde thing fit for dance class or netball practice.

I'm at once paralysed by

Fear

Envy

Meanness

I try shaking all three free but no joy. Not yet at least.

"Hi there! I'm Adele, Daniel's intern, pleased to meet you." <strange little handshake> "I have your emmess," and she hands me a thick wedge of paper, seemingly not *too* thick.

"My *emmess*?" I ask.

"Yes, your ManuScript, there you go... is it *really* the only copy that exists?"

I look at my title page. "Ah, yes... well... everything's a copy anyway, right?" and she nods or shakes and smiles and I get her inside and she's come in Kemp's little foreign sports car. "You and Kemp, you fucking each other?"

"Hah! *No*. What a wheeze." (My saying, and she uses it, I swear.) "He wishes. Nah, I play the shy new girl with him and he buys me lunch and lends me stuff, that's all, you know the score."

Childlike, nearly beautiful, tiny skinny hands, the whole shape not fully developed, yet truly confident.

"What happened to your leg?"

"Saw a sign, had to give way," I explain. "Care for a drink, Adele, Daniel's intern?"

"Sure, anything wet seems about right, wine would be good, no work for me till Monday, whoopee."

"What day is today?"

"Saturday... all day long."

I get busy with some cold Spanish blanco and keep conversation trickling along as best I can, considering my lack of practice, and I suddenly wonder where the old girlfriend is now, maybe dead, maybe not, maybe deliriously happy, probably, yeah.

There's a sublime dignity in the intern's eyes looking me updown, pondering, calculating, whatever it is she's doing a-swish with Viña Sol now.

"I love your novel," she says or she doesn't say or she's just about to say. "Ooh, I like your dog, I like your cottage, I like your balls, can I touch them?" What's all this writing on the walls how old are you are you single what's your inspiration why don't you have a television there's no wireless connection here do you have a smartphone a dumbphone any more wine what about some pot do you like to get stoned?

I show her my drawer full of pinks and blues and oranges galore and violins and harps and La Vista possibilities. She lights up like a dog-damned fruit machine on the brink of a sizzling payoff. This pre-woman lilting little lollipop strobing fast and we get discussing Nabokov and Henry Miller and PerSpecTive like Simon Schama or Keith Richards or somebody or other's Frostrup piggy-backing piss-taking hackwork versus celebrity, all that funky gambol gas.

I get her. Quick as that, quick as dogs, done, downstairs still, classless hot and come fun.

Chet Baker Heike Drechsler Jesse James, I can still manage it, I can do it. Now it's *my* whoopee.

"Who are you?" she asks, prone, wet, developing right in front of me, warm and light pink.

"Don't ask," I answer, "just don't even bother."

Then *she* gets me, just as quick, in total control this Nordic youth and kiddy skin, tiny frame, scratching and yelping, and who taught her all this? Oslo girl guides?

The dog's asleep, printed-out sheets of my *emmess* for a bed. All over the kitchen floor, a massacre of careless beast and words and just how much work and mental sacrifice has gone into this messy scene?

9

I hop out gardenly for the billionth time and curse skywards to the gulls and their one BASTARD in charge, "Ah, fuck you... I got my novel back, and it's called an *EMMESS*! Ahhhaahaaahahaa..." like a true lunatic. The purgatory elm waggles its mad fingers and thighs in agreeance I hope, and *The Man Who* issues out the speakers for Travis or Trent and it is surprisingly fair, and peaceful, and I feel good.

I happen upon a letter from the hospital instructing me to attend an MRI scan on the pot leg, but I've heard about some dude whose face blew up during one once because he had a few loose fillings so I may not attend, not sure. <run tongue over teeth> Anyway...

I'm so relieved I've got the bestseller back. No I'm not. I am. Maybe I'm definite. Perhaps I'm absolute. Don't be a prick.

Adele's a tiny myth up there, showering now, *yeah – showering*, apocryphal, mighty, big as Picasso's thumb.

Yer damn straight I'm an island I'm a railroad I ain't Hollywood I'm *emmess* MS:

Mucho Sancto Muy Speziale Manky Spiritus

Who'll come to my funeral? What hallelujah hymns to sing and who the fuck's in charge of the wake? Back to the question of helmsman, ah whoom ah whee, a soliloquy rampant bare and, "What you writing in that tatty little notebook?" Adele's back out in the garden again, wearing my *Hooters San Francisco* T-shirt and I just smile-release a huge great recycled thing, and off it goes, to spread the word... *JUDGE ME NOW.*

"Is that your real name?" She sits at the table next to me, this outdoor scene full of subtleties, bendy me solitude, and kinks in way-too-bold beaky bloody nature.

"What?" I ask.

"*Saxon Pepperdine*... is that your real name?"

"No, of course not, silly."

"Well, what is it?"

"What?"

"Your name."

<Pause, then...>

"Vivian Weepinghawk."

"*Vivian Weepinghawk*?"

"Yes."

"What the hell is that? Native American?"

"No," I explain. "Drunk Irish," and we share-swig the big punchy lemonade she's brought out.

The sky up there lets out a truly forgettable whimper and some *thing* winks down, some body celestial and massive and the day-star markers etch out a control panel with buttons ready to press. All the while a sign reads, *Do NOT touch stuff, else you'll be shot.* But honestly, not a single soul lids an eye-bat at such louche.

I've said it before, I'll say it again: if you're on the make, keep your sails out FULL. Thanks, Granddad. Cheers, Cecil. Greetings the rest of forever. Now let's get busy...

"Doing what?" she asks, innocent as unseen rivers, yeah, unseen and undipped-in, not even with a big young toe.

"Anything at all," my answer so fly yet heavy as a cubist's dream, copying Goya, quoting Hawthorne, sampling absurdity before the censors and publishers and advertisers and PR gurus stamp it all out and shoot the menfolk in control of the pen, the brush, the sweetheart plot frenzy, and there's lines of queues and lines of DIGNITY at Waterstones because they don't quite understand that the artist is *possessed*, not the *possessor*. See?

"Well, no... I don't, to be honest."

I say nothing and I think my face reacts with indifference but I can't be sure. (I strangely check above me for a mirror. Not there.)

"Shall I re-organise your *emmess*? It is a right mess, that MS... ahaahaaaaaha." <real kiddy giggle>

I look at all the strewn pages and paw prints and some spiders having a get-together on Chapter 9.

"Ah, it's up to you," I say and we sit there, sunnily, sillily, exchanging face game rituals like drunk cousins at a backwoods backwards dance. That scarlet colouring returns to the roofstacks and skyline and the sky pig silhouettes smatter about also at hungry play. All things feed.

I consider informing Adele about the gull lunge and fob swallow (Dan Kemp hasn't told her the full tale) but opt not to. Just doesn't seem right. She simply finishes the lemonade and ambles easy as a girlbreeze back inside where glasses chime out their well-practised songs and papers shuffle and drawers pop open shut. The radio joins in softly.

Everything feels alright, even a distant police siren and a clunking clutch. The dog's out here again now, snuffling and sniffling about at ease, at home.

"Why d'you have so much frigging Tabasco, man? There's boxes of bottles of the stuff. It's EVERYWHERE!"

I take a wineglass from her and allow my senses to fill gently.

"I like it hot," I explain casually and then, honestly, have to stop myself doing the Kemp *click* wink thing.

The afternoon eases its miscreant ways about us and not far off dusk-hour she reckons Kemp's car suddenly has to get back to Kemp and the village tonight, and London is Calling and all that so see yer later and I'll come back if you want and hope the leg gets better good luck gets better lud guk gets better *zoom*gone.

So it's me and the dog and the gull up there again, back us three, silent reverie and acceptance and melting timepiece cajolery. Jesse fucking James. Every mortal cage and key chain rattles its own tune and my cerebral orchestra clanks and churns mournfully. But, again, I feel just fine. Unbetrayed and bang-on.

I drop one more pink, crack one more Bulleit seal. This time, I strangely salute Scotland blam! then England's gorgeous little handbag itself, Wales. Britain's in me, I know it, I love it, ask my granddad, he's from bandit-Strabane. I continue this fingery-wrist notebook shuffle of resonance reasoning and down left crackpot *satori*.

Cheers, Kemp.
Cheers, the world.
Toodaloo, Reality, *wwwhhWhWHHoooooOOoooomppp!*

10

I've never told a soul about this, but a few years back I slammed a nightclub bouncer right on the jaw after he'd ejected a beautiful red-haired angel like an animal, just for being a little tipsy, and ripped her dress in half and left her in the rainy mud-sodden cobbled street squabbling about with her pride in tatters all hurt and embarrassed, but then the bouncer was too, so I immediately felt better. It was then I decided to be an artist. Or maybe it is now, this very *now* that I've decided. Yeah, it is. Or was it when I cracked a hundred in a second-class cricket game at the Oval? or when I sketched a self-portrait and it moved my mother to tears? NO. It is NOW. The dog agrees. The gull nods too, seriously, then swaggers along the apex into the future like a high-flying burrito brother keen on kismet and Californ-Aye-Hay.

Everyone's in the know, I know it. I think it. But what's the difference, Bobby Ford? Betty Ford Gabriel Byrne Sylvia Plath David Niven Calvin Klein Roger Waters Speedy Gonzalez AA Milne.

Reckon Sam Rockwell would play a good ME in the BESTSELLER adaptation for HollyWool-over-their-eyes. Intern Adele mentioned rights or somesuch (*Rights of Man* Lewesian Tom Paine in the ass), which means a movie, thinks I, so yeah, Sam Rockwell. Bit parts for the quivering Portman, Amber Heard, Ralph Macchio and Sting (*Rights of Man*. Know your rights, Man. What fucking rights?).

I once shared pizza with the Fonz.
    Played piano next to Elton John.
    Used Ted Heath's toilet.
    Got tip-wet at the Proms.

(Hey, so what? you're still a nobody. You don't know the market, how's yer piles, remember? Just WHO ARE YOU, huh?)

Malaysia, China, they all still hold their heads and extricate all their own hearts in agony and wretched loss and utter disaster.

Morally bankrupt MPs still slinging rhetoric about like public-school sepias intent on sitting still, devoted to The Middle, overjoyed at the price of milk.

War marionettes dangle.

Thieves flee.

Footsteps peter.

Whosoever dances a two-step, desperate to impress, disparate in classic sportswear, yet whistling beardy nu-folk songs to prove just how cool.

Shall I just grab this opportunity and run with it? What about Adele, my fresh young sweet little Norway pink-petal wet, there could be a love story in this, dying to get out, to blossom, you know, FLORA and FAUNA and don't forget to put your roses to bed.

The re-organised *emmess* sits ragged and pretty atop the living-room table now, paw prints, dog ears and all. Reborn.

My mobile skips and hums its key-of-C ramble and it's *Dan* fucking *Kemp* flashing up on the screen. I let it ring out. I'm a bit numb. I get back to some Bulleit action and shoot some strange relief down my nobody throat and my ticker gets back to clicker heaven and my thinkers back to kick back, feet up, beautiful Calypso-if-you-can.

A celebratory BOOMBOOM inside this pot leg suddenly, as if it has mended early and is ready to hot-step of its own accord. I'll leave it in its prison just the same. I'll attend the hospital MRI. I'll get in line, tick the box ✓

You know, for me, to tell you the truth, I mean, like, do you know what, to be honest, like, well, kind of, in my opinion, yeah... no; blah de CENTRAL bastard blah.

This March is just about over, placard ink is fast fading, masquerading as brute.

(What you saying?)
    (Shut it, dog, you're just a dog, I love you, dog.)
    (Therein lies plot. Stir it up and see.)

Kemp's calling again. Adele must be in London by now, surely. I let it ring out.

FUEGO *blam* to the *blam*blamma... .dot. There's melody in all things, not just the covers, taste it, I swear!

I need for nothing yet still I'm on the verge of selling out. Relax...

Mother... Father... will you forgive me?
    Please will you? could you? would you *like* to?

Follow your heart, son. Trust your vitals.

There's a gentle little *raprap* at the front door, a familiar recent code. It's pitch black out there, peach black peal time ah whoom ah whee... and I let her in, my sweet little nu-found engine tickling over, purring... developing, about to lunge... just who, who am I?

PART 2: LEISURELY MOVING WITHOUT HASTE

(rome)

11

Just imagine if the truth wasn't so hideous. Then look around.

I stepped out the shadows, all naked, shiny and keen. She just stared and blushed and stared and I swear one of those two little untilled mushroom cups swelled or pulsed or primed itself at me. I got hold of her and saved her right there whether she wanted saving or not. Mine instantly.

Easy, my mouth went off everywhere, tasting and gushing, and isn't it always like this?

Her lightness soon darkened and sleep and sweat took over, the swelter of Italian night plundering through the old windows with the centuries of spent dreams and deaths. I left her twined solo like rope and rinsed myself down next door where the taps whistled and the crumbling walls winked.

The moon was high out there. The faint crackle of the river a constant reminder that life goes on, no matter what, and however hard you try convincing yourself you've made it, you are never in charge, and never will be. So don't even think it. Something far larger is at the helm and Christ only knows if we're all heading down the right path or up the wrong river, and Christ is only *Queequeg* anyway, harpooning the eyes in mirrors the world over. The hunt is on, but it really is lunacy. *Time will tell*, but can you ever really trust *time*? I have once before, and that's just brought me here; damn nearly lost nearly damn.

I saluted the real glory of the mischief of the stars and crept back into that hot heaving twist of youth and shut-eye wine and wet why not, we're miles from home. Don't know her name, hardly ever do, but this one now so small and soft as a damp mouse that I could just crush to bits. I felt that first tear on its way but soon drifted off, helpless to the fools.

"Trumpet Man," she called me, giggling.

"I play the horn," I corrected her, then slipped her out the door. A snatch of a kiss and a sketch of *Sayonara Jack and the Goodbye Girls*, all she gets.

That strange, simple, stunning novel I finished yesterday sits bedside, in a weird kind of loll; it's done its work on me. I can tell. *Dear Father, dear Mother, harps & wolves*, all that spontaneity is provoking me into, well, I don't know what... has anybody else seriously been moved so much by one small thing... EVER?

I cracked the veranda wide open and that was it, another unbearably young standard done and there she goes, the prep-school rise and fall long gone, just a shuffle now and a sliver of hope, maybe happy, maybe not, and the supple Rome morning rubbed her out at the bridge.

Up to the border for me today, the festival, where things can really swing. I packed my stuff slowly and stoppered some wine from the communal vat. My pulse was up to something silly but off I went, perhaps carefree, most likely careless... <pause... pause on the exit stairs a little more...> I went back in and jammed the novel into a tight pocket. The author's face on the back cover creased and winked and grinned.

The noon train trucked along... Cava, karma, Cannery Row... Cava, karma, Cannery Row... to a beat, a rhythm. Some soldiers and sailors climbed aboard, played cards and joked quietly. Epaulettes danced.

Drinks and ideas and books were snapped away shut, to headphone-hide, sunglass-shame, the beat most civilians naturally tap, and think it a winsome whirr.

Do *civilians* actually exist?

The train lumbered uphill now and round the bends, busting, busting to get us there.

12

Trieste, that's when things turned lucid. *Lucid,* that's what real writers use when they're expressing depth and clarity and their perceptive coolness. I mean all loose and acidy as if I were a stretch of water looping around, swallowing up the tripping masses and life. I'll think up a new word for it before long.

Colours were all vital and the air fizzed with fishing toil and dusk looped around madly now, not me, I was sitting, folded, calm.

Glad I was here, even though the wine was gone.

I studied the boys down on the quayside scrambling about with ropes and orders with nothing but shorts on. They were the happiest little cretins I'd ever seen. Seabirds snapped away and fork lifts cranked along, busy. All knew their jobs: the captains, those sad fish and scraggly nets, everyone and everything, machinery. I wanted to be one of them, any one of those damn idiots doing their shift tonight, knowing their roles. I am here, my instrument and me. The only thing I have ever loved and held with true joy. Is this my role? I know it gets me vast sums of pay when I blow and spit into it and smile at the gawping faces and go *whoosh* with the form like I can. But can't I just sweep the scum from the holding pots tonight, or drive that truck and really sweat? Just once. I'd probably hate it, but I may find something else to properly love and start steering again, like I'm sure I once did. Let me try, at least.

I grabbed it out my case, stood and hurled the blasted thing with the built-up conniving power and surge of decades behind me and in me and off it sailed, a brass-bronze beautiful arc to a velvet slap and wet. Gone. And the tears came but a strange magic immediately got hold of me, gripped me tight, and walloped me up, and I suddenly felt *whizzing* high, then and there, up where I haven't been in years. It was serious head-tilt and body-surrender... just exhilarating.

I pranced along to the hotel with just my tiny case now and took a bottle up to the room via kindness from the front desk. The rest of the band were already gathered in the foyer, bleating the same old pre-gig notes that truly dampen the fire. They always arrive before me. I scooted past like a thief and got into the ruby quick as that.

The balcony was surprisingly bright and cool. Ten-ish. The threat of night.

Work-weary boats groaned and moaned their aches down there and the men and boys collected their wages and scuttled off every which way like jostling happy blood through thirsty old veins. I could see their homes in the back streets, tiny and lovely. Honest food and kisses off the family.

The sprawling warmth of the city hummed with this reality all over, pulsing right up to the piazza where I could see the festival fitters busy with scaffold and canvas. Humming and tender, then clatter and ugly coming together like war.

Christ, *Queequeg*, I'm suddenly not well. I can hear the paper whine and the ink howl and I can't wait to see their faces when I tell them about my piece. It's probably in Cairo by now, bent and smeared in the souks.

My head booms daft. My thinking's not right... I am suddenly not well.

I busy myself sketching *Peeper Stanley and the Clapper-less Bells* and the rest of the ruby helps. The night goes on and on without me, that high moon even higher, and the sneer of my helmsman etched in the stars.

Forget it.

A new day. My head heaved a bit, but it was miles from brutal, that brutal *mmmddddhha mmmddddhhuuurr* of morning after. It was more frraaaahhh frraaaahhh and something in between breaths like *kkhhree!*

I recalled bits about the train and the fish and fork lifts but I dared not read my notes, so I sloped out onto the balcony and sucked it all up as best I could.

All crisp and quiet. Saturday, June, no, July. Oh, the festival. Wonder what went down. *Oh, man!* I've never no-showed before.

The morning blues bleached across to wary ochre and those retarded boats smiled. There was a *crack, crack* of lap on the hulls and small harbour moorings, and the fed-up seabirds picked and pecked at anything, though swill-bellied still from the scraps and mulch of last night's pay-off.

Salt and hope dappled the air. A conniving sense of happening.

I wonder who else has seen this, thought this, been here and rubbed this handrail, awaiting that spastic stab of a wood splinter, that *zat!* of pain and realisation.

It'd be straightforward to be in your own right mind; where's the mystery and the gamble in that? Finally... I'm thinking like I used to.

I like it here. None of the true city choke. A constant tickle of breeze, pastels and gentle flesh and all those blues galore, inviting as virgins' veins and throats. None of this here has collared me before; I have been here before, yes, definitely, but it's all just whizzed on by, giddy with the autographs.

This beginning has me fresh.

I'm asking... what now?

Next room's bed suddenly *rat-tatted* away on the walls like a sickness so I *bra-brapped* back with my fist and heard...

"*...ah, Va Fangoo!*"

It strangely made me deliriously happy.

I ordered up more ruby and stared out, way out, laughed a bit, guttural, sly maybe, and in flashes thought about that latest blush in my bed back in the city. Don't know her name, hardly ever do. But something had a hold on me from inside out. Like the pulse of these back streets, real and fierce, and full.

Reckon I was starting to make sense. But out of what, only the magic of the vastness knows. Or Christ. Or *Quee... hah*, I laughed some more, like a ridiculous lamp, and I hadn't said *lamp* in years. I hollered it out loud over and over, *Lamp, lamp, maybe I'm new light, maybe I'm free...*

Then it was all *ratta-tat-aaaahhhh, RAT-ATAT-AAAHHHH-WWWhooooaaahhh!* through the walls from next door and it's pathetic and hilarious.

Sketched out *Officer Blonde and the Bed Plugs* and before long that fine ruby was oozing on down and I was alone and happy as this gloopy carafe.

I licked it out.

She, her, that one pulsing cup and that youth back in my loopy Roman bed had started this beginning here, my *satori* unleashed, so a love story must have started smearing its mushy, quivering, roomy-sick lips all-me-over.

Another get-in-line lunatic with a love story; hideousness, I realise, but it's the truth, blind eyes and deaf tongues, suck-sucking at the senses until the silent inner roar gets busy at the veins and strings, dying to let go, dying to SOAR! so tell me, what am I meant to do?

13

I took to the calm golden streets, ready for the next novel bit.

This is the loveliest story I've ever told or heard, I swear.

(Quickfast sudden check of *Light & Dark* portside pocket, and then agreeance maybe THIS is the actual loveliest, mmm...)

Agreed, my head's been like trapped mice lately. Then utterly numb. Then back to the riot. And so on. But now I feel sincerely new, truly delicious.

The cobblestone café gobbled me up and I settled down outside, everything the colour of decent fudge, and chinaware and glasses rattled out their songs. Defined bodies moved in and out like the finest oil. The ruby came. All this cadence and my new me and it's *Buongiorno, my masters, show me it all, all you've got, are you mad? thrust it on me,* and I decide to write for twelve nights, see what surfaces and see if I can make it.

Then she came gliding right up to me, sunglasses, beaming, and just brio.

"Didn't think you'd turn up," she said.

"Well... neither, I don't think... hi, how are you?" tripped out my lips... *easy, go easy, be calm...*

Another glass appeared on the table and we were there, right here, and this was actually happening. My heart heaved, all my insides swung and yeah, I was alright, but *Queest* alive.

I stared and she stared and blushed and I could taste her. Now I needed some answers.

I needed the real deal... the **hideous** truth.

That smile was the same. The blush too. Definitely her.

"Don't look so damn confused, Trumpet Man," she said. "It doesn't suit you."

I sipped at the ruby and my memory is getting worse but I reckon she winked or something because I felt disarmed, very much like a child, but *she's* the child, just look at her!

Meet me Saturday, the café on the cobbles, Trieste, and she has.

"Knew you'd be here," I lied.

"How come you didn't play last night at the fest?"

"I've lost my horn."

"Lost your horn?"

"Well, tossed my horn actually."

"...mmm, I see..." and her refined little eyebrows skipped now.

I took a long, true breath.

The world and each one of her sumptuous purling waterways calmed to a tiny ripple, like the first and last kiss of ALL life.

Now tell me... who's acting helmsman now, huh?

We are here, *saved*, *hideous*, maybe neither, maybe both, and I like the feel of this quasi-*enlightenment* very much.

Reckon she does too.

And I sketch utterly nothing at all, think nothing lewd, draw zero glib seer conclusions, just rock back in my chair, right here and now, allow all my senses to fill, sweet and easy, and out of another mad timely magical place some gentle Mahler trickles perfect, like the sun, like expensive oil, like the *Perfetto Cattura*.

Just imagine.

14

I mumbled some *fumble*talk but something was swelling in me and around me and then suddenly, strangely, I needed to sluice and get rid again and fast-purge.

And the gates de-latched wide, wide open...

I regaled all about the quayside last night and my feelings, how it all welled up in me as I discarded my lifetime's only joy. I told her about the other recent bouts of weeping and the feeling of being utterly alone but without any peace whatsoever. I told her about all this in such pitiable colour that it all sounded shocking and brilliant, hardly anything in between. All a very pleasant experience for me, as speaking anywhere near like this was something which hadn't tickled my buds nor rasped through my malady valves in years now. Liberating and just bang-on.

She listened and turned her head gently every now and again as if allowing all my words to run through her dark blonde curls evenly.

Locals floated in and around the place, knowing exactly where they were going and timing casual tardy to perfection. Tourists squinted and got in the way. The sun was up and at it, and just above the mass of old cobblestones, a haze climbed lazily like forgotten ivy.

The words came spilling out, on and on, so I let them. More wine came and everything was OK.

"What is your name?" I finally stopped to ask.

"Celine," she answered. "Celine Faurlain. I'm nearly twenty-one and from *haute couture* Paris... ring any bells?"

"Notre-*damn*! Of course I remember," and then I thought, *how could I lie to her now?* "Actually, I didn't remember, no. But now I shan't forget."

"Well, that's nice."

Some klutz three shops down dropped a glass and a few scooters skidded and hollered abuse. I immediately thought about the band and how I'd let them down. They'd be scuttling off to Venice by now for the Ska-Jazz with half the Republics. I did *not* want to be there.

I wanted this *here*.

Weird.

"So you quit the band, then?"

"Yeah, I suppose I did."

"What you going to do now?"

And I took my time, watched the waiters down under the canopies and redwhite parapets, whatever they are called, sweeping and arguing the spilt glass away. All the scooters had disappeared and then I saw him... one of those happy little wretches working the incoming boats down the quayside last night. Still just a pair of shorts on, thirteen or fourteen and dirty skin and bones, rasping away at my horn. My old joy. My gone piece. Trying, trying to get a tune out of it, but getting nothing but cawing hell.

We'd both spotted him. We laughed together. This lad skipping along, rasping and *vvrraarraaackking* and *bbbbwwwaaaing* and Celine and me laughing. Far side of the cobbles off he skipped, sounding out those *hhwwwaarrps*. Disgusting and awesome.

I got back to her, there at the table, here, that skin, honey, and the complexion of wild daffodil and gems for teeth.

"You are a comely little thing," I finally said. "And I'm nearly forty."

"I know both those things," she replied, eyes half-closed, pleased indeed.

"Who are you, Celine Faurlain? Just *who* are you?"

"I am *seulement une fille*, only a girl, here for you. We are both miles from home, exactly where we should be. At this table, me and you. Right here."

"*Queest!*" I said. "We've only had a night together and you know this so definitely?"

"Actually, it's two nights," she purred. "One at the Arras Blues a couple of years ago or so, and the other night at yours." She casually waggled two caramel fingers in the air, then quietly applied lip balm. I got a vision of me pawing at her, playing on her, tickling and exploring until she came again and again, the tiny little thing.

"At this very moment," I said, "I am extraordinarily full of new joy. And you, this beautiful baby flower, who doesn't know me, and I am happy like this! Why? I am a child again, I feel truly free, but where have I been all this time and where am I headed? I need these answers desperately, yet I feel so much joy. How, and why?"

Blithe as this constant sun, she took a sip and simply said, "We'll figure it out," and that was it. She was rather delighted with this and I reckon I was too.

Then the most hideous of howls rose up out of a horn from near enough under our noses and that little cretin held out a grubby hand for a euro or two.

Ridiculous. We barely believed it.

I dug out a note, a ten, gave it to the boy, and Celine Faurlain roared with such delight the table and chair creaked, about to buckle. A waiter appeared and shooed the lad away like he would a vermin pigeon and left some bread and olives for us, all in a single swish.

Something was in the air alright. And there went my horn again, whistling badly through the backstreets, scolded and true.

It was all a sordid brand of particular insanity and we both knew it. Don't suppose any single other speck in the entire world recognised this, but for us two, it was pure sass, fateful, perfect, right here, and we loved it.

The afternoon took a breath and exhaled some crippling heat. We ventured inside the café for some respite.

15

"So what's all this about, then?" She slowly unfolded a scrap of paper and tossed the sketch of *Sayonara Jack and the Goodbye Girls* onto the table. The air-conditioning vent made them all come alive and ripple.

"Just dumb sketches," I explained, offering her my notebook, and she swept it up, fair enough, and pitter-patted those lissom eyes along the words and curves in there. That impossible skin and the lips of sea-sky. That shape and hair and neck. And...

"...ahhup... mushroom cups... the moon... karma..." she whispered out.

I snorted a small sarcastic thing and got into the ruby some more. A ton of giggles came out of her, a simplistic wheeze for sure. Considered saying something about fate and destiny but didn't dare tempt *Queequeg* in there to smash us and this sparkling place into bloody stinking steam and mess.

"Love it," she went, "love it all," and ordered up champagne now, that irresistible French pink tongue twisting Italiano, lulling and lulling in that mouth like a curse.

Done for...

"Control, *lah-dee-dah*, why do you need to know who's in control anyway?" Her voice was a little cool stream over a day's hot rocks. "Just get on and let it ride. You have it made anyway, with your music, surely?"

I told her yeah, for money I'd be **OK** for a while to come. But I was after what the **O** and the **K** actually stood for. And who decides if you get them.

She threw a load of *O*'s and *K*'s out there and we cackled a bit, like giddy kids on a rickety bridge, *ooh, ooh, I dare yer, I dare yer*, but then she goes, "...maybe I'm here to make sure you get there. Maybe for you, *I* am in control." Again, she seemed completely impressed at her own trickle and discourse and the confidence got me pulsing daft. "I mean, here I am, cultured and marvellous," she continued, "and here you are, just setting off on your new journey, your new life. Of course there's magic involved, and decisions you are not used to making, but it is simple, *c'est tout*,

facile, easy. And you must get hold of me and off we will go...
OK?"

I swear this is how it all leaked into life. I scribbled away like a madman during her trips to the backroom just in case I forgot. My imagery and ideas crass and daft were streaming in my head and across my internal movie-screen flicker ticker-tape. This notebook getting near full; enough space, though, for a quick *Chet Black and the Gutless Brawl*, not knowing what in the hallway it's still all about. But, oh man, I was now *up* for whatever it is. Everything so damn fast...

hoo-der-babaddaah-Hoooot!

Back she came and I got hold of her and kissed her full and loose and heavy as this whole day. We came apart and cared nil for the absolute everything else swimming around us.

I witnessed myself unravel like chain and find my chair, just.

All new to me.

"I may need *saving* again today," she jibed. That tender blush tickled at her cheeks, then dissolved back out of there in a blink. The looping tripping masses were back gulping everything down in blues and sparkling lights, making the edges of bottles and cutlery fizz with electricity, ready to blow. "Hey! My sister's getting married to a writer, you know," she went on. "Yeah, Élodie, engaged she is to a novelist or an author or something. Maybe he can help with your new adventure *notebook* thing, get it published and let it flourish perhaps..."

"What... this stuff?" I asked, waggling this thing about. "Who'd wanna read this?" & I swear every man Jack about this place, this land, this country, all its breathing pulsing waterway doctors birdmen hothouse flowers & *fishermen*, the LOT, well they all raised their dandy hands and chuckled. It was good. (*I hope someone's writing all this down*, I thought, then I wrote all of it down and felt like a true sensationalist just like that other *LUCA* feller in *The Restlessness of Virtue (Light & Dark)*, and considered being a sell-out best-seller (again) just like the others, and pat-patted the bloody sweet *ENLIGHTENMENT* novel in my jeans pocket, *there there, rest awhile, I'll see you in a bit.*)

Somehow, through all the madness and careless heat, we got back to the hotel in fragments of the chiming church, and the rest of the daylight, with the sheets in knots and the fans on full, had us throbbing and intense, devouring like dogs.

16

Lying. Sweating and finally thoughtless. It could be death.

"Is this death?" I eventually mutter and darkness swills in.

I got the shower cleaning all the sex and slumber off me and reminded myself to check my notes, see what had gone down.

She had upped and left, still the night, her outline left in the bed hollowed out by the prying moon.

It was relief or sadness or maybe even death that had me agog now, wasn't sure. I knocked the fans off and sailed out onto the balcony for some natural breeze and there it was, kindly sighing in from the idling harbour.

I wrote *JAZZ (brackets (the only thing that's ever moved me) and BLUES)*, then crossed it all out and listened out over the town for a lamenting horn.

Sweet silence. When all I had ever revelled in before was <NOISE>.

I turned a few pages and, yes, she'd drawn her very own *Celly F and the Bulbous Cups*.

"Love..." I said out loud and felt fully weird so quickly added, "*love-ly*, that's what I said."

Out there was partly green and blue and blue-black. The sky and sea were planning stuff, clearly dark. June, no... July, HELL! It could be September out there for all I care! I could see animal haunches and teeth yet maybe even some of that other-world stuff: hope.

A lizard or some such other beast made a long scratchy call like a slowly snapping branch and it sprung me awake. I searched for it. In the corners of the room, in my tiny case, under the bed. No joy.

Queest! it's daylight again.

That little beast again *ccraaaahhhkkk* and it's at the door, behind it, I slung it open and there he was. A green gorgeous little thing, yeah, a lizard I reckon, his heart going *pump pump* and looking all lonesome. Just still like that on the floor, staring up at me, really quite effortless and at peace actually. I instinctively tossed him some leftover pizza crusts and he climbed up on them like they were a podium, proud as hell, biting not a morsel. It was intoxicating.

Then *swooooommpph!* the display gone, at the ugly rush of an old broom, and the porter going, "Filthy animals," and, "Need any lunch? It's noon."

I could have *Quee*-damn broken down right there and then, with nothing but shorts on.

I looked up the hallway for a sign of lizard-skin life or crust or crumbs at least, but the whole lot just gone like that. His poor little pumping heart.

"Wine," I said, burning. "Just bring me some wine," and shut the door on the sheer ghastliness of the whole scene and that bastard porter's cold horrible face.

I would normally think up a classic and blow and blow for an hour when I felt like that, but I didn't feel that urge at all. No horn anyway. I didn't mind.

Got back into bed and studied over the *Bulbous Cups* and my mood improved smartly.

The wine came.

No tip.

Ultra-different things were moving me now. Different forms and childishness. As if I weren't mid-life but a teen who hadn't come of age, who hadn't moved over to seriousness and responsibility. Crisis? What crisis?

And the ruby was back up and down like a fine horseman in fine silks, the mare under him flexing and eating up the ground in a fervour. (I attempted a little horse drawing but quickly scribbled it out and laughed.)

After a quick pocket-novel flick-through, yep, still the same restless magic... my insides were humming just nice, so I ordered up some more fuel with today's paper, maybe sneak a glance at last night's write-up, see how the band got on.

The thing that was hunkered down behind my eyes somewhere was: *How can I be so removed from something that has been so ultimately vital to me for so long?*

I rubbed them a bit, my eyes, but the mirror just shot back veiny threads. Least the rest of my face sparkled like renaissance, so, contemptuous of death, I slapped at the reflection, giddy as a loon.

That's a few nights done of the twelve I've set out to scribe.

Leisurely moving without haste, I'll call it. That just fell out of this pen, and *Queest* what a pen! Just a throw-away but it is dear to me till it runs out, then merely rubbish.

Who's going to type all this rubbish for me? Why don't I have anything electrical?

Then a blast of unadulterated biliousness and I threw up massively and got the shower head busy on clean-up. With thanks, it all disappeared down the drain. Then I felt fine.

What was it? ...*Leisurely moving without haste*? Ah, yes.

I had to get out. That damn hotel. So I did, my case and me, all last-glancing down the halls and in the nooks for that beaten-down pumping animal heart. No joy ever, any more, for that feckless skin.

"Your paper, sir... your paper..." ignored.

I wondered if I was due a mass sweeping and crushing sometime soon, so I drifted into the Beausejour for a livener.

Yeah, somehow, Celine Faurlain's here.

17

We said nothing at all and remained tables apart. For ages actually and it felt like it should be in a book, a novel, a Conrad, or an overtly proud Brontë for the old skin dreamers.

She had a burning white T-shirt on with *BLONDIE* all across it and I saw the Small Faces smashing up Clem Burke's drum kit.

My tired feet in tired shoes rested atop my case and I probably looked just like a dreamless hobo. My imagery finagled through the shallow and tawdry on to Marriott and adding my own horn section to *The Universal* and I coughed out, "...What horn?" and that made her smile, I saw it.

The juice got busy playing havoc with my lust switch so I tempered the she-bang by stepping up and sliding into the majors and digging up some starved miners of the piano, which seemed to stop the waitresses and the wide wide side-streets in their timeless tracks.

I tapped and tickled out whatever wanted it and a crowd came in, crawled up to my back-side like cowards, and awaited an ending that would never come.

The lid smashed down and I crashed on out of there without settling up, smiles turning to sneers, but I liked the feeling of my case bashing into knees and thighs. What a show. I got to the quayside and lay on my elbows to watch nothing at all but the sea. Quick as that.

It licked and occasionally growled.

Seabirds flecked in and out, perverting justice of course, cawing harsh, and exacting common assault at will.

Those bastards.

That hotel porter bastard.

What are their journeys?

"Wow," she said and plonked her case next to mine. "Some exit."

And all I could think to say was: "You ain't seen shit."

Her faultless skin was hers and we were here again.

"Just us two and our bags."

"Just us."

And we both watched the sea slurping now and the odd boat putter past.

"Everything moves," I said.

Then nothing... nothing... till, "I paid your bill at the Beausejour."

So I said, "Cheers."

"You know your name?"

"Mmm, yeah."

"In English, it's nearly *Ceiling Falling*."

"...OK..."

"Not sure what I mean about that."

"Right."

<PAUSE...>

"Say, fancy going to Spain?"

She hovered a second on the idea. Then, gay and fleeting as one of these connivery salt-birds, said, "Absolutely." So we got on the boat for Barcelona and that was Italy over in a hot breath and a *snap-snap* of her heels.

"Bet you didn't pay my hotel bill."

"Nah," she replied.

18

Some of those soldiers and sailors from the train now sucked on tall beers and played the fruit machines on the rumbling ferry.

"Mustn't get enough gambling done whilst on duty," I quipped, yet strangely willed them to win jackpots and maybe get undercharged at the overpriced bar. Better still, I paid a round for them all, discreetly, but just loud enough for Celine Faurlain to hear.

She threw me a blasé look and fiddled with her pocketbook mirror.

We secured an overnight cabin and every single man alive seemed to be staggering the narrow passageways and chattering like they only had this one night to tell each other and the old bulkheads all their limp secrets.

"Sometimes things are best left unsaid," I said. "Why do people feel they have to talk so damn much?"

She just nodded and slipped out of her dress and that sailing smudged out in a hot soft hungry blur.

Boats and crests and on and offs. Where does it all end? Whose port is calling, and why?

We disembarked and *The Others* drifted opposite, against our tide, legs swish-swishing with bags and some were drunk and crestfallen. We are here in Spain and these are all back to Italy or lined up to hit rocks and sink down, down into the fettered unctuous depths where it all began.

Barcelona loomed up on us like a mighty spirit. Enchanting and frankly full of spooky.

Bad buzzards hustle everywhere but the joy is in the tongue rolling, "Bar-*tha*-lona," and recognising the odd place from years past spent wound right up and funless busy.

I've played in there. And there. It's all a lifetime ago and I kissed Celine Faurlain on the Diagonal like administering a rare stamp on a gaudy postcard where no one lids an eye-bat at such louche.

We scurried our feet and cases round and in the side of Miguel's for ruby welcomes and dusty seats inside.

She spoke pretty good *Cat* too, so we swip-swapped lingos like haphazards ablaze with abandon. Sounds crass, I realise, but hey, needs must. And we were somehow *free*.

A kid, just a kid, came up for an autograph. Obliged, naturally, but then recoiled as he scampered off because *she* was sitting right here, watching. It seemed ridiculous.

That smile spread across her face, though, and I recovered quick as a sluicing conman.

The juice came, some tapas, hardly a murmur between us and I think I loved her.

"Is this *love*?" I asked, straight up.

"Well, we've only known each other *one* night," she mocked.

"We'll always have Arras," I said back. I spotted a stand-up piano, an old boutique, in the corner but refrained like a bad poet in a puddle of free fun.

"You are scribbling an *awful* lot in those books there."

"So very true," I answered and skipped an olive off the table-top into her lap. She picked it out and popped it into her mouth, brazen as a bullwhip.

"Behaviour," I commented cheerily.

She smirked and chewed and spat like an untouched whore in a fake church dress.

"Who's a whore?" she quizzed, stretching to read these overcooked notes.

"Me probably... I love you."

And this is hard to take but she started to cry, silently, otherworldly, sipping away, crying and faceless now, sipping and beautiful.

She is new *MUSIC*

She is *MINE*

I wrote.

And for some other reason added

ONLY

and got it going down my wanton throat before I broke down too.

WE ARE HERE <ARROW TOWARDS>

I'm ugly. I'm old. I'm quite senseless. She is ALL I'm not. Yet I've got her and this thing has us glued up and I want to sit here, Miguel's, for years and... another autograph, I forget the big following here in the *'lunya*.

I had to ask her: "Where do you have to be?"

"Where do I have to be?"

"Yeah."

"Nowhere."

"What about university, or your job, or your *life*?"

"It is all here, in these hands, right here..." and she cupped them, her soft long hands, and gathered some of the local ether, rattling it around like a mad alchemist's shuffle, and then *poofhh!* blew it all up with a gesture of letting go a balloon. Then she just took a drink and it slithered down gorgeous.

Her golden neck jigged.

"So you don't have a job?"

"No," she answered. "Do you?"

"No." I tried to slither it down the same but it got stuck. I coughed and swallowed hard. "Not any more."

"Good," she said and suddenly I knew she was something special. And *shot* rich.

"So you just go around Europe making musicians lose their minds?"

"Only one."

"What, never before?"

"Nah."

More tapas came, lovely old recipe vegetables and oil and cheese. Fresh herbs and lots of garlic and I got the cascabel chillies clicking in their passion.

She hummed along to the bar music, a gentle Catalonian thing, fit for supermarkets and hotel receptions. I briefly considered a middle horn section but shrugged it when...

"You took my cherry," came out that mouth. "Back in France two years ago."

My frame and system and sinew bubbled like a sick mass withering.

I'm weak, weaker than that, nearly gone. But wait, now it's... I'm coming back, yeah, now... coming back, I'm back, big and surging and bristling.

Got her in Miguel's back room, not even the toilet, a sort of passageway area towards the kitchen where pans crackled and chefs swore.

It was over in seconds. *Seconds.* I mean it, 15, 20 *seconds*.

There was no tenderness or shy or prelim, just hurting fast and hot and good.

She cleaned up in the toilet and I poured back to our table, speechless, dustless, and Miguel served the wine, on and on.

Celine Faurlain, I visualised slowly, trying to negotiate and understand every little swirl and bend.

She waltzed back and nodded, mostly very suited, I thought.

I ached gladly and rose to salute some boys outside on their bikes taking photos. "Blow!" they shouted, "blow!" and clicked their handsome machines like a goofy bunch of Kerouac's Deans.

I hollered, "No!" back and gestured to Celine Faurlain as if to say, *Look, I'm busy here!* and they accepted this and melted away into the Barcelona shadows and reds.

I wondered what it was all about and the soreness and crazy somehow got me hard again.

"Let's find a place to stay," I suggested.

"There's always my cousin's," she said, eyes all a-hoot and those teeth clicking now like searing seeds in a too-hot pan. "She's right in the centre of town."

"Is she right in the head?"

"Hah! Nope."

"Let's go."

The cases groaned again and rattled along the unreal painter streets.

19

Cousin opened the old wooden door topless and she had the very same near-nippleless cups swelling at me. She was overjoyed at our arrival and her skin was the same but the hair black as night and long, real long, like an animal.

A man was sitting in the huge lounge area scoffing peanuts and Greek-looking and big, with bright clothes tattooed on. Oh so pleasant, these two, and warm as the hills and they got the spare room pillowed out comfy, all ready for us in a blur.

For surprise guests landing at their door, they were tremendously well stocked, the fridge and cupboards crammed to the hinges. Some local football crashed out the TV and I tried to recall when I last had one of those pounders switched on in the same room as me. Couldn't.

Cold beers cartwheeled down and round like a helter-skelter, a trophy parade, a gone-nuts holiday, and on a toilet visit I noticed a *Bodega* and an arrow pointing down some steps. Off I trailed, bells ringing.

A wine cellar, big as a dance-hall, old as a bullfight.

I was dreamy and bent, totally bent. They soon joined me down there and we all mangled into the racks, friends for life.

"There's an old guitar down here somewhere... yeah, here it is. Pick out a tune for us, will you?"

"*Out-a-tune* is about right," I snickered and got some manky C's and F's going like a wild prison break. I whooped and howled a bit, kicking the chair legs and knocking the guitar head on the rack stands and they got clapping and happy as cats down there, lovely and daft.

My voice was thunder but on it went, nuts as them, and those alarms rang out with the wine, oh that wine, swooping us all up.

The endless night careened on through the bones, up the feelers, and out the proxy. It was the ONLY thing that mattered. Anywhere. And we happened to be here, where it mattered... and I barked it out and got called the "craziest fuck" by all of them, like a banging chorus, and we got stripping down and dancing, glistening hot spinning tops down in that Spanish magic box.

VIVA ESPANA and the blood of bulls, VAMMOOOSH! and still in the key of the prettiest damn SEA!

And I got her, the damn cousin, fast as that, whilst the rest of Spain and the entire world slept.

20

The best way to say this is, *aah, tadahh,* and two excruciating little golden mounds this way, and two the same that way, and thank *Queest* and movement of order and ships that there was no Greek driftwood bobbing about in here as well.

"How come between you both, there's not a correctly formed breast-head?"

"Just like Grandma," one of them said and breakfast whispered us back up to what normal folks assume is *The Real World*.

Strolled on up we did, to a beat, a rhythm, and I recalled that busting bitch train, so long ago. A few days only, but years and lives ago it seemed.

Tapperdah-clat-ttyah

Tapperdah-clat-ttyah

and some blues sound out and it's me, my sounds, that old record.

The Greek smiled bone-white jewellery and *Queest* he was handsome and I'd just had his wife.

"Nice music or what?" He two-armed out for us all, flexing and preening like a myth. He shimmered like old gold.

I wanted to explain immediately, so I did.

"Us three just slept together."

"Of course," he said, flipping eggs and bouncing to the track.

I looked at the girls and they were so utterly unmoved by the entirety of all this that I simply got hold of a green kiwi smoothie thing and slaughtered it with some thick-back Spanish toast with rubbed-on garlic and tomato flesh.

I found a pen, just a throwaway like mine, and scribbled

LIFE... on it goes...

And we all bopped now, all of us, the whole world, and agreed

This is the ...

"So where are you two heading anyway?" asked the Myth, gracious as straight roads to equanimity.

"Now that is a capital question," I answered and had a kaleidoscope episode of Austens taking turns in gardens, aspects considered.

"What sort of answer do you have?" he asked.

I shimmied up from the granite top and replied, "One most fitting."

Those two cousins grinned eyeless little things and we all *knew*. Magical? Only a lot. And all those interior browns and creams began their intentions on me now, quite decently, considering. I dozily retreated to the creaseless guest pillows and crawled on in and disappeared to the other *Real World*.

Now is this Death? Answer me, hot dogs and God damn. Is this my Death? am I over, am I gone?

I've done my time, and it is curtains for me, right?

Nothing.

So I slept and slept and dreams wallowed like hanging fish, salted and scored.

The beat went on, a familiar rattle miles away now, but will it ever leave my system for good?

batatt battah fferap frappah

KCCAALLOOOOSSHHH!

My shoulders heaved at all the rolls in there and my soreness got stinking hot but I was ancient music and ended. *Queest* those cups, those *CUPS!* Am I so bad? Or am I just *found*?

I used to want it *all*, I wrote.

Now I just want *half*. This half.

"What is all that you are writing?"

"Just words," I explained. "Mainly in half."

"Ah, OK."

The coffee machine gargled its hymns and kind old mantras but that busting fridge *eeked* at the seams and with kind eyes alone the Greek knew and cracked the mighty *schloooping* door.

We both got into the gentle and pondered like calm statesmen with fresh agendas.

"Do you... I mean, have you ever, well, allowed..."

"No," he popped, "only you. Celine said you'd be together here one day, and this is it. *IT. And this is* US."

"What does that mean... US?"

His face was like mousse and far too acceptable.

"US is temporary," he proscribed. Prescribed. Perhaps both. "*YOU*, that's permanent."

The Acropolis roared.

What is going on?

"Just let it ride," he said and I swear I'd heard that before but the juice went down and down and we sang trite little folk songs together like brothers as if the barricades would come down tonight and the suffering and flaming injustices would all be quelled. No chance. So the Pernod and Metaxa appeared and that was that, harpooned, lampooned, and prone as landed rays.

21

Woke up ropey as a raggedy collar going *whelp!* but one of us got the Viña Sol going and I was quickly alright. Fruit started flashing lovely and bright and ripe as well so we all forgave our senses and eased into today's heaving mouth.

That TV machine spewed out basketball now, all slam dunks and sponsors, but the girls and me soon wafted outdoors to the early sun and the squeal of the city clattering and whistling out on the balcony.

I had a thousand things to say, but said none. They, rich and careless, lolled and slouched, tones glowing, and I snatched glances at all their expensive lines and flavours and the palpably moveable swells on offer.

"After Arras, we've been to Munich and Montreux and Galway, you realise?" one of them said. "Even some backwoods Wales-place called *Hay-on-Wye...* WHY? *Don't ask me...*" <strange little elbow-in-ribs type jokey move> "...and all you did was *blow* right past us." <Two-girl giggle time>

"Ah... OK, and...?" begged I & yes, even squirmed a bit.

"Yes. And finally, right here & **now!** you are Celine's. So, tell me, Music Man: do you **love** her?"

And this blew me away for a while in a NU-world new ME rush and a surge of swords and sashes crunching. I caught myself tap-tapping at the barbecue lid in a fretful twitch.

"Well...?" Cousin urged.

"Yes," I ultimately confirmed and they hugged.

"That's that," one of them qualified and they tossed their cigs over the balcony into the streets and hotheads below, and trotted back inside.

It's busy down there, and up there all over, this city. Built old and brash. Reds and yellows crash into stretching get-there and vendors galore hawking their wares and coffee on corners and the burn. Sun looping up and ready for hot gush and the tight streets already sizzling and neighbours barking at one another with such flint, it's no wonder the place stays in flames.

Mad gorgeous Barcelona, pumping like that little heart, let no bastard sweep you away, for me you are *Knee Dead*

Bent Silly

Needed

and I trailed back indoors too, enough suffocating hot hoolah for now.

They were all eyes deep into electricity, cheering and picking at melons and pips and flesh.

Greek cooked up some steaks now (forever kitchen-preparing, this one), busy away and somehow cool as blue. I writhed at the girls, four cups, the glory, and sneaked off and got rid solo like loose thread. Guilt used to then swarm up on me like a horrible fog, but not now, doors open, it mattered not, so I took a snooze.

Soreness teasing me bad, and good.

Woke up again and again and everything stood still, silent. Silent as rags.

"You want a fork?"

Pause the stillness...

"Oh yeah, please," clacked out my auto-lips.

He sat down on the bed. "You know, I've had a history too, you know?"

"Right," I said. "You know you've overdone the *you knows*... you know...?"

"Oh yeah... funny."

Little strips of meat and fine fresh salad with rock salt.

He told me about Laos and Eastern Russia like a madman in charge of booming magnets and oh, what a thing rolled out of him, it was beauty and sparks and passion and it went on and on, not missing a *click*.

I chewed that steak down and it was gone glory and I think back to it now, that plate of pink twisting animal and green leaves, and whimper.

"Who is Celine Faurlain?" I asked him, seriously.

"She's *Celine*," insouianced back to me.

"She's *Celine*..." I mimicked, "and does that mean *crazy*?"

"Oh yes." He sucked at some ruby... "Ooooah yes."

I said nil but thought *All right then* and sketched out *EV Love and the Blazing Lamps* right in front of him and the wine now, and then the *bodega*, the lot of us scorched and branded and I thank the systems it's just me and the mounds in here again now, resting, looning, legs and bends and tidy heat, with no Greekness. Gracias, merci mercy, Ευχαριστώ,

and the fools in the dreamery then lured me back into their unthinkable chaos. The actual *Real World*. Where every whole little bit exists and sweeps and plunders and sincerely helps.

I'm learning truths and learning them fast, and I'm *OK*.

22

Another Spanish morning soon had its cape and bull-rag about me but I snapped out of it and found a bar on the corner, just steps away, but definitely out of all that lusty meld for at least a breather. I had to think. Is this true? And is this hideous?

I had to have a look around.

True... yes. But hideous...? More like silly, maybe even sublime. A definite change, and a change for the good.

I am here now and a few smoking craggy locals spying on me from behind their coffees and plumes.

Just a face, but this new life in it has them misconcluding my relevance.

You don't know me. You recognise something, but you don't *know* me.

Queest, I don't know me yet, but I'm starting to truly learn, I reckon.

Flicked through a newspaper and spotted the band would be here next week. Then I checked the date on the paper and it's a month since at least and, yes, I'd been part of the gig. Just down the road here. I remember the warm-up band got booed and bottled. But we made it swing, I swear, and all was grand, yeah, it's coming back to me now.

Got the barman to frighten a couple of coffee beans with 'buca, then cordially ordered another as Celine Faurlain came floating in on a warm breeze and all those crags choked.

"How do you do it? Just appear like that?" I asked, casual as I could.

"Some sort of magic, I guess," and we got into it all again.

It felt good.

Turned out she didn't catch our gig round the corner, she was busy back in Paris at the time. But Cousin and the Acropolis did, said it was a pitiful night.

"But we played a blinding set," I assured her, "yeah, definitely."

"You may well have done," she said. "They were busy at the hospital most of the night helping fix up the opening band... his brother nearly died... think he plays drums."

"Ah, hmmm..." was all I could muster. Then I pondered over the providence of the circumstance and the meaning of it all. And got nowhere.

"I know stuff about you, background and what-have-you."

"Oh yeah?" I asked. "How?"

"Internet and all that."

And off she went, rattling through my life, a lot of which I had to second-guess myself, then concede it was all true.

Chet and Davis and the Beats, the igniters, naturally. The solo and experimental bits, the touring, movie spin, Dizzy, that Paris project, all the funk.

"But that's not *you*, is it?" she stated, in a question. "*THIS* is you," and she pressed gently at my chest... "and now *THIS* is you..." and she pressed at her own.

I tried to say nothing but probably said *Wow* or *Phaa* or the lurid both.

She was gloopy and the truth. I knew it.

"What's the deal with your cousin back in there, then?" I asked.

"What do you mean?"

"What do I mean? Well, the last few nights and days of, well, sweat and sweet frenzy, and all the food and the Greek and his bodega, me and you two girls... maybe *that*?"

"Ah, that. Yeah, it's cool." And she shrugged.

Cool. What the fuck is COOL?

I slotted a 'buca. And studied her lines all over again. Slowly.

"We'll have to try it sober," Celine Faurlain proffered, grinning away.

"Maybe not," I concluded and off we sailed again, to feel the daggers and primes of this magical place.

Spirited away, spooled in, by beautiful oblique, siroccos and chimes, no question.

Barcelona gulped us up and my new word for *lucid* came out

was boRne

got boRn

...and the Ceiling of the world started Falling all over the lot of us.

3a or 4th or 5teenth day here and my mind is tumbling giddy as bugs and it worries me about the twelve nights thing. Can't keep up. And her face here is like lake-water in a dream and another unbearable dress paper-thin and perfect.

Looped and looned, I had a hankering for nothing at all. Not the band. Not the music, *my* Rome, the cities and towns and touring, my life. None of it. Here *I* be, right here, now, and I tried the cupped air trick, rattling around, letting go the balloon, feeling spot-on, and we danced effortlessly, to nothing, no sounds, just the occasional gust and odd glance.

All the old walls and shutters and bits outside were quickly ablaze again, making everything sear, so we cooled off by some pretty fountains and whinnied and shook like old stable-mates after pushed-out gallops. Considered trying to sketch another horse. Didn't dare.

Queest, what is all this? What have I been writing? Yeah, life, it goes on, but what life? What of this new me? So many damn questions, probably not enough sluicing time.

These two words are out, children, now that is for sure:

Truth. & *Steerage.*

Everything was moving and we decided to head for Paris.

"Lovely," one of us said.

"Lovely."

Leisurely moving without haste, a few nights left without doubt.

On and on.

23

Sometimes shit just doesn't make sense...but that's quite alright, etc., and *crank*... the aircraft doors bolted shut and that stewardess looked about 14, all full of hope and energy drinks and probably on her fourth flight today. I got at the champers before take-off and then sit-back, thwacked-up, miles up and gone.

Easy.

That daft wind was out there somewhere, lusting at the flaps and heads and bulk and gear. The sky bubbled its sick broad palette and I scribbled away, comfy as a well-versed pretender in this sweet class, just like the rest, and that sub-growl rumbled away at all our curves and lids.

Striking Barça shrank and shrank into dust down there, the coast vanished, verdant reams took over, and we were both alright.

Just a quick hop and a skip to the history bank and razz of the lovely French left and we discussed the Cousin some more and the Greek and both their effete delicious manner with everything.

Then Celine Faurlain took a snooze and I watched her pour off elsewhere so softly. And Charles de Gaulle charged into this thisness all blurry and stamping. An autograph hunter took the edge off somehow when she said *Thank you* and *Farewell* in such a manner it had me near melted.

Celine Faurlain got hold of my arm and we made it out of there and heading for some or other *ArondisSSsemenT* like extras in a wild movie experiment with Polanski hopping at the helm.

And Paris, *o Paris*, it got me straight away and the Faurlain residence dotted magically against a city horizon, sparkling against late-afternoon fuzz and smoking violet embers balling across the sky and lines and concrete and wispy boulevard tree limbs.

The estate didn't sprawl, it more or less lounged out over a few acres of tended greenery and a decent pool shaped like three crop circles. I suppose the actual building was like all other magnificent old-money French piles: sweeping staircases and wide hallways with stunning paintings and relic books everywhere. The only things missing were the maids & manservants, explained away with "Dad let them all go, then he died the next day. Haven't got around to replacing them."

The place was ours, and ours alone, and it felt weird, yeah, but quite fair, considering. Hah! Right.

"Want a drink?"

"Oh yes," I answered dreamily, and continued adoring the walls and doors... still fairly impossible to take in.

So I stopped and got back outside by the pool as evening toasted us and there was maybe a dead animal floating in there by the slurping drain.

"The gardener should be around tomorrow," she said, unfazed. "Just left him a message."

And so the breathless humming night soaked our skins, hers so caramel and tender, mine old and had-enough. Still she got on like a kid gymnast and calmly moved up, down, up, up... down till we both ended hot as hell and slept, drinks at the side, ice cubes *clomping* together as they dissolved to their happy demise.

24

Woke up with Celine Faurlain still astride me, still as night, and my arms wrapped around her, holding her into me. My hand behind her felt a tickle on the back, by the wrist. Breaking dawnlight allowed me to see the bug, a bee or dragonfly-thing, with long flashy wings and a head too big for its spindly haunted frame. It was still, too, but then suddenly fast-stepping like crazy and I knew something was about to happen, and yep, I remained motionless, let it do its worst, can't change this *natural selection*, and he looked at me, this bug, not so flustered, just a bit *busy*

& *SLIDE*

in it went

a bastard barbel sting.

I stayed still, accepted the stab, let it ease on in and it felt now – alright – I tell you, and he looked at me again as if to say,

"THIS – in you – was me, and now, I'm *YOU*."

"I am *YOU*," I said. "I am *it*," and I wrote AMANUENSIS and finished his tale.

He was dead now, fast-stepped and tapped-out and some strange amber clouds quickly gathered in memoriam, heads bowed, bald, toothless, tired.

"I am *you*, too," whispered Celine Faurlain, wiped her bottom lip and dozed back off.

I stared at my red sore wrist and that little black needle in there pulsing now. My head was all spinny, but vital and new, again. I started breathing in time with the beat of the hurt, all agog like that, like a *Queest*-alive lunatic. The lifeless body of the bug on the ground now, in a still pose like a rampant bucking horse and smiling.

I drifted back off.

25

A huge bullmastiff or a Burmese or some such busting brawling animal was lumbering towards me and Celine had gone and I was definitely awake. I could smell France and see Paris in the stucco.

Lumber, lumber, slobbering jowels and all that bounding fur... "Whoooaaa!" and I bolted up, unsure whether to launch into the pool or scarper on t. firma.

"He's OK... he's OK, very friendly..." and the gardener, must be, appeared in jeans and straw hat, brown saggy chested and happy. So I stayed and received the beast into me like an old pal. *Queest*, a beast alright, a ton twenty *pp*pounds easy and it took all my strength to stay in *cchka*control there by the mocking pool and arches and alabaster plant pots. The gardener just got busy fishing out that other animal from the water at the other side and said no more.

Hadn't stroked a dog in years.

Hadn't seen a dog like this *ever*. Maybe in a book.

"*Dieu*, what happened to your hand?"

and I looked at it now and it really was a flagrant mess. The gardener dropped the furry lifeless gunk and sifting rod and took up my arm, inspecting it real close in his hands of decades of hot outdoor toil.

The dog just sat at my feet, awaiting something from his master, maybe a dire prognosis.

"Wait here, I'll get my tools..." and this made me hot and flash and blur like a horny hummingbird. The dog followed him away and I got inside, flapping wild, to see about a drink, see about Celine, my hand and arm now throbbing and flashing.

"Good morning!"

"Ah, morning... I've met the gardener. And his dog."

"Aren't they both gorgeous?"

"Yeah, so, he wants to cut my arm off..." and I showed her the bulging mass growling and growing vermillion sore to the knuckles now.

"Wow, what the hell?"

"Some bug had me this morning."

She took it up and eyed it all over, rolling my arm round and round and it made my head heave.

"Gaaawd, I need to sit..."

"Sure, yeah, come here." She led me into a different room, full of brash colours and ancient tapestry weaves and far-flung metalwork holding it all together. I lay on something soft and expensive and slipped away without noise or fear, just a bit sickly and gone but quite OK as her face looked down at me and that impish complexion of Sunday school and those teeth and all that other... hair and... eyes of...

26

...the loom of booming underwater hauntedness; that swarm blue-grey swoon and wispy with needy reeds. Gloop and cling, all dreamlike, annoyingly retarding every last little detail & dim as cupboard space inside bad wet wood.

Sunken-chest and heartless I get up and stagger and write all this down
with some other bastard's hand & bones & pen as my stung limp limb is
a stump, digit-free, bloodless and stubby, yet weird and cute.
Queest, I hate dream segue fang, but this can't be, it can't! Look-see,
there's Celine Faurlain out through this sad French window.
And the gardener with his saggy chest and hardened gait, wait, he's
fishing dead folk out the pool now, that faithful beast at his feet, nuzzling
dust & bugs, and yeah! it's the band all face-down drowned dead in that
vein-blue pool, MY BAND, my boys I'd left with their dicks in their
hands and their pieces of joy flat without my love & lurch. Hah! What a
wheeze, as if I'm needed, knee dead, bent silly, like towns and dreams and
cocks and cunts and lips of mothers and autographs and miles underfoot
like harpoons in the soles, the Euro soles, the worldly souls, and Queest, I
hate souls too!
My stump-arm, I just can't make it bash on this Gallic window glass,
it's stuck somehow, so I try to shout at Celine Faurlain out there but
nothing comes out except a pathetic mournful child-moan, loud as a
swoooomphed-up lizard.
Uselessness in these sick treasureless depths, my eyes heavy as sin down
here, this gone room, all the pictures on the walls soggy and books and
stars.
This crazy bed, Gats-ornate, gilted and quilted with such finery I want to
smash it to bits.

WHAT IS NEEDED? Why?

The sun out there pokes through as if I'm in a mammoth treacly ship,
drowned inside somehow, portholes about to gape, floating about in this
old-money Paris sea-garden swilling in rotten mossy nonsense and then
rain out there, RAIN. It's all leaking out this ship, my boat, it's cracking
up, I'm going to make it... I am! Do it, crcraaackkkhh up, flood out as
rain, oh, that rain... each drop a single different form, a musical note, a

word, a snapshot of my life, a glimpse of my scenes, this book, ink and howl and sex and tossings and heavery. It's pissing out there, slashing into that sea-garden, the world falls, its ceiling, the lot, a deluge of ALL that is, clock hands and ALL that matters,

You Crazy FaaFuck!

I see it all and I've got my horn back now, my old joy, raised to my pursed lips, ready to BLOW, but it won't, I can't, I've no other hand, just this stub, my life is gone, over, but I somehow manage a holler out loud:

"...BE with me always

Take any FORM

Drive me mMMmmad..."

...torturous and craggy and that old brown wise gardener is now giving it to Celine Faurlain from behind, over the lounger down there, like a mad soldier or a sad sailor thrusting hard and that huge dog is now a massive dragonfly bird-bug hovering with beastly wings stabbing at them both

STAB STAB

PRODTHUD

SOKJAB

ZAP ZAP ZAP

KAVvVvvooOOOmM

& there's blood now and come and sweat spewing in all that endless rain, spiking up and through it all, cupping & mixing that mad palette daft and that rain of faces and cobbles and strings and Italy levers and miles of Spain red and lust and wantonness and all that pastness, Hellenic glory and boats gone fucked and I'm ALL OVER

again.

Finally...

now is this Death? Answer me, hot damn and God dogs. Is this my Death? Am I OVER, am I gone?

*Because I reckon I **want** me ended. I demand this hideous truth. Over and done for, finally... now, come on... this is far too much:*
LET ME GO...!

I see the novel, there, somehow in its usual *LIGHT & DARK* loll on a bedside table, that writer fellow grinning away at me, and me alone, now how is this the end for me? I have so much more to do... help me, I need you, I, I... I don't yet even know who I am...

PART 3: PEACEFULLY SOMEWHAT SLOWLY

(sussex)

27

The motor of life is desire (I think I recall).

Hot innocent bloody *bangbang* vital (I damn well know I write).

I begged my pot bones and normal bones, flesh, sinew, curves and lids out the bed. Some kind of memory foam dreamslab that came with this place, but I'm a real nightfreak – so full of solo slithering and wriggling in here – no wonder it can't remember my shape quite right; there's another little shape in here, is it, can it be? ...a heavenly warm caramel bundle though, and it took a while to engage any sort of rise-rise-gear, but someone said begging wasn't his business, tuneful and oozing Pure ♫ bedside ♫ Suchness and my frame and system eventually surfaced and hop-whinnied awake and the alarm clock whizz-smacked the floor like war and a felled colt and caboodleclIasssh. (A sudden signal-loss with the radio alarm resulted in a torturous squeal which in turn resulted in the machine being ended.)

Abluted, coffeed, let the dog out for a piss. Watered (not sure why, the clouds were full and mean-looking) the bare elm-roots, the last of the tomato plants (why so many dead *so* soon?) and the dog's muzzle (got to force it in her mouth a bit... getting mighty grey and wearisome in her not-so-old age). I am ridiculously glad the dog is back. It is an extreme relief/release/abject elation.

That lazy old moon had forgotten to make way for his brother or mother, the sun, and the two were in a.m. cahoots with the early caw up there, chaos breathes! *Where are you now, Culpable*

Gull, WHERE? But I reckon it's plain to see... peace is in the offing, somewhere, damp rainy peace, yeah, probably, and maybe some answers as well... finally... we're hopeful, sinful, keen looking up and all freewheelin' endless busykid sky...

Coffeed again and got the new Apple-lap-machine whirring like a top and it seems that the novel *The Restlessness of Virtue (Light & Dark)* hasn't so much sailed up the bestseller charts but rather cracked up into flotsam, drifted aimlessly, sunk gone down to join Ahab's snapped head-valves and coils and *Pequod* crew, glugging and planning and reforming and gathering all its unctuous unseen unfathomed strength, amassing nuclear intentions, and launching up into our very own life-space and pulverising the planet into an immediate realisation: real writing CAN best-sell. See? Finally?

Virtue... pah!

Wait... what's this?

    SEAMUS HEANEY – DEAD

    NO! and I was instantly excessively sad. God damn *the news*.

...my father digging...

...and I had a decent little cry there, the damned old young dog staring at me, weeping a bit also, water and spit and yellowy weepage drooling down, Seamus Heaney gone.

"We'll be gone soon," I announced, but my pathetic voice made zero impression on the dog. "That means you too." Still nothing, and the postman handed me two letters through the kitchen window, shying away he was, probably on catching sight of the wet spots on my shorts. Tears, I swear.

The dog curled up, I opened the letters, I threw the letters in the bin, saved the unfranked stamps, the radio played the Wilburys, and rain started its tirade out there.

Ambushed by all this sadness, why so much for me, all the damn time?

BASTARDNESS

Monday, *all day long* it seems cool to say, and pelted by all this, so I dressed quickly and rousted the dog to join me down the Wheatsheaf.

Still a chore, this pot leg hooming, my temporal lobes surging, the news, all the disaster in these otherwise tender, refreshing airwaves. (Will these product placement pricks *ever* pay up? <Blackcurrant, any currant, no fisticuffs, take a leaf out of Tabasco's best-seller, man.>)

28

"How's the novel coming along?"

"Oh, great, just great, thanks," and I paid my small fortune for just the one drink. Not even a small discount for all the gratis hot sauce I've provided this place.

The dog curled up. I decided to get drunk and write poems all day in memoriam of goodness.

The barman kept at the *how's the leg looks like rain* English-talk so I sloped into the back room where the log-burner fizzed and some between-job draymen idled and chuntered at the *Sun*. One of them resembled my late father: miserable and dirty and hair pouring out his working-class ears. We nodded at each other nearly politely and thankfully they engaged me in nothing further.

The dog upped, took a few tight turns, then curled up the other way. Noon was on us and I fumbled about with the word, misspelling and crossing out in a frenzy.

Tranquillo, man, you'll never get a blue plaque like this.

Then she came blundering in, tiny & soaked shiny, hooming and heaving in strange hooded beauty, and every last little washed-up immediate thing changed, and changed for good.

"Wow... how did you, I mean...?"

"Oh, it was easy," she interrupted and explained coolly: "You leave tracks like a wounded bull."

Then nothing. Nothing.

She brushed rainwater from her mad brash boutique rain-mac layers (must have brought them with her) and dripped all over the place. Attempting insouciance, haughtiness, recognition.

"Drink?" I eventually asked. "Adele? Celine? ...whoever you truly are." I almost whispered the last bit. An in-gag with myself: magic.

"Sure," she said. "Anything wet seems about right."

I got her a Campari out of random surliness and winced at the cost. Still no discount. The dog hadn't stirred, I popped another log on the pub fire and the draymen's cups had left sad Olympus rings across gibberish headlines.

I finished my beer and fastened up my notebook of poesy gutshot sketch scratch spillery, then leaned back, two-leg schoolboying the chair a-creaker. Warm. Quiet. Nice.

"So..."

"So... I got to the bit where *the Musician* is out cold. A coma, I suppose, after a bug got into him."

"Ah, well done," I said. "You lasted that long."

She looked half-bemused, half-who-cares. "What? It is very nice to read."

"*Very nice to read.* Excellent."

I looked her over.

All the same, really, maybe a couple more visible lines round the eyes this close up, and a tad more tillage at the rump than last night. No. Impossible. She is holder of little flesh, and less muscle. Still that Nordic sass and arty little angles everywhere, a caricature of a girl who's cool and mysterious and lovely, someone definitely alive.

It put me in my notsoright banghouse mind of my leaving gesture poetryscrawl I'd left my ex as a parting shot... a salvo... a salllooooo:

I walked & laughed and tipped my hat
To the freshest blondest baby
She winked an eye crystallised
My legs shone still beneath me
Oversold my opening line
A crack my knee Achilles
She'd turned a grin
I'd fallen in
Bouquet'd by the fiercest lily
I'd failed lost she'd turned and fled
Her petals strewn stiletto'd
So I fixed my hat
Walked on and laughed
Oh Fuck the whore this Ghetto!

(Interestingly, I had all that memorised deep in my lobal fronds somewhere, word-for-smiting-word, I promi...)

...she looked me over. I cared little how I now appeared; in fact, I was rather glad I had my worst jeans on and a tatty old T-shirt from Wales. Bush head, footpath face, yeah, care-LESS.

"You have your way with me all night, then leave me in your bed in the morning and come to the pub...?"

"How awful it must be to know *everything*," I replied, almost without even thinking. Without looking, without much at all. "How's the drink?"

Her face clenched and she made ripping and scratching motions at her throat. "Appalling. Just appalling."

I smiled then.

We got back to mine (in fragments of the chiming...) for some lunch. Some cerebral pill-down. Maybe even some...

29

Rainwater gushed at my front steps and down the little path. 3a or 4th or 5teen rivers, an ocean at the road. June, I think it is, or was that months ago? A fitful summer was here or is finished for us all now, the brooding up-theres confirming that with their masterly mercury elephants and winking weird-blood juggernaut doom. Timeless.

"Thought it never rained here," she quipped, "the Sunshine Coast..."

"Me too," and I got us and the dog inside where two humans shook like dogs and one dog scuttled straight to my very own petering fire.

Got some pasta going and opened some cheap wine, boxed stuff, pictures of Australia and giggling Speedos, Frisbees, a golden beach.

"Headache any better?" she asked, edgily, kind of feebly too.

"Oh, it's getting better at being a headache," I said. "Must be all the practice."

"Probably a tumour."

"Yeah, cheers..." and we clinked glasses.

"To tumours everywhere."

"Tumours."

She zipped questions at me then, like an old aunt at a family do. I felt obliged to answer, given her recent naked surrenders.

So, you sleep around a lot?

                                          No. A bit. Sometimes.

Seeing anyone properly?

                                          No. A bit. Sometimes.

The novel, then...?

                                          What about it?

A best-seller, you think?

                                          What I think matters not.

Hear about Heaney?

                                          Yes.

Upset?

                                          A bit. A lot.

Is this wine Australian?

                                          Yes.

It's terrible.

Why's it say *Timeless=Primeless* on the wall?

                                                          Always has.

You find that T-shirt in the street?

                                                            Clearly.

What breed of dog is this?

                                                      A confused one.

Aren't we all?

...and I left that unanswered, just finished my torrid Oz and got back to the whole-wheat penne.

The bubbling pan was just like all those puddles out there reducing my garden and plants to dark mush. I thought about Dan fucking Kemp and London village, all this muddle and mud-confusion, wrapping and swirling its lashes and licks and dirtsome urgesome get-some ideals... and that thieving bastard beak (ha ha craw). Over-the-road Rob too, his simple geniusness, and, well, everything that has happened so sluicing fast, ALL this hideousness, just like I said, but I am hard-on keen that it is definitely the TRUTH, yes... yes it is. And real truth is beauty, don't forget, which fetches with it harmony, shudders, life. (Feel that? yeah – something has a hold on me now, something fresh, something good.)

30

"So, Monday, what about your job, your life, London and underling-ing for Kemp, all that?" I asked, casual as I could. She took her pasta bowl, did a little kiddy sneer at it, forked at the surface parmesan, then her face softened slightly; *it'll do*.

She nodded lazily. Ate some, considered a silent munching notion, nodded, smiled, tissued her lip, *hmm*ed a bit, then said, "I don't fancy going to London today. So I shan't."

We both smiled and creased our curves and lids and pasta pouts at one another and I directly thought about her naked lines, her movements, that brown-gold curve of back. I recalled them all lucid and clean. O for Chrissakes, hold on, we two are turning into the Musician and Celine. O wow. O no, we can't be. O bugger.

"No television, non?" she added. "Against your religion or something weird?"

"I have no religion," I answered. "And no TV." I watched as she worked her keen eyes & mind over bursting bookcases, the stacks of notebooks and scraps of reminders stuck galore. An old Tanglewood guitar leaning in the corner like a Beat at the *Wha?* jamb, bits of newspaper articles sprinkled about, a few empties and shoes, an old manly Kahlo print, and the dog resting, tongue slightly out, warming dry now, seemingly content. The room was amber, was scarlet, was definitely unreal, flickering and fizzing, dreamy & warm, very warm.

She sipped her wine and tiny glimpses of naive girly magic dotted her cheeks and smile, innocent ringlet hair and impossible magazine skin, not the patchy, acidic noose, Campari-coarse and killer, girls so often quickly become (to me) (therein lies a truth alright... etc.).

"Why'd you sleep with me?"

She took her time answering. Sucked a final sip, gave no obvious emotional clue, and just breathed out... "I adore your book. It challenged me. It made me *feel*." A camparibanrockbreathslap winced my winkingeye and I deserved that, what, wah, and all that.

"You haven't even read it all yet."

"I know." <head tilt, long smile now, soft soft face>

"Perhaps you shouldn't really read any more," I suggested.

"Why the hell not?"

<PAUSE then pause... breathe, then *breeaathe*...>

"Well," I explained, "things start happening that probably should *not*."

<...>

Adele, Daniel's intern, Dan fucking Kemp's sweet gorgeous little under-fling, she just eased on out an egregiously nonchalant body sway-shiver-dance and said, "Tell me about it." Her hands now fluttered and jiggled as if panning for gold.

I went upstairs for a piss. "Aren't most things better off left *UNSAID*?" she shouted up at me playfully.

31

Everything moves. Then everything is moved. Nothing is meant to sit still, not even you. Now work it out.

Grandad told me that when I was 12 and struggling with early algebra. Thinking back, he probably just meant, 'Clear off, I'm watching snooker.'

But something triggered something in me and I wrote:

Gotta keep moving, keep on keeping on, don't look back, move forward, no stillness, blow open the mind, get on the road...

and somehow I figured and lettered out the correct answers, as if distancing myself from the problem and re-attacking and allowing different forces to apply and be applied had eased a sliproad out, a comfort break, a mindcrashtest for dummied and stinking beatBeat thinking.

"Why don't you stay here a few days?" I suggested to her. "You know, kind of let the dust se—"

"OK," she fired back and slopped her half-empty bowl down and got to her feet. "I'll get my stuff from the car," and off she flashed, quick as that.

The rain had eased out there, but still her footsteps splot-sploshed noisily. The dog uncurled now and stretched out long, allowing the fire to warm her grey belly some. Her tail wagged once. Then she closed her tired gluey eyes slowly, made a tiny little whimper, and died. My returned best little pal, yeah, she just died. Returned to die, suppose. Man, it hurt. & it hurts; present & past alike, *hurt* is *hurt*.

I buried her out the back, right in the top corner, by the elm, slopping and sweating in the mud as Adele showered, yeah – showered, and tottered and creaked around up there, I saw her shadows and shapes fast as bats through the upstairs windows.

I carved *RIP* into the thick soft flesh of the lonely old tree, not for the pious, however, but for her name, *Riptide de la Mer*, named after a scare down the beach when she was just a pup. Been a good dog, loyal and decent, considering. Hasn't lived very long, maybe a blessing.

What a tilted jilted Monday this was turning out to be. Magic, then empty. Fresh, then churned-out insane covers. Truth. Hurt. Beauty.

32

I tossed the leftover food, pans, plates, bowls and forks and graters, the lot, smashed in the wheelie bin. Don't really know why, it just seemed the right thing to do. Then I showered, cried a bit in there, too, and it brought me back to somewhere near normal, wherever the hell that may be. Had a quick flick through the bona-fide BESTSELLER *Light & Dark* (will I ever... etc....) to spark some further furthur now-here energies about me and into me. Climbed into some other old clothes and scribbled away at a sad little poem, moving on to the other shore, afterlife, afterdeath, journeys, whiskers and warm fur, all that. Thought about that bastard gull. Laughed finally. Went downstairs, down to nubile heat I want, I desire. The decent radio played ELO.

"You sure Rip was dead?" she asked.

"Hope so now."

"I hope so too," and we finished the gash wine, bolted through some half-decent port and our bodies made a sad lazy X across the sofa and we mumbled about being in relative bloody peace now and slept.

An hour or so of slumber drifted by. Then, without words, our X became Y became X became H h H and equalling (=)1 and always moving and dear Grandad and that gone-old maths syllabus could both finally claim a semblance of *here&now* usefulness.

Then more slumber, curtains drawn and the frequency oozed perfect Chet now and Christ! that Bose system was expensive but the sound is so very good and full (does this make me *MIDDLE* though?). Aah... I looked over Adele, saw Celine, no, it's Adele, yes it is; again and again, sleeping, yes, her firm little chest damp and murmuring beneath thin cotton, aah, what have I gone and done?

Christ! I'm the shittest shallowest person I've ever known... what have I done?

I got to the kitchen and steadied myself and my thrumming cage with some of the good stuff: old hearty Italian ruby-red, full of history and help. Rain sliced down again out there and dusk threatened to slip through its shapeless states real fast and morph into true dark, booming.

Sure enough, half the bottle in, sitting there solo in my small rented cottage kitchen, here in lolloping Sussex, dog dead, family long since dead, my damn leg still potted and stiff and sore, she's here, this reet petite child machine, this tiny Celine agog on my sofa, the thunder roars and only then I truly miss Rip, she would've bolted to my bed, shaking, I would have comforted her hours if need be, and the garden back there jolts and volts from deep within.

Still this awful Monday claws on and on and what have I done? what am I? but maybe now I can finally make it to a version of wealth, the dripping luxury of buckets of my very own money & respect & *freedom* I've always chased & craved and lusted after, virtue regardless.

P<Aus>E

"Damn right," I eventually confirmed, then reclaimed more celebratory maths while she gormlessly dozed.

(Mozart's redcurrant facefriend then fisticuffs.)

33

From the bedroom window, the vista affords me gorgeous little whitecaps inching across the Brighton marina wall like worms. Not rough as such, but I reckon you'd choose a good hat if you were on deck. But on a superyacht you'd stay below deck, playing roulette and sipping cocktails with the tanned beautiful & retired heroes and wealthy braindead serfs. That'd be me: shallow and shit and rich, louche beyond louche, below deck, grinning. Wait! Haven't I already sunk gone down into the swooning leagues, gazooming heavy and gone? Restlessness, virtue, what... the horn is tossed, that Musician is lost, been bugged, we ALL have, this novel is my bug, surely, that bastard gull up there (where are you now, thief, where?) BUG OFF! Poor little Rip, gone, just what, what is it ever all ALL all about?

She sleeps now…

Ah whoom, ah whee, and I climb into the shower. Pot-leg cover performing its duty admirably, it's finally Tuesday, I'm a fool, yes, & I lather up, humming myself towards a brighter mood, maybe sanity, maybe further truths. She still sleeps. I lather up, more wash, more clean, further furthur.

There is no exquisite beauty without some strangeness, Poe-diddly diddly-dee.

I lie down on the bed, pot only slightly damp, my persona cool and clean and talcum powdered with nothing but fresh cover shorts on, the faultless blonde child *still* sleeps. I pick up some bedside Joyce:

Rapid motion through space elates one; so does notoriety; so does
the possession of money...

...and loop into a strange fast Continental caramel dreamery, as I
often do.

34

Awoke with a real monster going *Bad Carnival* in my head.
Instruments of illness giving it wallop! in there, temples ablaze
and my eyes surging to shit-God algae rhythms and fury.

Quickly decide to source some necessary down-swing-pot-fix
from over-the-road Rob, he's on an Oriental delivery mission
down the mighty coastal road, and thankfully that salacious
foreign sports car of Kemp's is lurking outside so I hunt down the
keys and jump aboard and whizz off, head clanging like a loose
gate on a secret riverside gunman's path and this German-Jap
machine sails lusty and true and stealthy & stick to the road, you
gone blur beauty head-spinner system rollicker, ALL is a blur, toss
me about, take me wherever, take me... I LOVE YOU! I commit to
YOU, and YOU ALONE!

Whhhhoooohhhooooooooo! out the open air frolic a madman
time.

Mesmerising, the bEnDs of the superficial Cuckmere.

The Golden Galleon car park holds a few tourists with cameras
and ice creams, and shaggy old dogs wet and happy, slobbering
over stiles after their masters, and there, at the back, over-the-road
Rob, and a casual handover, snatches of conversation about that
novel I lent him (*Light & Dark*) &: *You are on the right path, man, and*

do NOT worry about the outcome, follow your vitals (direct quote) and it's off, kicking up dust and back along the coast road, quick as untamed Haribo whores.

Used to fetch Rip on these Oriental jaunts over the road. Not in a car like this, though.

I pull in at the Smugglers for a taste and my head eases off to a faint snare, the radio purges the effortless Pixies and I wonder if all this mad-trapness is actually happening. (He truly is a genius, that kid... he knows something... he knows the LOT. I'll try to smuggle the meaning and all that right into your deepdeep thinkers before long, worry nil, Percy Vere, a helluva right hand.)

I wonder about all these folk in my life, the new, the dead, the gone. All those brotherly gulls up and out there eyeing up all us souls down here, it is quite clearly directional chaos, a madness of survival and desire. And she didn't finish my novel.

Back home in the garden, scene of SO damn MUCH, that stupefying motor car whispering and lowly whhhoooshing its come-down hum, I roll another smoke with unfamiliar hands and I notice the terrible firmless mudslides have convened at the southern edges like rotten old sandbags in retreat, but at least today holds the sky clear and youngblue and, dare I say, full of new hope and warless and somehow chest-out proud?

I lean up against the elm and take in the good green in a massive long draw, the last gulp of the world, this swirling burly bulging Earth bursting at the seams. Exhale long and slow and skywards and my face and head swing lovely and daft and my body folds and I pat the damp grave: "Fare thee well, Riptide de la Mer... rest thy bones in bully peace..." and rub my fingers along and within the letters *R... I... P* in the soft tree-flesh, negotiating each carve and swirl and curve and bend. What does it all truly mean...?

...& I mock-salute the celestials and the cawing gulls and their one flailing Napoleon and over-the-road Rob for being a genius.

"Where are my car keys?!" I hear hollered from the kitchen window. I take another huge long draw, allow every last little thing to pass

and just

L

e

a

n.

& all about me this very now is one ONENESS I can lick... every last little thing makes sense and tastes bang-on but only to me, right here. S-L-A-K-E-D-R-E-A-M-S-T-I-G-H-T-H-O-L-E-H-U-R-R-Y-smudge.

I don't need fast. I need no haste, none at ALL. But I ain't sitting still. Who are you, Oslo sweetling? just who are you? and reach down for the notebook, it's just there, an arm's length away, avoid the springs and broken bells and reach down now and write, but I'd have to put the lamp on to write and that will disturb her but I have to get this down, so reach and switch and write. NOW! you lamp, NOW!

35

Now I keep having this sinner's dream (instead of my sweet Continentals), where the two words

tolerant and *tolerable* (the Mendy Q's have fucked off)

are having a fist-fight. There's never a winner except maybe the referee – Notion – where Notion is the fact that my imagination has become so unoriginal that even my dreams recur.

But this new forage for answers and discovery

RE: BASTARDNESS;

this exercise in The Now

that referee – Notion – matters very little, as I am just here writing exactly what on this silly planet actually goes on, and therefore why diverse magical imagination is totally overrated and utterly not required.

Reach down drop the notebook an arm's length away, switch off, she just turns the other way, passes a little derrière gas pop! and that's it back to the memory-foam mind-meld of forgetful unimaginations

side-by-side

worlds apart together

in sinners' bedly tidal

alonemanship.

Then Wednesday came with a bump and my head damn near smithereened. Rubbed it sorer then repaired to the Wheatsheaf, I suppose to get fixed. Head. Ache. Grain. Fix. All my own doing.

Scribbled away Rip-less. I promise to explain everything to her. Every*thing*. Christ! If she doesn't understand through her very own mental discourse within a few hours, then I shall think her no more than a simpleton. A cute tight-hole sweet baby blonde simpleton, yes. And pliable fun too. Desire, my motor's a-slake, purring a-through, now that *IS* vital.

I do wonder what everything is still all ever about, as usual. My search for answers continues, no doubt, but somehow I am this very now more learned, spiritually, viscerally, and feel I am getting somewhere. Sure, I'm still hopping swing-leaning on crutches (pot off very soon) & my confusion switches constantly *clickclickclick* (hear them?) but there's the Best-Seller problem (no selling out), sell-out in its very nature (wow) naturally, the whole world knows that, but my control panel is right in front of me with lights a-flash-bang-snap like a gambler tuned up, ready for a sizzler indeed, yet here I be... here she be... & I just feel ALL things and bodies and stuff, ALL about me FOR ONCE makes sense, here in this Day-Glo essence, this bubble, what a sensation, and I let out a huge great lionised *RRrrrrraaaaaagggGGGGGggggg-HHHHHHHhhhhhh!!!* for anyone, absolutely *anyone-soul* who may be intriguingly involved.

Drew further furthur immediate sparkle-light thus:

I always wanted to draw and sketch. I always wanted to play music, the piano, the trumpet maybe. Got to be abroad, Italy, Spain, wherever... & I always wanted to be rich beyond rich, to wallow in wealth gleaming, and perhaps be splashed

hitherwhere42

with fame like

Brut

on a broken boxer.

I just don't think I can sell out like this. Seriously, *I don't think I CAN*. This new light has me sparkling and chipping away at the harshities of

BASTARDNESS

with new chisels and force – no plot, just truths, hideous or not, Christ! I'm new music and I'm cackling alive like a gone beautiful careless river unseen and undipped-in. O cover, cover me up!

The stars and wounds and mouths gaping open to every other new WORLD have finally cast me free, free as flies. Guideless with my own hook and barbel stingless and no more poison and yeah, free as flies, all things move and fly, free as words, my how judiciously *NOVEL* & what happens to the Musician, Adele? and are we in the same DAMN boat?

I
AM
READY.

...

"Shall we go to France?" she suggests and I immediately say: *Oui.*

36

Newhaven. Not new, no haven. I wonder who else has thought that or been here and choked on this ghastly vision. Best just to look south and pray time to board swoops you up and delivers you to the horizon, thirsty and keen to driftbound beyond and maybe the ferry bar is serving already.

Sure enough, cold French lagers pour lively and she exudes pleasantry now. Soft pleasantry, yes, somewhat rueful in shades, & this Channel-borne soft early summer sun pulls the *Mor Breizh* tide and the eager bow is on the make and hopeful smirks and I reckon these grand euro fruit machines are due to pay out (tax them, tax them, think of the fishermen).

(Contemplatory moment having seen a backpacker. The original Tentmaker, the Rubaiyat, warns of: the danger of greatness. The instability of fortune. & of being too intimate. My, how my boat-going neighbours give me funny looks when I announce these virtues and hence give birth to a true vibrating sense of mentality meltdown brotherhood here.)

She talks and gestures this way and that all over, the icy whip-snap on deck abbreviating most the pithy sentiments and it's out here, hands on rail, when I see the holidaying family starting their adventure and it triggers me to say:

"What is your story, Adele? Just who, *who* are you?"

"Well," she replies, hair and scarf gallivanting daft. That head-tilt, that sizzling smile and kid-chin, those eyes, ah, yes. "My story, well. It seems you have already written it."

"What... you think I am making you my Celine?"

"Yes. But maybe my very own Celine, for I am *me* after all," and both us stare out at the blue-grey future and mist billows and spray. It's biting cold now, yes, and enchanting. "I feel this love thing brushing up against my head and heart."

"You do? Christ!"

"No, not Christ... I'm in love with a real music maker... an ALL nu-beat artist journeyman, a leader, a man who is going to *play* and lead and then *truly* live. How he wants to, how he should do. Hell, how we ALL should!"

<Pause... cold swill fresh salt bluesky little fish spray-hope>

"Well, who is this musician?" I ask.

"Actually, I've never heard of him," she explains.

"What's his name?"

"Hmm, not sure."

"No wonder you've never heard of him."

We get back inside to the bar and small-talk with dancing children and junior linguists on university exchange. There's some town mayors too, PAs in wrong heels, and army cadets with shiny faces and shiny boots, and oil-rig paramedics exchanging up-down tales with some boatless Belgian fishermen returning on foot after a run-in with the Eastbourne (damn righteous rulebook prick) Coastguard. The ferry is steady. The cold out-theres froth and the windows steam up. Everything seems OK.

I write and drink away, happy scrappy notebook, joyous free mind warbling and diving and realising... she rattles on about Casablanca or Tangiers*absolution* and *empti*rubiness and fake real fires that cost a fortune. Ah, cost. That spiteful label forever in our eyeline, forever in our hearts. Perhaps for me... no more. Perhaps for *us*... no more. (wow. ouch. all that skerching deepdown thought...)

All us journeypersons aboard this vessel get ourselves giddied up and raring to go to new lands...

<ANOTHER TALL DRINK – GRIN>

37

The ragstone carve-outs and snobbery of England dissolve in the spume and wake. Britain's in me. I know it, I love it. Just need a damn break.

Take me, harridan wet, take me, I love you, swill me through, boss me about... and I consider leaping overboard right now.

She's still inside meeting folk and keeping her shoulders back, eyes square, and understanding everyone's ways and means instantly. O she's at it alright, and she's *good*. I'm not losing it again, I swear. O gull, is that you? Is that really YOU? I see you there winking – hah! BUG OFF, you winker, I got it made now, I AM FREE! – you Trenchant Hector – FREE! – you understand, comprenday, HAY? finally? do you? yes all of you... ALL of you <arms flung out here, further spray flow salt time this vessel trusted to paydirt gainsay make its wet way to a destination bold> me and my BUst buST leg have got it made, see! <hop smack point at now un-POT leg with crutch display to omni up-there control panel ship-steers, world steers, harpoon-guides> We are on the mend and honest now, bones are crying out for new lands, yip-yippety *yahoooo*! & yes, look-see, there she is, that fresh new petal child, bursting with ruddy dash and life, there she is, back solo now and, wait, she has the rest of the *emmess, THE BEST-SELLER, my MANuScript-novel* with her and is about to tuck in to the rest of it, allow her mind the freedom of the muddle, the conclusion, the rest of FOREVER>>>...>>>

& I knock and bang feverishly got to must do HAVE TO *bangbang!* on the wonky Perspex view window from right out here into right now there and she looks up, drink on table, MS in hands, ruby of cheek, juicy of mind, ready...

"Come here... quickly, out here... NOW!" and I two-arm gesture like a lunatic and loud & realtime lustful, to ensure she doesn't rip into any of the rest of the words and pure magic gone maybe-too-crazy in her hands. She appears all jokey flustered and *OK*-acquiescence shoulder shrug drink finish hula-hula what-a-life.

Out she comes, hood up now, scarf tight and brazen face like that, so willing, so open, even all wrapped up tight like that. "What you doing, crazy? Sketching a band... the Musician would!" (ha ha sarky)

"What... *Giddy Wet Truth & the Best Sold Covers...*?"

"Yeah, crazy, yeah..."

<PAUSE>, pause.

"You know, there's going to be a delicious surprise for you in Paris, you know?"

"Hmm, two *you knows*, you know..."

"I swear I've heard that before."

"So what is this surprise, then?"

<PPPPpppaAAuse...> sea spray continuance full-gullery follow and dive-hover-observe-scowl and grinners-AWAY! this ferry boat making waves and crimps and purls and dreams still, yeah, look out, dreamers, do not ye awake, I warn you!

"O just you wait, Adele, my captain-ess, my tiny No-way Norway Celine... just you wait... I fully understand now it is MAGIC at play, I can't explain... just you wait!"

I gather the full MS from her soft half-gloved hands, doll's hands, arms and shape and delicate head to match. She grins, warily. I full smile no-wink, just calm and overseer *natural*, the helmsman, the seer, the control panel brinksman, *Pequod* Queequeg Ahab sharp-shooting NEWS corrector, yeah... ME. Forget the ills, listen to the rights, know them, feel them, be your ultimate SMASH-house self. ALL of you!

Arms out horizonto, bello, this beautiful PEEL of paper as the gulls peal out their songs, their cries to the heavens, and each single *ffflliiip*flutter of page of words, my words, off they go to the heavens all *fly* like that, to the whirly-drink and *pop!* swim and sink under water, through all other-life-form depths, to the mass unctuous undersea garden ready to build and gather and SURGE, surge the nuke-power up & UP! the paper unfolds itself into its own free beautiful joyous wormy cunning wind-space swarm and swirl & beautiful capricious art-flow MANuscript tornado whipping a frenzy of gulls and spray and the captain of this vessel even unleashes one ALMIGHTY *WWWHHHHhhhhaaaarrr-RRrRRRPPPPPpppPPPPP!* of the ship's horn, disgusting and AWEsome, mind-blowing, revelatory, unsung, blow, baby, bLOW! and the whole *beat* lot of paper is GONE<<>>gone, it's finally out there, free, released to spread its power of the wet wide word, the magic of the EYE-word-SEE-sea dance, right here & now out my hands and arms of decades of toil and loss and heartache and Rip howls too, out of nowhere, from bang underneath our noses and off it goes now, the full *EMMESS, the ms, the best selling hyphen novel,* go, fly, enjoy, grab at souls, linger, change, affect, breeeaaathe, be ALIVE... and this sea-BORNE whistling magic gets a-hold of me, fat, *fat* & violent, wallops me up, I cry and wail and cry but o so SO beautiful it is and how it skinside inside-feels and IS! *RRRRaaAArrrrGgGGhhhhhhhh!* each pretty parting page a single sniper-shot of my life, *ppppfffttt,* take it down! this past-life, a snapSNAPshot of what's gone before, weeping, feeling sorry, purling of white reams and LOUISIANA dreams and, and... fizzing with HOT SAUCE vulnerability and lucy loose sass maybe, & parental loss. Now it's all...

GO! ¡vete! Va via! Merde!; Putain!; Bordel! (in vino veritas)

GO!

38

Adele's face is staring out too, listening to my wails and moans and guttural deliveries of tongue and daub and she now – finally – joins in the fun, the freedom fun, and starts her own howl and tossings and get-rid together we rise up in arms, in alms, us two here now this very moment, this SNAPsnapSHOT in time of life as it is, this being as we are, this *thisness*.

39

Listen and revel In Horace, In Heaney, In Virgil, In Ishmael, in the sweet sweet *lifethought think-time REaL VER\dad-time producers...*

Skies change, not cares, for those who cross the seas.

When he had said all this, his eyes rolled
And his teeth, like a dog's teeth clamping round a bone,
Bit into the skull and again took hold...

We faced one another, hardly knowing each other, yet nothing else came into the now here reckoning whatsoever. O poise, *o prepare...*

...the latent heat gathering, so vast a palette, so much speeeed, increase in knots & warmth & true piston power. Feel the intensity of growth, feel it? do you? hell, I don't really deep down know what it collectively means, but I sure do like this feeling, these revolutions, this developing urgency, this UP-down *here*now pulse & swell. *PhhheeewwWWEeeeeeee!* let it ride. Raw. Unmissable. Loud now, most lik(e)able, e-less or not... what was it, yeah, yeh, get it... ah whooom ah wheeee, we are getting somewhere indeed.

All these reds and blues, whitecaps rolling, everything moves, pops & swirls, sure it does, every last little thing, encouraged or not, off we ALL go. Insanity? or simply the *REAL* DEAL? Check all the angles, perspectives, perceptions, yeah, check them all, consider the HVA-opinion of Tracey Emin, and then UNDERstand the universally true-fuelled concept of this whole ART of life.

On it goes... a familiar beat... without it, you die.

And the crutch now, this fake limb I been relying on, well, it's time to go. And up & off it goes, more than decades of power and conceit and connivery potential *WWhhhhhoooSShhhHHH* off it goes cartwheeling UP & gone! a tomahawk slice-slicing through this mass celestial backwash, clean into among the throng, the bull-gullery, the savages, the hunter-gatherer airborne get-some flash & blurs, take that! use it! ride it! eat it! *RRRrrraaaaAGggghhGGhh-Ggghhhh! Yip-yippety yahoooo!* & I holler out: "O my dear, ugly, beautiful chaos..." full of joy-release, an exhilaration of senses and elation, and then quickly turn my back on the whole scene out here busy-gone-nutso.

We smiled, quite calmly considering, kissed, slowly, ventured back inside, out of the actual past, the past Gallic Hellenic Thoracic-deep breath out-there madness. Didn't even see if the crutch ever made it to its new wet world.

Slim pickings. Whole. Some.

Slake, slake, power.

One more beer perhaps about now, and look at all these poor poor souls all glue-eyed & guessing at us two magic fools, all their unlived faces blown wide open, and all grabbing kids and partners out the way, let these hideous fruits on by without any fuss, oh my! what a life!

"Drink?" she asked, making graciously for the bar. Onlookers were still stunned inside here and utterly moved to a stillness, in true hearty *bangbang* Jesse James absolution.

"Sure," I replied quietly. "*Sometimes life is merely a matter of coffee & whatever intimacy a cup of coffee affords.*"

"Ahhaa! BRAUTIGAN!"

"O, such a beautiful coveree, coverer, and natural caresser of lies and hearty TRUTHS you notoriously are."

Inward cute giggle time. <small pause but then quick think time auto snap> "Hey, I've nothing left to read now, crazy!"

"Best you have this, then," and I instantly picked out my pocket-borne answer manifesto & slipped her the torn and tattered *Restlessness of Virtue (Light & Dark)*. "This'll move you some, you'll see." The author's face on the back cover grinned and creased and damn near *click*-winked.

<miniscule shy schooly grin pause>

"So you want a coffee?"

"Hell no... gemme a beer."

& all about us ♫ SwoonS in its NoW shackles ♫ a-rat-a-tat*aaahhh!*
I can almost smell the cobbles and charcuteries, oh la-lahhhh!

THIS IS THE END

{for nOw}

PART 4: VERY COMFORTABLY
(paris)

42

This has taken me days+weeks+smokes to translate (language and scribblejam) from my scruffy little notebook, so forgive me for any wrongthings... I am patient with correcting and procedure stuff normally, I must be in my professional life, but with this, I have not been, but there you go... etc., anyway, it is all mighty and true so read on... I must share my story, NOW (under a little new-friend duress, sure, but it feels important all the same), as I just believe something is going to happen shortly herein thereafter, etc....(^), something abundantly bouncingly relevant, so go>>>>>!¬:

I started the translation weeks ago, when happenstance nature & life (pro-guess) threw somebody special & prone into my life.

I place my hat, pink like a berry liqueur, on my head, for the first time in years. No, wait, I think I recall wearing it briefly yesterday... yes, yes, I did. Something told me to do so. And now I know why. It feels good.

I am Dr Patrice Sagan. I am going to the beautiful Faurlain residence today, to see my coma patient musician, and for some reason, I feel that magical writer I met on the train this yesterday has something else to do with the rest of this event and happening. Words and plot in juju-motion (I had heard even the English refer to *juju*, even though I believed they did not truly comprehend its meaning. Nor its power)... & that girl he was with did seem familiar, too... I guess. And off I trail, to the sumptuousness and history of that place, this place, hell – my tense-work is as putz as theirs! – and I feel just about fine and the rest of the world is here in my footpath, clicking heels and toes and sparks... my doctor-bag swinging at my side and the streets coated with lavender and scurrilous mist. The air is pipplin & popplin, rife with hooks, rife with signs. I whisper: 'RIFE.' *rife*. it **BL**o**WS** away, répandu... off it goes, gone. It is nothing now, that rife.

I am Dr Patrice Sagan, mother a teacher, father an exiled Moroccan poet. Today, finally, I feel truly on course.

"Ah, doctor, welcome back," and that true beautiful woman-girl with honey hair in waves lets me in. "Still the same, I think – the COMA beautiful man, but please *please*, do all you can. I feel it must happen soon, one way or the other." She offers me coffee and such like. There's another girl's voice back there somewhere, they laugh together and chime cutlery and chinaware. (Are they serious about the coma-man musician? or just ultimately blasé about ALL our fates?)

I think and have thought about 'the other' (= death, I think) many times since arriving here and tending to this bizarre situation. But today, somehow, it bothers me not, and I swing round the corners in this mass timeless stunning mansion, and up the stairwells quite full of peace and maybe other-world karma. Sufi ṣūfī Dharma. Both. All of it. Realisation, destination... I'm here, at this time, where I should be.

Yes, I know about the musician. But mainly because I have researched him over the last few weeks. Weird circumstances here? Unquestionably, yes, but it's a question nonetheless, and my answer is ridiculous but obvious; I am merely doing my job, caring for my patient. This I must do, and in I go and what I see before me now, in this bedroom, is disturbing and extraordinary. It shocks and steals my full breath, like thieves, like unexplained magic when you await nothing but the norm.

"Pat?" he blares at me... "PATRICE? the train, the taxi, ahh, yesterday?!"

"Oh my..." is all that comes out of me and we kind of embrace, like ancient friends, yet we've known each other very briefly, almost not at all. It's the writer from yesterday's train. "I am his doctor," I try*try* to explain and point at the comatosed bed sloth in wires and sheets and bleeps but we don't look his way, just stare at each other, calculating what the *faa*fuck (new term to me).

"This is all getting too much," he says, patting at his own reddened cheeks and nursing the back of his head a little. "First him" >>>>>>>points>>>>>>> "and now *you*. We are here, now... is this happening? & you're a doctor? we shared a joint on the train!"

"Ah, yes, yes, indeed I am. Ah... we are on the right path." I try to expound, but really, I can't. Strangely, it's exhilarating. And we start laughing like a pair of fools. Then a sudden, startling, sense-stopping child-moan groans out from the bed...

"AAAhhhhggh... am I dead? am I gone...?"

...and us two non-coma new friend weird-out fools fall frightened to death in a tragic hothead weeping heap.

43

My *doctorliness* takes over. I scramble bedside and gently bring bedsloth to. He is alive. He moans some more, but he's alive and eyes all crackling unsealing blinded and I get the curtains drawn shut and he damn near shits himself in that bed.

"Am... am I in Rome? is there water? I see stars, where's my hands?"

"Here, here, drink," and I angle the glass up to his old-rag lips. Water goes in. "Paris," I say. "You are in Paris. Now be calm..."

He adjusts everything he's got in that rattling famous head, and he is quickly very alert, considering. His body shuffles and squirms free of the bedclothes, free of CNS lapse, void of paralysis, that state of inert manifested human-gone. His black skin is patchy and tired. Doesn't look like his posters, the record sleeves. Yet he is brimming with substance, a tiny sort of magic perhaps, and I wash his face down a little.

"I know you," he says.

"Yes, I am your doctor..."

"No...him!" points past me. "I know you, yes. LUCA?! I love your book, man."

"Ahhh, wha... what?!" comes back from behind me. Then: "Wow, thank you. You know my book? I love your music..." & it's a crazy situation, that's the easiest way to explain it, and if I overthink it, I may perhaps explode or implode or neither and just wither away as this right path has brought us three here now, this very now, and we all try explaining this riddle like set-up kids after a plan by the in-charge folk, the supernatural powers-that-be.

Music man. In bed. But by strength, by belief, with care, now alive. "I truly love your book, man. *The Restlessness of Virtue: Dark and Light. Light & Dark...* harps. And wolves... raw, whoopeee!"

Writer man. In this room. By belief, he's here. "I've followed your music for years, seen you in New York, in Italy too. You really play, man. I heard you were here, RIGHT HERE! I just *had* to come."

Me. I believe I am here.

Two girls. One, so beautiful. "Who is the other?" (A different kind of beauty, less obvious.)

"Oh, that's Élodie. My fiancée."

"Élodie?"

"Sisters. Celine... Élodie..."

And two of us men here go, "Ah. I see."

And supposingly so, that is that. *C'est ça.* Unsurprisingly so, we are all still playing fate & mathema-tic-tick-a-tack, but it feels alright now. We're getting somewhere. Somebody shouts for the girls to come up in here at once and this unfolds...

Faces are thrown like clay and spun wicked, curves, smooth, rips, harsh, all truths as it's all honest reaction stuff. And touch. Heady old air, ancient music, all starting off, but very familiar. A beat; *ttttssss ttttssss... whhvvvbbbrrhh... and roll24...* ttttsssss (that's a fresh*lucid* influence-borne nu-NEW juju manifestation).

Celine dives and gulps up Black newlife Music, tears go and come and whoops spill, it is love for these two <*I thought you were gone*> and the other two <*how absurd this is*> are in another love, but real and good about it. I don't know what to do, but I've done my doctoring for now, and still I feel I have to continue my ON COURSE bit, but Christ! what is that? It is difficult to explain for an unwriter, you try if you dare, and I wish my father would help.

Au fond, ma vie ne changera que de forme mais j'aurai inauguré une nouvelle voie mystique, celle de soufis élégants.
After all, my life will only change in an outward way, but I will have paved a new path towards mysticism, that of the elegant Sufis.

I administer all requisite medicines, updates, inform all other souls that need to know (visiting locum(i) and hospital people(s) etc.) and normalness doesn't descend, far from it. But becalmed non-order falls on us like the sun through the old windows now and that gardener (strange collapsed chest, post-op perhaps) and his dog down there are so happy and joyous in their work, dirty-limbed and keen. Even a wave and a wag up at the busy window here. Some cool air arrives in, too, it livens the place even more, smiles and laughs come back, and, "I'm just *so very happy* I still have two hands!" howls the Music who must have been suffering horrendous dreams in that coma time, and he skips about now, tenderly, yes, but free. Now what am I meant to do? My lovely unique hat has been shifting hue like lavalamps ablaze, or maybe it is merely my perception/perspective that is changing angle on the colours of life, my life... what is it yearning now(?), and music pumps easily in, like water... "What the hell is that?"

"It's Mahler, doctor, Mahler number 4... *Sehr Behaglich.*" The two French near-royals shimmy and gleam and we three boys, men, children, we watch and, guardedly but *tellinstories*-like, with eyes melting, learn.

Cloudless, dreamless and dreamlike we continue, we drift by one another, 5 of us, five, thisfive, just checking we all exist. The music ♫ flut-ters ♫ about like exquisite wings and juiced.

We are all just arty little pieces of lovely caprice.

"We have a mutual friend," the writer had said and we both sang out, "GENIUS!" and somehow we all just knew... (Some sensible explanatory type wants me to put here: over-the-road ROB, apply some thinktime about storytellers or something, man... PLOT revelation time maybe?)

They get to their lives and comparing what they've done and played and written and how similar their lives strangely are, and all random together vibes (*WHY THE HELL ARE YOU HERE... MADNESS... I AM WITH Élodie WE ARE IN LOVE we are to marry... BUT LOOK HERE IS YOUR NOVEL I CARRY THE DAMN THING AROUND... OH WOW... YES BUT WOW DOESN'T DO ANY OF THIS SITUATION ANY JUSTICE... AGREED* etc.... *I NEARLY GOT TO MEET YOU AT HAY-ON-WYE... HAY-ON-WHAT?... YOU PLAYED THE BEST-SELLER EVENT, AN EVENING SLOT, I MISSED YOU BECAUSE I WAS SIGNING SHIT ALL DAMN NIGHT... OH, THAT PLACE!* etc.) and some wine pops – "But not for the patient," I oblige and these two men or boys or twelfth-night newborns (somebody else mentioned this) (getting tired of brackets and all this really) are falling in love with each other's styles, they are one-and-the-same souls. Oh my! But aren't we all the same mortal soul in any single snapshot anyway? Oh, my father would be proud. I hope he *is* proud, dearly, I do.

Something delicious is going on, literary, mystically, otherworldly probably. I roll a smoke downstairs now, in one of these magnificent rooms, so utterly moving, it's dangerous to walk and gaze about in. So I sit down.

There are inscriptions on the walls. Some seem disgusting, scrawled as they are on such lusciously decadent styles and coverings:

Mutatis Mutandis... Eridanus Supervoid... AtSwim2Birds... DANSU DANSU DANSU! and other nuances of gauche. ***But the truth is, it's not the idea, it's never the idea, it's always what you do with it***. What words. Even gauche is beautiful here, today. There are quotes from books too, *Wuthering Kool-Aid Shakespeare* & *The Leisurely Umberto Eco* & *The Spirits of the Dead*. And cool tiny sketches of supporting bands and girls in awe. And what the fleur-de-lis is ALL this *Light & Dark* business?

Sometimes shit just doesn't make sense. But that's alright.

44

New music plays, blues, cathartic and rude. Things move upstairs. In that renaissance room. Those new burgeoning love & life people. Fawning and loving whatever it is they want to, or *have* to. (I feel tremendously relevant with all these souls here, just fairy-tale I suppose.)

The sun is up fully now, it's early summer I think, or is it autumn now, is it September the 14th, already, seriously, is it? whatever it is, I reckon it's *birth*days for us all, real birthdays, we can live from now on... and outside these bewilderingly old bricks and frames and glass, the misshapen gardener rests awhile, the huge dog gives him a paw and gets a treat. Outside the property walls, a football loops in the crystalline sky with aerobatic fearlessness and searching and playful and children wail in fun. A trumpet sounds out. A bird sings. Cute little clouds scoot along. I can smell *happenings*.

I have a little inspection of my strange*strange* hat (nowhere near normal, this thing, perhaps I should tell you more about this, I don't know...) and, quite simply, I wonder what all everything is ever all about. Something lures, something reels, something lands. Waterways, fish, journeys, felt-tip milliners, vermillionaire discovery... now who in the hell organised this little get-together, this nutso jamboree of occasion and birth? This forging AND flow of delta pure sweet torpor time? These words are sluicing out of me and somehow burning onto this paper, and they are truly not mine, I swear.

The boys growing into gentle strange NEW MEN upstairs asked me to write about today, about my hat a little, all this thisness. So I do, here. Man alive, they'll probably ask that gardener fellow too, in their catch-the-moment idea spin that is going hooola in that house. I sense something special about all this. Yes, yes I do.

Then I head off home. Feeling fresh. Feeling *ME* again, what I used to feel like, when I was full of hope & I believed I could achieve anything in the world. Yes; ANY DAMN THING I LIKE. Ahh youth, youth & freedom... DRUNK ON IT ALL, desire pumping through me, IT SWILLS ME ABOUT AND I SHOUT, SHOUT IT OUT: *WHIP-whiPPPpetty-yahhoooooOOOOOOooooooooo!*

Wow. What a day. Then, with no time to set thoughts truly clear & straight (is that *ever* possible?), I see two figures walking towards me, in a weird sparkly elemental mist, a sort of human-cloud CONJURING fascination. Ancient *williwaws* begin whispering among the treetops and these two characters notice and spin their heads and eyes up & round at the skies, their arms linked together like chain and comfy and still coming straight at me:

"Hey, oh! hi... ah, sorry to trouble you. Does anybody live up this road... ah, back where you've come from?" and this man, this happy, free, on-course-looking soul, well, he points back the ways behind me, as if I don't know where it is he means.

"Well, yes, somebody does," I say. "Who is it you are looking for?"

His partner is a tiny little headscarf girl, all child-eyes and shelter-demeanour, leaning into him. He ponders a moment, then it's all: "Hmm, a musician and a beauty, that's who we are looking

135

for, I reckon." He favours one leg more than the other, this man. This searcher, well, let's face it... this dreamer. You don't have to be a doctor to realise ALL this. He and she then say something like *ah whoom ah wheee*, in unison, you know, together, honestly, they do. Do we all sincerely speak this way? Then he mentions over-the-road-HYPHEN-ROB, I swear he does, as significant as air and space and time and *RIFE* old perception.

They both then kind-of smirk (he all *I TOLD YOU SO*) and body-sway and way friendly, *really* friendly, tinily tired maybe, but magic & real safe like, well, I just point out the Faurlain residence back through the trees and assure them it's not far at all. Man, nothing ever is... ***right?*** *and off they go...*

...and off I go too... feeling, well, *absolute...*

{fin}

?

THE RESTLESSNESS OF VIRTUE

[{LIGHT AND DARK}]

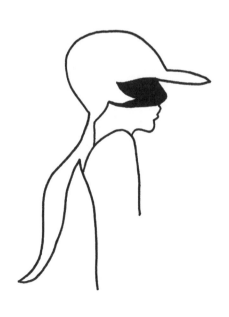

BEGIN...

1

Dear Father,

I miss you.
I never even knew you.
I love you, I think.

(it's ALL about me)

A small, black, simple, Jewish-looking reggae kid knocked and banged feverishly at the door and the home-owner hollered out the first-floor window, "Bugger off, coon. You're not welcome here."

"But your house is on fire," the black kid called up to him, "the roof and round the back."

"Beat it, COON!" and a wise old dog jumped past the bellicose white man and clean out the window, quickly gathered its legs on landing, then scarpered down the road at full tilt, no looking back, as did the little black kid, the pair of them pelting off into the distance, gone, and the home-owner fool in his burning house perished along with a well-known prostitute and rammed shelves of romantic poetry.

Charred bones and bricks and ash now at the scene. A few teeth and spines.

I don't particularly care for this short report, this beginning here. Still, the local gazette ran a rather dumbed-down version with a lot of sub-editry and polite conjecture. Not long soon after, I was commissioned to write: **No more news**. Instead, editor Bob asked suggested instructed ordered me to: take a couple of weeks off, find yourself a little, go surfing, whatever it is you like to do, yeah, find yourself, maybe come back in a bit with an insightful touching travel piece, fit for the middle classes, yeah. He seemed very pleased with himself when he'd finished.

It was all a bit strange I suppose, but Cornwall and the sublime heady rush of *SURF* did sound pretty good so I pushed off to Newquay and to Mousehole and to St Just and back to Newquay for a week or so and found just about everything except myself. Perhaps, though, that particular discovery will come, in time, so I said *balls!* to the gazette and *balls!* to the middle classes and I wondered if editor Bob and Local Newspaperland would ever really miss me at all.

I like it here in Cornwall. I have enough money to last me a month at least (a week in hand off Bob and got £500 for my '04 Getz), so I'm happy with this decision. And I've started sexing the hotel receptionist, an English girl called Jess who surfs and smokes, has tattoos and calls me Luca, not Luke.

I dream about that burning house and that friendly leaping Labrador-cross. That word *COON* makes me feel truly sick. And I question whether it all actually went down like that. Well, of course it did, I WAS THERE: the prime witness. And I think about editor Bob and his prickish ways. Life, I suppose. It's all such a massive damn test all the damn time. Does it have to be this way?

Mum seems to think I should see someone like a therapist, but I only speak to her a few times a year, so I won't bother.

2

(COON! that cretinous bastard was shouting. Retard and simpleton and all that ugly name-calling business, Christ and Godman and Buddha, I used to get quite a bit of stick back in school for being a little different and I got into fights an awful lot, but I'm an adult now and get into trouble far less, but still, it's all so very unnecessary, right?)

Anyways, this is my bestseller I've decided to write as getting another shitty job in any Local Newspaperland doesn't quite tickle my buds anymore, so to all of that: SO LONG! Bah-bye! Besides, all these best-selling authors are positively well-off and screw any damn thing they fancy and all seem particularly at one with their own little lives and plots, so hey, why not indeed.

A Croatian surfer down here, Stanislas, and his sweet girlfriend Jaime (pronounced Jamie) are my and Jess's best friends. We beach and roll and drink a lot together. Occasionally I sex Jaime and Stanislas sexes Jess and it's all very friendly and actually life-affirmingly JJSL invigorating (say that out loud, it feels good).

Jess has quite a few shifts at the hotel. Stan works at the Surf Shack. Jaime and me just drink and write and sex, smell the outrageous sea-air, take in the raging views; she's a poet and she draws too. Here's a few of her cool little sketches:

(If this space is empty, they've been fleeced, and in a way, so have you.)

3

One particular random hot-crush juju night at Fistral, we got a huge bonfire blazing with tons of other flinty heroic surfer types and I chose this moment to tell my new close friends about the fire and the black kid and the dog incident. It didn't really affect the girls but Stan openly wept. I comforted him. Then he told us his parents died in a fire on a boat and we all then comforted each other and I reckon we were very definitely friends then.

Jaime's got lovely little athletic tits. Jess's are different and rather saggy... for a youngster, that is. Stanislas is a good lad, dark eyes and strong and honest. And I'm just me, probably hideous, but I don't know. Random and weird... endearing? Not sure, I reckon I used to be, for a while at least, but hell, I'm not a kid anymore and I'm not a spastic. Bah-bye.

A small black simple reggae Jew. What a way to start a bestseller. Jesus, wasn't he a Jew? Whatever next in this searing hearty spontaneous thrust? Don't know yet... read on... write on... I will.

It's been longer than a week, wait, nearly a month down here already, and personal funds are running low but Stanislas says, "Don't worry about that, Luca, I have insurance money coming soon," and he smiles maniacally, connivery almost, stunning. Could be a character in a book. Should be. "You just write your bestseller," he continues, "everything shall be beautiful," and off I go into the decent breakers today, he gets back to the Surf Shack all sun-tanned and happy, girls aloof with smoke and wine and I silently thank that prick Bob and his gloryless life and decision to send me southwest with a week in hand. He probably never even wanted the travel piece. And finding myself, pah! The bloke's a gutless bleg and deep down I knew that the whole time.

These right-hand breakers cut nice today. I'll switch, ah, the rhapsodies of me-goof, WATCH ME SOAR!

Sister nature brotherly sun my new friends and sex fun, a new life (is it *NU*?), a fresh start and my writing shall show that and yeah, a bestseller still sounds pretty sweet. Sweet as good summer.

Another bonfire tonight and Red Stripe and dark rum and it seems the whole beach is one mass juiced-up party. No trouble. Just vast stretching youth and freedom and get-theirs, get-ours, holler unforgettable soul-etch and carve-out, hot night beauty.

Some lovely kid exercising his right to be captivating picks and plucks a beaten-up guitar and sings out something like, "Shut the folk up, dumb 'em down, chain their ideas fast to the ground, HOW DARE THEY DREAM...?" and the melody is so gentle and most of the people here know the 'HOW DARE THEY DREAM' bits and ravenous love for one another extends to the town and to the sea and far beyond the simple existences into deeper sweeter truer realms like visions and not just dreams but realities, right

143

here, right now, & I say, "HOW DARE THEY DREAM?" and I dare you too.

Us four JJSL sleep on the beach all close and warm all night, smile huge and it's stories and surfboards, fire down to a low black crumble glow, sea-sigh idling in... and out. Cool the milky moon, lolling an arc, its own righteous celestial swing.

I wonder if I'm copying Twain or Coelho or Jack. I should read more women writers. Just glad I'm not confined to any trained form finally, yeah, that's it, I'M FREE!

(What's that little black lad up to now, you know, the fire-warner? And that poor old dog. Oh, me old life. Balls to it, I'm now nu-me. Nu-life. I AM ALIVE, and partly delicious, and I slide into Jess all gormless. Warm and easy.)

(I strangely thought about Maggie during that nightslide. Editor Bob's wife who once looked at me queerly when she came into the office to hand-deliver iced buns to all 'n' sundry because it was her (*yeah, I know, I don't look it, do I?* she insisted) fortieth birthday. Massive tits. Massive legs. A bulldozer.)

Here's some photographs of the morning after that big one on the beach (you can just tell how special, right?):

(Again, if this is blank, start asking questions.)

4

It's still thatthis morning, Leonard Cohen's mumbling quietly about gypsies and flowers somewhere and Stanislas still sleeps with roaming closed eyes and I think of his parents burning to death on that boat on water.

I never *really* knew my dad and my mum's married a Moroccan feller who's very friendly and wears a well-kept little beard. But I only speak to her a few times a year, so I don't think of them that often.

FDR had his Warm Springs. Perhaps this down Cornish-here is mine... fixing my mendable insides, my skerching thinkers, my (dare I? dare I?) SOUL (ouch).

The condescension I've come to realise, Christ, I do it to my fatherless self, hah, how raw... whoopppeee! Christless cocksuck, I can say anything I like. This is MY bestseller, right? *Sunday Times Culture*, they do lists – check it. (Don't mind about tenses and plot, brackets & ,comma, commas, or look-back, jump-for'd passages of time, lovelifeloss, just write HIDEOUS TRUTHS... but I need a detective... I am a detective, no, no, that's **defective**, OK, oh well, I feel good...)

My balls ache a bit, but I do feel good. Serious.

"Mine are a little sore, also." Stanislas is quite candid too, and he reads my notes here I make and the girls snortle-laugh hearing him explain. "So what's happening in your bestseller, man?"

"Well, kind of ALL THIS, I suppose."

"All this?"

"Yeah... everything that's going on and a few thoughts and plotless plans really."

"Ah, OK," one of them says.

"Hang on..." I suggest breezily; not sure why, but out it comes. "Let's stop calling it *The Bestseller*... from now on, it's just *The Novel*, OK?"

"Yes, sir!"

"Blam blam!"

"Oui, oui!"

"Hai, sensei!" and they all bowed at the waist like the Japanese. It was pretty damn funny. Meaningless untoward bestseller blues, still funny, and we toasted today with sun-up rum. Then we all four surfed and a hundred others joined in slowly, casual as popping up. Some remained on the sand, painting and taking photos, and the headland swelled and everyone laughed and that lad got busy strumming again. Reggae played later, a local band on a ramshackle stage, quasi-suicide speakers smokepillsbooze bestsellerBLUES writerjourno prickBOB shoulda tried his wife coulda tried his wife really smokepillsreggaregga hypnoZOOMtime blamblamhoomingBASS racksteprackstep hop-up howlersswingers goodtits badtits titstits boy voice girlsong dog scurry SURFSURF summer beats reggaregga RED Stripe rumbaccy blowbabyblow smokeboozeSNOOZE fireBURN blaze snooze smokehead... HEAVES... SWIRLS... and rest now...

5

It's quite simply a question of VOLITION. Ah... *VOLITION*? Yeah... and off we go... that's how our conversations start, or something similar, and I feel I am growing and growing *up* and beautiful open discussions ensue. Answers parade, coconuts shy, crests of waves giggle. Stan pays for most things. Jaime suggests we all go to her parents' holiday project place in Biarritz soon. The weather is decent here. I'm called Luca now. Jess's tits are the same.

I know I'm not normal. I'm thankful for that. Oh brother, oh Bacchus, I am drinking a lot. I'm thankful for that too. But whom shall I thank? God Bob? Mum Dad? Doctor Gopher, whom?

I thank myself. Thank me. Fuck you. Fuck me. I will. And she did.

The hotel is quite sad so we sleep down the beach a lot but we use the hotel room and shower fleetingly, the TV can go to sweet hell with all that bloody bad news in smashing hyperbole pouring forth whenever it's clicked.

I saw an Australian girl today with ridiculous point-up tits and zero nipple. Some guy had undertow scare on the other beach and Paramedic Sam got busy and all was OK. We're OK. This life, now. This novel. Here. Hup! what a wheeze, this, my act of FAITH. Faith? Yeah, and this is that is *us*. Friends till the end. The end of what?

(Art. Craft. Imagination. My pocket pen wrist brain finger MANIFESTO to explore and exploit, repletely break it all down... yes.)

6

The sea in its whispering glory:

Come get some... eat me up!

...and I really carve up for a few hours, spilling and careening, pushing, PUSHING as far as I can. I've reached a point; this crafty natural wholeheart pin-through. I am this. And this is what we toast tonight. On & on. Surging timeless wake-up artistry, forever been on the prowl, now lime and light and fire bright. We dance the body electric all damn VOLTY night.

(Contempt for ingratiation, Rembrandt's heart, Slater's hooks, Hank.) Luca, it's you. Grab the light, step on through the fire, and surf it out. A thousand whispers, when one holler will do: be you,

LUCA, be you! I shall, and I went between the Australian's legs and Jess adored me for it, watching all the while, and kissed me so wet and heavy afterwards it felt like whatever LUSTLOVE should be, if only for 5–7 seconds which are all over now.

What a day. (Carpe diem for all the bestseller listing humps and hacks. This is now just NOVEL.)

Woke up hungover from good dreams, not the booze nor the other goods. Wistful inside hikers on the happy clamber. I felt good. It was fast becoming a usual feeling.

I got bakery coffee and sweetpains for us all (Stan's cash) and we sat clustered voiceless munching and sipping, early herald singsong animal sky violet streaks and look, airborne claw-marks in blood and flesh.

Crunch, the hikers went on and up for the view and snacks. That sky up there is full-on angry somewhere on this planet right now.

And fires rage.

Maybe murder too.

Ain't no maybe about it, hon.

Yet we are here.

The four of us.

Maybe happy, maybe not, but I sure am.

Hey, Luca...?

Yeah...

What about your home back in Local Newspaperland?

Oh, it's still there, no doubt.

Then we got back to breakfast and skygazing, all T-shirts, ripped shorts, skirts for the girls with little pleats round the edges, the Australian had disappeared, surfboards for sofas, random ember snap, this was our planet, and we could do anything we damn well liked.

"Wow, the Australian's tits are something else."

"Maybe we should become existentialists."

"I maybe need to beat off."

"Hey, I'm being serious."

"So am I."

"Or sensualists, yeah, man, real wake-up artists, celebrationists..."

"How much money you got coming in that insurance bundle, Stan?"

"Thousands."

"Great. But you can't keep spending it all on us."

"Why not?"

...and he just seemed so defiantly inexhaustible and truly sweet and full of carefree joy, we all left it at that, rum appeared, smoke, tattoos started their ubiquitous *woowooh* dance and Stanislas Western Union in town and OutbackBillabong or somesuch and discussions on Biarritz, other France, Spain, Hemingway, Switzerland, New South Wales and Big Sur.

We exist. On this planet which whirls around like a whirlybird eyeball and only the real artists are set to fly and see whatever they like, and then, and only then, will they go on and truly plunder.

"How's your NOVEL coming along?"

"Oh, fine. Here, have a read... write something if you wish..."

"Hah, OK..."

LUCA IS A PERVERT
But I love him
We all do. Bye-Bye.

Some kind of symbolist hero act took form in Stanislas then as he bought a *Daily Telegraph* and set fire to it in the main street without reading a word. All the while a huge salacious grin balled out like a huge great firework shooting across the southwest heavens.

I found it just about fucking hilarious, there in the car-less street, passers-by gawping incredibly, Stan dancing his salient madman dance with this newspaper torch belching and crackling and burning like the sun.

Wake-up artists for real now and the side-streets and sweet shops and lollipop kids all laughed fresh-eyed and wild too. One kid super-soaked us, water bombs & pistol shebang, choking out the *Daily Torch*, still we made giddy and an Argos box-van ran over the dying flames and paper ashes. The only vehicle we'd seen and the driver blared his horn and shouted WHOOPWHOOP! out his window and whizzed on through to Marazion or Penzance or HMS *Seahawk*, happy to have been party to real-time celebrationists, if only for a breath.

"Hey, Luca."

"Yeah?"

"Say, I don't like the beginning of your novel."

"You don't?"

"No... all that black reggae Jew business. It doesn't seem right."

<pause... then...> "I know, man, I agree. But it's what fell out the pen at the time, clunky and violent, but all heart and caprice, so it stays."

"Ah, OK. I understand..."

and that was that (teeming with oblivion).

150

8

Back at the beach, the two girls cuddled like sisters and gently slept.

Very close, the four of us, so very quickly to know each other. LIFERS maybe. Somewhere, the Australian girl smiled a brave little shameless smile, I knew it. Then I went and administered some rapido self-relief and my balls felt better, and this wake-up artistry was starting to tickle my idled buds again, stirring them into a cabal dance of real excitement and *HOPE*... for the first time in years.

Stanislas reads a sad-looking Norwegian book. I write. The sky stretches over us all, yawny and vital. Bob's still a prick. Maggie's tits and thighs grow & grow. Random surging burning visions.

The beginning remains.

I do believe something to be wrong in me. Reckon reader knows that already. These three here know it, for sure. Wrong, or is it just different, or retarded? aargh, sweetpoorchild awful tags and straps, man. Such destructive analysis, Christ, please don't turn me out a masculine bloody sunken Woolf, please!

Here's a poem by Jess (again, if it is missing, etc.):

There are harps and wolves at every corner
Even in these silly round rooms
My eyes
I see them chasing and playing

In a frenzied surly glow
Like a dying fire that could rage again
Like a cracked ship way down in the fettered unctuous depths
*   where it all began*
Like me like you here where we loved
And forgot how to hold on
Harps and wolves
Galore now
At the door now
Baying

She read it out softly and marvellous, and it really got me.

"That really got me," I said. "It's going in the novel."

We all dropped a couple helpers apiece, time for a fire, some fluids, noon surf, hook-back glide and lurch, friendly competition.

I thought about harps and wolves all day.

Back at the hotel for a bit, I watched two kids playing pool for nothing but kicks, and it struck me at one stage in the proceedings how it was simply a contest of safety shots, instead of attacking shots... waiting for a weak safe play to then pounce on, instead of a strong, brave foray in the first place. Besides all that, we had a quick beer together and toasted nothing but Cornwall.

Back at our beach camp, my JJS three nu-pals had disappeared, maybe to the shops, maybe to the hedgerows for some tri-sexing, leaving the surfboards and scatterings and smoulder all safe in their own rights, beach rights, surf rights, existential, I suppose.

I got on my elbows for a peace of flat gazery, the join of sea & sky across the exact middle of my eyes, my hair dangling bushbig long now, shaggydog, a few swimmers and dreamers out there in switchback tiny scramble foam, life, on it goes, golden thoughts &

plotless plans, just like I said, awful fat violent beautiful to die for unassuming walloping voomvoom elbow sinkhup sinkhup yeah! What's left in our makeshift survivalist sink-fridge? Couple Red Stripes and gummy bears to suck. Dropped a SOLO pocket bluey and enjoyed me own company Ltd and the Australian appeared and I charmed my little highway into her outback right there in the sand open kiddylaugh harsh&fast openair blue sky seacrest eyeline pink skirt whelp working-class Bruce's working life from muffled speakers somewhere faint and it's back out in the surf, gummy bear teeth dicksore now and man she can ride dancer balance Picasso shapes.

"Hey, where've your pals gone?"

"My pals?"

"Yeah, Stan and the girls" (her Aussie voice and young tongue like popping candy somehow).

"Oh, yeah, they probably went to town."

"They got in Mike's ute, you know?"

"Mike's what?"

"His ute... er, his van."

"Ah, right, yeah."

"They'll be back," she said, finally, eyes all ahoot, as if *what the hell, lah-dee-dah*, back on the beach, she somehow in tiara now, me thin king drip down *ah well*.

"Maybe they disappeared to France."

"France?"

"Yeah, one of the girls has a posh place in Biarritz."

"Ah, cool," and we cracked the remaining barely cool Red Stripes just us two now at the mini-camp, with nu-gone-friends' surfboards and all their bits and bobs and shapes and footprints still here at camp.

Mike & the Utes. This Australian child talks about Emmylou Harris or someone and this tiny skirt and brown legs and bare feet jet-white biggrin teeth and fruit gum lips. Doesn't really matter or concern this novel too much as I simply DO NOT KNOW how long she's going to be involved, this Australian popper. Everything's candysweet with her, carefree, maybe careless, but who cares? Seriously, who cares?

She took it in her mouth, oh that sweet tongue, and maybe, just maybe, my balls will soon dry up and shrivel raisin-doom.

"You're not all there, are you?" she asked. "You know, way weird kinda... but I dig that. And always scribbling away in your little notebook there. What is your story, man?"

"It's a novel," I explained. And left it at that, and she seemed most comfortable with that and took back to the lap-lapping sea with Jaime's board, nonchalant, quietly exuberant.

I started to think about getting more drink and pills but Stanislas the bank was not here and he'd been buying all the food too, except for the odd breakfast up at the hotel, and yeah, I missed Stan and the girls a bit. My nu-pals. My nu-close-pals, I thought.

I palmed and fingered their leftover footprints and elbow-marks in the sand and then carved out a little harp and a wolf as best I could and I stared emptily at them, totally unimpressed at my own beach-art.

All the rest of this day I devoted to a meditational technique Jess had shown me.

It involves three great big internal body-consuming SIGHS of maximum in-out value. Eyes shut soft. At the start and end of each sigh, allow the body and mind, every visceral pump and thread, to just disappear thoughtless actionless, just be ultra-NOTHING. Then stretch each sigh further, further till the three sighs take over your whole being, the whole lot of you, then allow whichever force wants to play, let it right on into your lifeforce shape and remain still, numb, still as death itself, relaxed beyond natural and meditationally calm, for as long as is necessary.

Try it.

Forget THE WORLD. Its ills and swings and TV news, Local Newspaperlands and bullshit. Black Jew beginnings, fire dogs, harps... wolves, yeah: THE WORLD. Friendless abandonment when you finally truly started to believe in real friendship for the very first time. Forget it ALL and drift, ride a crest, pop, shoot, caress, blow, think, dream, LIVE.

"You are so weird," she confirmed, the Australian child toy-mouth and I wondered how many cocks she'd sucked this summer, and at what karmic cost.

What are my feelings? They're quickly cold and selfish.

I light the fire back lively with fast hands and consider what the word *selfish* actually means. No I don't. Yes I do. No I didn't, yes I did.

Australia's gone now. Wonder what it's like in Biarritz. Mike & the Utes. They were my friends; well, not Mike, I'd only seen him and met him briefly, dancing with Australia he was the other night and Christ this is my last pill SCHLOP! gone reverie well-early stars out hungry lonely LONELY? how is this possible? in my new me nu-me here starscape moonscape tanned and lively and wake-up artistry? how? In what tiny capacity can it be possible now I'm me alone again? Little old LUKE?

And I lie down. Here I am, lying down down cool sands, gentle kisskiss sea spray happy noises from others non-lonely newfound goodSOULS and decent boopboop acoustic beats and strings and goodvoice join in Cornwall free-for-all except ME, LITttttle old Luke, young-big Luca, for me it is all perhaps frantic-dharma-dear and where my nu-friends go and WHY?

I think I know I think I cried a bit nightynight blurry.

Bob. Prick Bob, he could've been a friend. Maggie too. Any old Jew. Black, yellows, reds, limbless, hopeless... anyone, I'd be friends with anyone, I'd be friends with THE LOT, but would they be MINE? Truly? Or say yes and lie forever and then just leave me high-dry retard daft? I am retarded, I am slow, fuck you I am I'm not I am not I am.

Long gloopy sad night. Hard to write.

9

I woke up. Morning dark. Pinprick planning-stuff-sky. Organiser, *Manipulator Totale*. MT. The ignominy of powerhouse helmsman. Friend decider, up-there boomer, yeah, you up there, see me supine simple know-nil here, me, yeah, I know I am. But just who are YOU? Who?

"Hey, Luca!" and it's Australia arm-in-arm with cocksure Mike. Yeah, Mike.

"Hey, how are you? Seen Stan and the girls?"

"Er, no; why, mate?"

"Well, weren't they with you in your UTE?"

"My what?"

"Your van."

"Oh, yeah, they were, but we came back hours ago. Think they're at the hotel," and off they stroll to play and burst and pretend lovepop! with one another and maybe many others more.

I galloped up to the hotel half-happy half-not, what the fuck(?), kicking up dust and extraordinary dry-mouth throatlessness thoughtless, myriad matrices and mentality in all its shallow sweet bitter pillhouse garlandry T-shirt raw understanding music sex nu-life friends. Mike's a prick. Bob's still a prick. Maggie likes a prick. Australia likes dozens of pricks. I'm a prick. This is my novel. I remember my dad running so happy towards us that day and that German tourist bus full of secondary-school German kids smashing him to death into that British brick wall. I remember Mum breaking down. Then breaking down over and over again for years. Yeah, it's going to affect me. Serious. Yeah, I'm weird... but good weird... ssSShh... surely.

Where are my friends, my nu LIFERS?

Sprinting galloping raging lunge feet skidding up to the hotel entrance and I see a dog, is it that big runaway Labrador cross? and I quick-scout about for maybe a little black Jewboy kid as well and then think *oh my cavalry horses*, that would be true designer novel plot by (dare I? dare I?) bestseller writer in his/her writing office den with Post-it notes and iPads and Apple one-bites, with framed Sky Arts Man Bookers and orange & banana tree juicy holiday Bermuda with private schoolkids family lovelife LIFE LOVE!

Skidding in and through and up to our room, our come-&-go room shower in & out, sometimes bed and sex room and which floor? yeah, here it is and BANGBANG, "Stan? You in there? ...Jess, Jaime, hello?!" BANG some more.

Realisation I'm sweat-HOT desperation panting dog-rasping animal, actual panting! BANGBANG then quieter rap a little TAptap (is the camera on me? You know, the up-there helmsman camera-star Godman SighJew clicker?)... and then click *SSsswoooomphHH*, the heavy hotel door slides fast wide open:

157

"SURPRISE! Morning, Luca..."

"BLAM!"

"Hooloah-hoolah... bonjour, monsieur! Hola!" with streamers and such like early morning madness and life erupting.

My friendship Room 44 triumvirate JJS is back in front of me madmassive smiling faces and shouts. There's a makeshift dining table, a kind of half granite slab really, across the double bed with breakfast items, fresh fruit and whatnot, little bottles of fizz, meats and bread, fancy little packets of sauce and jams, the lot.

If it had been ordinary madness, I would've calmly taken the crossed-leg bed position and tucked straight in, but it was all rather suspicious and unreal.

Just what is going on, man?

"Well," said Stanislas, girls background grinning shiny-faced, expectant, "we are about to celebrate today, now, the rest of our strange-*strange* lives... we're on our way, we go to France, then Spain, ARRIBA! I am rich. We are rich. Now let us all eat, and really LIVE."

Bubbles and feed jostled down all our throats.

Stan's insurance payoff, must be.

We *are* nu-friends – I knew it. We're going to France.

"When?"

"Sunday."

"What day is today?"

"Thursday," and these four souls housed in four very different bodies here in Room 44, surfing love corner England, this tiny island, my little doubts peck-pecked at my skull some more, but I did feel bang-on, we all did, and we all held each other and we were WAKE-UP ARTISTS for real now, together, to get some! "It may be Friday."

10

"I got a new tattoo," and Jess, her leg up on display, winks and nods down to her ankleside. It's a HARP, with a friendly big-eyed WOLF entwined through its strings. Underneath is *JJSL*, all our initials of course, and a little golden star sparkling.

I admire it dozily, then perform a quickfire three-sigh meditation, deep, near tearful, and they all know, we all know.

Then back to breakfast joy and pre-noon wayward celebratory kid-fun. Brilliant.

"Just joking, silly Luca!" she suddenly wails and lick-finger-rubs off the mere pen-ink tattoo and we all damn near DIE laughing. What a hoot. The lot of us four, gone melting loons. Perhaps this is finding myself here, ourselves here, Room 44 magic like this, unforeseen, impossibly happening.

"Cheers, Bob!"

"And who is this Bob?"

"Ah, just a clever prick I used to know."

"Oh yeah?"

"Yeah. And here's to his big-tits wife – Maggie."

"To MAGGIE!" all four of us and we got smithereened: four spinning tops down in that magic Cornish box.

11

"Jesus tax."

"What?"

"Yeah, Jesus tax. For every single cross on a chain, in a tattoo, around the world, man. Taxed."

"Wow. Think of the earnings of that."

"Throw in Bible tax."

"Hah! Bless-you tax. Prayer tax, all the religions."

"Oh, for sure."

"Hey, I'm wearing a cross."

"Well, give me a pound!"

"A Euro."

"Yeah, pay up."

"Jesus Christ!"

"That's a fiver."

"'Like' tax."

"Yeah."

"'Do you know what?' tax."

"Definitely."

"Tax tax."

"Tax tax?"

"Yeah, man."

"How?"

"Not quite sure."

All four of us deep in giddykid drunk fullbelly stasis screw-eye smirk thought.

"There's a storm coming in."

"Let's hit it."

"Whhooohooo!" and away we chased to the beachcamp for the boards, us two boys leaving the girls in 44, and we lit a full three-hour set, a bulging burly lungbuster set. Dreamy. Drunksafe, fearless. Brotherly charmed, I'm sure of it. It was the finding: ourselves, inside, skinside, viscerals, face. Once more: the lot. O SWEET CHAOS.

We came back to the hotel in struck-down beatific woozy silence.

The girls asleep.

Then we slept. 4:4

12

Obviate obviousness.

Has a publisher got the cojones? The cosmithereens?

My, how novel.

13

"There's music everywhere."

"And art in all things."

"Tax-tax, do you hear me?"

"Yes, yes I do."

"I'm glad we are here."

"Yeah, me too."

"Girls, are you happy?"

"I am."

"Yes, I definitely am as well."

"Is this it then?"

"What? Is this *what*?"

"Does everything from here deteriorate?"

"What?"

"You know, we've ZENITHED. We must come down, sometime soon."

<PAUSE... pause... thought, all three of them & ME>

"I do hope not."

"Same here."

"And me."

<I nod calmly>

"*ZENITHED*. What kind of word is that?"

161

"Novel."

"Is it in your novel?"

"Yes."

"Well, what about this going in as well? 'Coming down is often the best bit'... think about a helter-skelter, a SKYDIVE, man."

<Peacetime nearly-deep thought snooze>

"Hey, come on, all of you, GET UP! I've something to show you in town. A Croatian close friend of mine told me about it. Come on! You'll get a real kick out of it, I swear."

Off we all trail ice-cream skedaddle weekend whistling sun-up again all us alive lucky souls playing this game. Stanislas leading the way ice-cream mouths messing around town buzzing high Main St low street side streets and then we're here, like some comic caper:

HECTORINA Schütz

Mainly just for...

Booze & Books (Croatia flag and all)

...and there's a ton of decent colours and shapes and art-shots on the shop sign. Man Ray-Jackson. PJ Harvey-Emin.

this is not a kid-joke (I specifically remember the words *kid* & *joke*),

it's raw, whoopee//<<>> I swear.

Brilliant, isn't it? and in we all four go, meet the owner, Hectorina herself, and the place is a gone batsocrazykook-dream cuckoo formula for sure with lunatic asylum pots & pans music and kazoo and a bad old keyless piano clunker pulsing and bounding and bumping and Hectorina and Stanislas proud as Judys the pair of them in cahoots show us round, looksee looksee wammo...

...WAMMsical awake now, I come to and headshake it clear.

This nu-artist of sorts, Little Old Luca, reveals his madnotbad dream to the Room 44, HECTORINA Schütz, all that.

"Luca?"

"Yeah..."

"You are the true cuckoo, man." <yet more ridicu-louse-mouse laughter>

(It felt so real) & I hate dream-segue stuff. Come down from there, come on down.

It was flying to France time. Newquay International. Yes, I know.

14

We gathered all our conveniently small travel bags in the hotel foyer and had a goodbye game of pool. Funny how not one of us in doubles match-up bang-ball played a single safety shot, oh no, it was all guns galore rattling those blazing fireballs down. Neither team won, and none of us cared a hoot.

Jess's tits are just as nice as Jaime's. Different, of course, but just as nice. I love all four. I love Stan too. But not as much as the tits. I tell them all this. Then it's Bye-bye Birdie Newquay we all four salute and taxi ride airport heading BA for Biarritz nu-life next step Jaime's parents' old money renovation place, we are welcome there? morethan welcome she insists and we pass the port wallop up into the skies miles up&gone and G&Ts and ready for the next novel bit.

"Hey, Tax-tax."

"Yeah?"

"Hectorina...?"

"Yeah...?"

"That was my mother's real name, you know?"

"It was??"

<PAUSE>

"No, man, Just joking, silly Luca."

SCHLURP, one more G&T, celebratory I suppose, and our giggling.

"Tax-tax?"

"Yeah?"

"Just think... everything is mental. If not, then it wouldn't be worth thinking about."

<the schlumping together of little ice cubes in little plastic airline cup>

Then:

"OK."

...a simple beautiful conversation the likes of which can only nourish the *Yūgen* goodness in all taking part, apart, impartially, or not.

[Surfing picture with BA plane flying above into the hopeful beautiful sun coin and all that...]

(If that's not here, guess what?)

15

Biarritz is a ripe little surf town, clinging on to France like a juicy signposted berry on a bush. Jaime's family retreat renovation complex, busybusy action dust... about ten minutes inland, a kind of sprawling mass of farmland really, with farm-building renovation projects galore except bang in the middle like a hum-buzzing roundabout, the nerve centre, already spruced-up sparkling modernised, nearly too much so, all mirrors and bright and angles with eco-ideas and such niceties. Don't complain, I won't.

"I won't either," says Stan, eyeing up my words all the way in.

"Her mum's tits are just the same." (photo on wall)

"Yeah, they are." (Stan again)

Workmen and farmhand labourers are busy on the projects all over with cranes and diggers out there so the noise is not the best for peaceful *Vipassana* mindfulness (been reading about it) for us to wallow and rest in before our next assault on SENSATIONALISM. But, hey, acceptable and schlooping fridge doors and drink stations heaven and snacks and oodles of *can-I-touch* impressive wines and music now from hidden speakers somewhere, a shiny new system, just heart-jarringly crisp. Reckon we'll be fine here...

...at least for a few days, you think?

Ah, oui, oui, monsieur! Paris on Friday. And Stan and me selecting wines as if we are connoisseurs not just of the here&now but also the 1974 claret and Pinots Egregious.

A soft hungry blur enveloped us whole, us four. Then

sexmaybeLOVEmakingnow notsure why not? me mine he his me-his he-mine singalong flow brown bodies like rich oil slaking, working, sliding all over. Then coolingdown liedown intricate ceiling upthere study makes 1&2 disappear like a seaborne see-saw kids in playpark with paints, mum&daddio 3&4 next door calling out to see if we're safe.

"Tax-tax?"
"I've no idea, don't ask."

Whoop-whoopee! ...and it's hypnoSNooZE time in way too comfy FRANCEfast, très content soon-future machinations let-them-eat-cake house, and all these fresh lilies everywhere tightening my breathers, yeah, but oh well who put these here FRESH FOR US?

One of the many stunning, truly stunning pieces of art here is a framed wonderful etch-thing, a carve-coal & chalk scratch evoking ease and tranquillity and, well, Christ knows what. I approach it closer & closer and yes, it's a HARP and, that's right, a damn WOLF licking its strings, sparkling, snarling. It drags me in face-first pphwwipp! & Luca, you are IT, see the light, SEIZE it.

This is no dream, I swear. It's just a realreal moment in this nu-now-factory, it's a-happening and I don't quite follow, but hey-ho, it's tasty magic. I consider calling Jess over to witness it all. But I don't. Not sure why. Wouldn't that just *BLOW* her away? I just stare and stare some more, drink it all in dry and blackwhite burn.

I know I'm not right, OK... I KNOW!

This is my novel. Still not sure about the beginning, but this nu-me has me light-headed and forgetful so I don't even remember it or what I like or not. Relax...

(Massive full-on interpretory ARTART for the louche which was so overwhelming I wrote all my immediate reactions down rapido mental mad and then strangely threw up little bits of sloppy airline feed and tried to write or make sense again, then stopped. Then I felt out of myself, expanding, understanding, sucking it all in and the one lasting *click* is one of Morality in Tin Cans and Jugs of Poison... I know, just ???)

Art new surprise novel. Jaime's father and all this collection lead me to believe he is Nabokov Constable Ice Cube with a pompous twist. It's going in the novel, but not the full describe-heart-sweep-ill-cascadery of visions and further vomit thoughts and half-arsed understandings. Just the surface, SEIZE it, Luca, & just checksee how *deep* you get.

"What do you think, Luca?"

"Just *wow*. I mean it. I can't explain..."

"Excellent. We're heading to town, check the surf, hit the shops, all that. OK?"

Yesyes, me in my mental suspension and languid for no other reason than *this*.

16

Both the girls skim off in one tiny roof-off toy car and all the nearby builders and their big muscly backs whistle and grunt at them like pigs. Not wolves. No hoods, a billion reds, even more heedless miseries and gestures. On it all goes.

"You found the secret room yet, Luca?"

"Secret room?"

"Yeah, follow me..." and we trot up and round this post-postmeoff-modern hopscotch madhouse ensemble taking in all the fizzbang colours en route and the dickie birds and petals and then orderly convention versus incredible and unnecessary to the extreme.

"In here, look..."

...in we go to a hidden back room and it opens out into a large flat low space with nothing in here but walls and walls and dark and darker still. But then blazing like a tiny beacon at the far end is one – yeah, just one – framed something on the wall all lit ablaze by mystery spotlights somehow. We stride on over. Taking care in this other-world dark and other-world weird clingy cloudy atmosphere.

It is a beautifully framed handwritten seems-to-be-FLASHING BLACK INK note on a scrap of brown paper-bag paper, like a lost piece of trash lovingly found and adorned and up-there heralded and life-stopping:

WHY DO YOU RULE AGAINST ME
WHY DO YOU SILENCE ME NOW
WHEN WILL THE TRUTH BE ON MY LIPS
AND THE LIGHT BE ON MY BROW?

It's just so simple & vulnerable in there, coy and crumply heartbreaking, yet in total control of this secret room, whatever the hell it is, this Dickensian backstory hullaballoo hideaway of one piece artscream poemjoy. Again? No idea. But it's delicious, it's *insane.*

I read it over, four and five times. Stan does too, he must do, he's right here, then we leave, slow-tip-toe the batso and gone out the secret dark room.

My teeth feel weird.

"What? Your teeth? Why, because of that poem?"

"Not sure."

"The secret room?"

"Maybe."

"Oh man, Luca, with you there are so many *maybe*s, so many *perhaps*. I hope there aren't so many in your novel."

Pause, then I go, "May..."

"Aaarggh! Don't say it."

"...MMMAAAYYY-make some drinks you Tax-tax COCKSUCKER!"

"HHaaahahaaHHhoowwey, I will, I will... TAX-TAX!"

...and he did, a good long mash-up bourbon ice thing, brown sugar and lime, two little straws; where he found all the perfect elements, I'll never know.

We discussed being there. How we both got there, our *journeys*, people love to say. Paths, rides, oiled-up automator belts, whichever you damn well fancy. Then we discussed where we might be headed. I mentioned (*perhaps* on purpose) Marrakesh (mum). He said something about Belgrade (cousin) and an island off Dubrovnik (parents' memorial).

"Where's your father, Luca?"

"Dead also."

"Yeah?"

"Yeah." And that was that.

"Here..." He gave me a little pink pill.

"Oh yes, man, you brought some?"

"No, man, Jaime did in her sweet little lovehole."

I tickled and teased it with my worm tongue and sucked it down. It seemed the right thing to do.

Of course I immediately thought about Jaime's tits. Jess's too. The BA cabin crew tits. titstitstits, I'm a tit, Stan's a tit. We titted ourselves back into the dark secret strange room, laid our man bodies down with boy-joy (don't think it) and that one poem in its spotlight glory EYEBALLING us two tits next to each other like this. Don't know why, we just did and I'm not writing this whilst in the secret room, no, I'm writing straight after, now does this still qualify as SPONTANEOUS ENLIGHTENMENT? (I didn't want to upset the supreme collective silent roar of us two tits in there.)

"Is every random thing that happens in life, you know, is it scripted, Luca? Plans, *journeys*, all that? Fortune, that sickening word *fate*. Is it all already set to happen?"

My whole body in its death pose here secretly breathing deep from toe-quick to sloth crown inout in out, each inch of skin and insides and hair breathing in out, even my eyes, growing big frog, then shrunken doll, ears pumping, throat&chest, veins, strings stretching and squeezing, pulsing and breathing.

"No. I mean – I don't know, Stan; who does? All this destiny and what-have-you. The mapped-out dance of fate, organised happenstance, *aargh*, ALL of it."

"Oh, thank God. Yes, thank God you don't know either." (real *relief* sounding)

Still dark here, obviously. That one poem up there, scorching away, in control, alone.

"How are your teeth now?"

"Oh, fine, thanks. Actually lovely and sharp and smooth."

"Well, that's nice."

<PAUSE, probably while we both rub our respective tongues over our respective teeth>

"Mine too, actually."

"Oh, good."

170

"And how are your toes, Luca?"

"My toes?"

"Yeah."

"Well, they're wiggling like worms."

"Hah! Mine too."

17

We could've been in there hours or just minutes, lots of peace and quiet and silent sigh inner meditation (Stan knew the technique better than I). After all the last few weeks of zipping about crazy, it was downswing-perfect, just what our systems and sinew, ballbags and brains needed. R&R, yeah. (finding?? whoa, slow the horses...)

We are good NU-FRIENDS strange NU-FRIENDS here in Jaime's parents' sumptuous art-house. Stanislas is good and rich. Jess is Jess. I am me. These four we are JJSL I know, bimbling about in this whooped-up sense of *now*. (Now just might be a dead cat. How do you put a value on it? Wait, is ANY art *good*? shouldn't it all be hugely subjective? contextual sexual concept-art, yeah, go ahead, TRY to be objective and then listen to your fib-switches go clickCLICKclick like frustration matches that won't catch light for days, then *fassvhoom* up all at once.)

Is art fire? DESIRE? being a liar? no. yes. absolutely. It must move you. OK, it's a jet plane... a see-saw, a memory. And it depends on the mood you are in today, the day you see it, hear it, taste it, gulp it down whispering, '...move me... go on, move me, I dare you...' SWALLOWED – then, 'I'm not moved one bit,' & 'I need the toilet,' & 'I object'... and, really, YOU'RE FIRED! & I don't damn well blame you, and, finally... *PUMP that well.*

"So, your dad was a hit?"

"Excuse me, *a hit*?"

"Yes, er, a hit by a German bus?"

"Oh, yes, yeah. That's right, killed by tourism, the old feller."

"Damn Germans."

"Yep."

"And your mother is in Marrakesh?"

"Yes. Living with a well-kept beard."

"With a what?"

"A teacher – no, a university lecturer. A nice man actually."

"Oh, I see. What does he teach?"

"Poetry. No. Philosophy, I think."

"Oh, wow! See, Luca... existing and thinking, you know, *existentialism*, fizzy pop, man, it is everywhere."

"Yes." <PAUSE> "Yes, Stan, it is everywhere."

"Not for your father, though, Luca."

"No. Thanks for that, Stan."

"Or maybe it is. Like my burned parents, too, on that boat. That's why I love water so much, see? They are always there, in the living breathing surf, wet and loving, watching and loving me, yeah."

...and then more laindown two tit men godly SILENCE together in endless boy-swish of flotsam celestial friend beauty striking matching darklight.

Naturally, I was thinking about Mum now. Is she happy, was she ever, was I??? You know, all that. Well, I'm happy *now*, I know that, you dead cat. But does head-high realisation mean I must come down? Man, all I see is paisley palette-mix swirling maroon and secret blackness eyelid smear. My fingers and thumbs twitch, fast-stepping like bugs on drugs.

172

"You are mental, Luca."

   "Well, at least I'm worth thinking about."

   <PAUSE, then> "Oh, yes you are. Yes you are."

I started thinking about crushed-to-death Dad also. Apparently, he liked Turner. Hooker. Kipling – wait, didn't *Jungle Book* have something about being a wolf in a good verse of that? Yeah, something about not being a scavenger, the beggar, but be a WOLF, the hunter, out in front of the pack. Yeah, something like that. Christ. I wonder if he would like me now, all my wrongs, my peccadilloes, my goofs. Maybe I'd be more hopeful if he'd been around. But wait! I am full of hope now and maybe he's something to do with that. All my doubts about fate and laurel kismet, ah, kiss-me-quick BULLSHIT, this is all of my own doing.

"Nothing is scripted."

   "Your novel is."

   "Yep. Yes, it is. But not a word is *planned*."

   "Well, there you go."

18

We clambered out the secret room giggling again in the happy dark, out, back into the unsecret richness, stairwells, beauty unthinkable louche room on floor on more rooms and doors dilly tanty fancy brash eyewide sparkling glory. What a house, a fantasy; some place, I tell you.

I got back to scribbling these words here and time had shuffled its slugs round Picasso's clocks and Dali's cocks, sticky trails slimy from those builders and muscleback labourers humping and thrusting into Jess and Jaime in that tiny dirty four-way roofless car and hi-vis vests and biceps and rigger boots and whooping French dusty come and sweat.

"You think so?"

"Oh I don't know, peut-être oui oui la la c'est ça, let's get some drinks..." and we did. I found some nu-to-me reggae and got it tearing out bouncing, bouncing fearless out the juicy system, all juiced-up of its own accord. French urbane reggae stuff at which I auto-sneered before quickly falling freefall headtrip into its brave cadence and Django trim. It really got me. I told Stan and he agreed, I think; he was all drinkstir coolhat skipping spilling big grinning in that suntan again. We hopped about like loons. Giddy. Free. Nu-music filled the place and all things thrive, on & on...

Yes, ALL THINGS.

Whoooohoooo, and all things move.

The girls arrived back, full of immediate samejoy and shopping bags, hollering above the music: "No surf, dead as a pond, we got snacks," and boxes of fruit and drink appeared and, "This music is insane."

"Aren't we all?"

"You are, Luca. Crazy king of the cats..."

"Dance, Tax-tax, dance!"

...all this kid-time frolic inspirational and some smartass would say JUXTAPOSED against the extrêmement adult ART in here and super elegant furnishings and seriousness and success.

19

Without any warning, I was lifted and pressed up against this delicious over-the-top ceiling, flattened up there, looking down at inherent geometry of this splayed-out action scene. A photographer artist dream of blur energy lifezoooom, which we all crave brilliantly strange; we all admonish and bully it outwardly (what a spastic space & time etc.), yet, like I say, inwardly we yearn for it. Reckon it's called honest truelove be you, be me, be *us* and I'm so glad I'm here, I've made it. But wait, I just spastic-slurred like all the rest... hah! see? finally?

Underplayed brash go gettum over-juiced hypno ZOOM time once more sounds bang-on and here I still am up-here, kooowheeee! looking down kuma-satra jawlines and swoop dense tonal hum harmonies darklight timeless movemove & there's me, look – Little Old Luca – arms flailing serendipitous know-all face now hooming in-out cheeks to the beat and rhythms and all over ONENESS with girlboy girlhim no one's knave no one's king, an unsigned letter, writing, written, non-stamping, utterly non-sending, non-sending, until, until...

This personal transfer of in-head and eye viewpoints is a natural pop-up for me. I see all this from other places other rooms, secret or not, it's NOT empty, apprehended solo-ism, NO! it's just easy winsome placement and positioning that I'm getting good at.

I feel at uptits downtits. We huddle and holler, I see it all, black & white photo negative strip-down hanging flash and tired flesh now and RREEEssstttt, yes, rest. Relax... puff out & breathe now loose natural organic animals in a millionaire prosaic banal Tricolore tin can.

Is this love, someone finally said, didn't *ask*, in a semi-suggestive soft bubble, yet it oozed and dripped and bled sincere.

"One day, maybe, & I reckon we'll be in the MOMA too," someone else said.

"Who is MOMA?" asked Tax-tax, nu-Tax-tax, who I think is Stan, and, and guess what broke out like snakes and plagues and nu-art pop icon craze? yep, hula-laugh-howl, the lot of us, spinning round in this continental box now, like fruits and slugs and tonic melodies.

"Pah! simpletons and retards and *black* spastics."

"You are black, though, Luca," one of them said, "DEFINITELY a little bit."

... then <pause... the stillness>...

"What is wealth, does it actually mean anything? & obviate the obvious."

"Well, it helps, that's for sure."

"That's obvious. What about deep down? You know, what would David Lynch say?"

"Who?"

"A film-maker luvvie artso *Twin Peaks* titsmachine type, much-loved kinda guy, he's pencilled in for the BIOPIC."

"Whose BIOPIC?"

"Ours. For we are ONE."

Salute! à votre santé (formal), tchin-tchin (drinkdrink pop pop one more before dinner time pinkPoP too). Gawping not losing WinWin stations for an hour or so. Original question sailed on by, unanswered, as ever really.

Becalmed. Sensible, dare I? In a way, yes. Mealtime meats and health-core vegetables and couscous, water, and yes-*oui*-si wine. Oh, that wine. Such heavenly juice, brought UP from a down-below cellar with racks full, dusty most of the bottles, even in brand new space, a sparkling Ikea-rack, dust and dirt on must-wipe labels, aged beauties in nu-world beds. Get some more, this is divine, try this, have that glory.

We chatter nicely, eat and sip gentle as if it's all so natural. We are adults. It won't be long.

Skim half-understood newspapers and magazines, discuss, sneer, mock, joke, cajole, drink peace DEBUSSY seducing dusk-time joy.

Jess gets to sketching away in quietude solo-station reverie. It's beautiful. Jaime and Stan kitchen-hover, pretending to clear away but just playing. There is a true ONENESS right here, this now. And I do realise I rattle on about this inexplicable sensation of NOW but you try, go on, do it. And if the magic is real, then you'll nowknow what I mean. See?

A comfy rich wave washing through all our soultime headcalm, this classical music is just perfect, the timing perfect, all this clicking together in our non-sensical mass of senses which is gun-barrel true, bent unruly as flames, but so so intoxicating it's shoot-'em-up mendacious-MAD.

Luca? (Me to myself.)

Yyeeeeess...?

Is it necessary to involve the wanking sexing swearing guttural think-out-loud winceyette boomer-foolish she-wolf sucking crass dumb-time writing in what is ULTIMATELY one damn fine novel?

Yes. Pull the rug. Then lie cool. And I sit back into a loll, smile, engage nothing but my own space here, nothing else, and realise that YES, stay true, be you, Luca, be the light, lead the pack, growl even. Feed on the YES. Fire on the uproll. From ugly to unacceptable pure beauty, involve it, become it, this is you, you are making it, so let it flow.

Then I feel an angel rushing hands and wings and whispers through my hair and head and this pen drops... & smacks the floor.

The bristling nascent seed is sown. Sewn finely into life fabric to burst and grow how and where it likes. Colourless, formless, free from any expectation. To thrust skywards, to bulge its fertile boughs above pathways and sidewalks, to shelter journeymakers from rain and thunder and strike-down slurs.

Retard! Black-death!

Beat it! You're not welcome here – and all the rest.

"Luca? ...hey, Tax-tax!"

"Yeah..."

"Did the novel beginning really happen? Or are YOU the little black kid, warning of fire, then running away?"

<REAL PAUSE think-time PAUSE>

"Yes. You are right. But the house did burn down with a real old bastard in it. I put my spikes into the report, though, yes, I did."
<tiny embarrassed flush feel>

"It's OK, Luca. I suppose you wanted to get fired from the newspaper."

"I think so, yes. And prickish Bob did the rest."

"Good old Bob!"

"Salute!"

"Salute."

Some seriously old bourgeoisie blood got raised and swigged then like working-class heroes finally coming to terms with raggedy strange nu-world (maybe)deserved success.

"Did your parents die on that fireboat, Stan?"

<short PauSe, then:> "Yes. Well, no. Three days later in the hospital. I couldn't go see them, though; my cousin said NO, it was very disgusting and bad."

"Wow. Very sad."

"Yes."

He wept silently, then slight noise, and gently we embraced and both cried quietly together, brotherly, and I reckon the girls saw us, left us a while, then joined us and we quickly regained our boozy cheery state, altogether that little more learned, bigger, better, constantly evolving and breathing fuller and meaning oh so much more, more in our connectivity emotion whelping cleave of these four humankindly kindred sorts.

"Tax-tax, JJ, let us go on and learn and blossom and celebrate as far as we can, OK?"

"Ah oui, d'accord, Sir Stanislas," and off we go again, walloping kindling amoureux seeds fit for each other's mutual bedshapes and windowsill sea-view plant pots, old troubadour smoke voice, full of lust and Gauloises promise.

(full of hope, this is real-time come, come along, there's enough for everyone...)

"There is nothing more truly artistic than to love people. Vincent said that, Luca. VvG himself."

"They fuck you up, your mum and dad. Philip said that, Jess. Old Larkin Bum himself."

"Knowing me, knowing you. Think that was ABBA said that," and Jaime snorted a hoot of milk and muesli at the table. BreakFrancefast tomfoolery. Conscious Larkinesque sun-up ease bodies swooning eating fickle marionettes trying to take or fake

179

control, grab the strings themselves, and attempt mastery of desires or at least the *understanding*.

20

O, I do wonder about these o's and the ponderings and the words, what I've been writing or thinking down inkily. But revision and sub-editry and look-backery are things of the past, right? I have turned for the good, and it's no apology. Am I a writer an artist a person a liver a potion an inquest a river? a puddle a wish a spastic splash? Just what, what am I?

Oh brother and sisters, I do wonder what I will write, but only the magic of the vastness knows. And fuck! FATE – it all happens too late, and I stroke the lovely soft wood carving DES OR MAIS above the kitchen door arch, smooth as this pen barrel, it leads out into the venturing free-for-all French sun garden wham! it's whips and snares of bugs and sun and vast Gallic sweeps of irreverent face clouds gallivanting pure white on pure blue, kissing up there, winking, twiddling moustaches, saluting their vistas, no doubt each and every one OUT to SEA. It could be just a continuation of breathtaking paintwork from inside. A sprawling fresco fit for Louis XIV, c.1701.

The builders lay their bricks and architects and the higher-ups chatter with ties on, getting in the way at will, wrong shoes and poor site-sense. This development space of a dozen or more similar glory homes spattered around, servile growing-up bees busy round their QUEEN, us, this place, the money shot! oh honey, all this clangclang shovel noise engine boom trowel throats scratching out instructions to the hods and cranes way up in the scaffold gods. I scamper off and through it all, coolly as I can, to find me a little peace.

All that ear-smash utterly erased the sky paints easy as that, senses compete, hear me, see that, lick me, fuck that.

A scratchy overgrown track leads the way round and down towards the yellow gold town, the sea lisping and purling and tittering away, swishing out there, preparing to take completely over or to slyly charm and forge a memory or maybe just to smartly back back off and disappear for good. S and the Js remain in the house. I look back to checksee if they followed me out. Nope.

(Wait a sec, do beekeepers keep bees just for the honey? Or is it a power thing? a being different & daring friends to try it thing? to pump that handle in and out in & out, pumping out that smoke, whatever the hell it does... is it for that? Or is it to care for a QUEEN, to not get stung, to hear the buzz feel it, that flutterrZZZZZZzzzz latent power, unused power, then when it is used, you die, and the QUEEN just shrugs her little buzzers and moves merrily along. (Thousands of others to pick from, you noisy stripedom knaves.) zzzzzZzzzzzzzzzZZZZZZzzz)

T++ho++se billowy sky faces trundle along after me, my only followers, no bees, no friends, back alone again then. But it's a different again then. Little Old Luke look at him stroll down there in this new place, Little Nu Luca, his nu-face an explicit theatre of boyman stasis split widewide open staring at the water wild out there, streamers of spirally parched slurrrrpy cantering manes...

No anger no grief no abandonment, it's NATURE and progress and growth and development throat-shakingly real, ride the horse, surf the break, keep on keeping on, boy, fuckdamn reel 2 thrilly-reel.

Following my feet round further and farther, this fatherless ? man, so full of questions ????? I reckon they leak ??? out my eyes and ears ????? and trickle down?? this raging s?unny dusty hill, tongues out like? slobs, eage?r for a we??t themselves. Track-side trees thin into even spikier hedgerows, more human life down here, young and old arms and legs swishswishing and mopeds and pastel pushbikes scuttling about merrily. Tanned faces and necks. Lightwear shoes.

Then a very beautiful momentary hush fell about the place; even nonchalant Chansonnier birdsong and bakery sounds, clinking glassware and exhaust putter were shushed away by the white lips of the bluegreen chevaux sea. I quickly grabbed at a dry chalky wall lest my !toes &knees and ?torso collapse and melt away and my skull was to calmly dissolve at the sheer *satori* of it all. The view dipped and gulped me right up, crumbs and all. Then all the noises eased themselves back into the scene, one by one, politely reintroduced one another and coyly took their stations, each to patiently await their chance, their invitation to dance once more. I fell for the bright brazen one marked BAR and held out my hand.

The beer was cold, is cold, and will be cold for a year I'd bet. The skinny little paper coaster soaked up the fallen foam thirstily. The rest was up to me. I gladly obliged and fast felt back near normal again, wherever the hell that may be.

Love all Trust a few Do wrong to none, a wall-hanging insisted; that silly old genius Billy S gets everywhere.

The half-full ashtray was shaped and coloured like a ravaged lung. Vulgar and perfect. The whole bar coughed. Someone at the fruit machine squealed BINGO! his craggy lines bulged and voilà coins ++tippled++ and ##splashed## out the pay-out tray, a fortune. The place old and new, French, very French, nearly French, Basque, tourist, passers-through & me cheered, we all did, and the happy old sot railed on & bought beers for all and music now, bangers and whistles, and what a decision to choose this place for my première Biarritz whirl.

Whoops and clatter and Sweetheart Rodeo banter (tattoos and Byrds), the language was ONE: fresh. And plentiful. Funny what free stuff brings. And not a single speckly throaty cough in sight! What sensible reasoning. What a payoff.

Out past the bouncing shoulders and sunhats, the bicep beach flexed its wares, rocks at the elbow, left-hand cut, sliding, a few rough-shod slap-happy types, more concerned with labels and stallion gaits and filly kerfuffle. Ah, beachwear gods and merch fools, a lot to answer for, you model capital citizens, and it's all about the *look* and muscle and no cracked teeth nor scars of the testy seas or the ART of surf, no, and whoa GodmanBuddhaBaloop, one more fruit crag beer for the place and everywhere I go seems to make some sort of capricious nu-me sense.

I sucked it all in. It felt good.

A raw, simple realisation slipped into my thinkers: I didn't consider any lewdlust thoughts about all these gorgeous young girls, hanging skipping around nubile, sweet, happy, Little Old Luca realising this, SURE, I saw them all, bright young dazzlers, locals, tourists, Americano blue jean pristinos and Italiano some still life, slow-mo, speeders now, oh raw, whoopee, I could paint them all, I can't paint, I can: YOU can't! I just haven't, now there's the difference. I can write – see – but is it any good? will it sell? who are you? (Don't forget when it sells best, then I really would've made it, yet alas and ergo and that, I won't forget the little people, multi-coloured or dreamless or LIFERS or not.)

I would normally hit the waves, I thought to myself, score a board try lip and curlbacksome for a few, but I didn't. My rods and conductors rested a while observing everything whistling on by holidaymaking grinning, the swishswishers prevailing kings &

queens galore and the bright red white parapets (is that what they're called?) rustling and roadside chains rattling.

My dad gave me only one gift I remember: Jimmy Baldwin's *The Fire Next Time*, and in it, he assures his little nephew, James also, that: "You come from a long line of great poets, some of the greatest poets since Homer. One of them said, 'The very time I thought I was lost, My dungeon shook and my chains fell off.'"

I just recalled that so lucid. Can't wait to tell Jess, she'd dig that, oh boy she would, that's what I'll do, I'll get back to surging Gainsbourg honeyed-up Bee buzz-house and tell her, yeah...

21

En route, a dirty big old campervan, real old-school thing, beige and cream and neutral all over, parked up peaceful, windscreen full of nasty-looking packets of parking tickets, and a big hand-made sign:

THE BEER RITZ

all welcome

...hanging over the swung-wedged-open door and six or eight guys hanging around there with Neil Young or some such playing and they're all smiling and smoking and so incredibly open. "Hey, how are you?" in broken English, then "Greetings, brother!" in perfect English and gallons of free cold booze flying about, Hullo, this is Charlie and Des and Jürgen, and whoever other breeds and smiles, this is a six-berth and there's 12 of us... we figure we can't all be sleeping at the same time, right? so what the funk... and boards and pushbikes strapped and clipped in and so very warm, Hey, I'm Luca, all that, I'm finding myself, all the medium talk and it's try this, smoke that, want a dream tablet? game of chess? Wait, I says, a dream tablet? Yeah, here, what kind of dream would you

184

like tonight... sexy or violent or deep-treasure-dives, what do you want? Pick a colour, pick a dream...

I just grabbed an assortment of rainbow sweets and these guys were so damn nice it made me feel special, then inadequate, then really up and good, and then scooting back up the hill to the house all foolish but bells ringing perfect. Crazy, I realise, but hell, this hideous juice-truth went down just like I say and I hope I did the scene justice because it won't come around again, not like that. Then it's a traffic warden, very serious and hot greasy shitjob face on him, sneering at the campervan and writing out another ticket for those sweetsweet guys BEER RITZing so I sauntered by and six or so cars up, the ticket man's scooter all angled on its pegs, local authority flags on it, and I just eased my foot on out there, resting on its little seat and yes, incidentally lolled it over past the point and over to a *cruuunNCch!* and a wing mirror flung-snapped away to the other side of the road and the *screeeech* of metal and plastic and tarmac all sickly and brilliant. I didn't lookbacksee to deeply observe the driftsong smokesmackerie reaction, oh no... my saunter sprang into sidle and upped further to a full-on hurtle, low gear, gone, whooohooo!

Little Old Luca going bananas (could do with some vit. C slugs actually) – think my chains are off alright. I swear it's happening this quick. FUCKDAM quik (no time to correct. good boy Luca) fast as bats just a lot less dark more light than dark yeah, feed your headlights, be the seer. Keep up I write I'm UP.

And those damn architects still in the damn way (crane-driver up there looks like a madman ready to snap) all this union countryblue and drygrass brown dustcake drownscape for the lot of us; us branded down here and looned.

A good measure of quotes and songs and lines are impacting me; suppose you feel this too. Good. And all the ART is creeping importantly round the membranic clusters as well. Toss in some overdue freedom, new thought, nu-friend-type freedom that is. Lust has morphed into sweetsex. Tax-tax cash. Mil(e)age, with or without any (e)cstacy crash and yearn yearnsome gutsome cover the ground humming and run, run, Luca, keep on going until Bob's yer ex-boss, sweating in a UK cheap suit (frayd so) and DESTINATION is now key and all the locks on the whole of Canal St are getting mended up *real* fast, I mean it. Book nothing, plan even less. Just go.

Glad I'm writing all this down. Will make for a fine novel. (But what for the small, black, simple-looking Jew coon or whichsobleeding ever beginning? What a hook, may need a sharpening, but that's not the point. The point is (remember?) it's CAPRICE. Spontaneous enlightenment production, not sand prime paint paint and one more coat for winter, no! Let it on out, looped and looned, and never felt so unquestionably In Control, helmsman, no screech, no HOWL, brinksman, yeah, you! I've got you, I've got you ALL>>>>!)

Cheese fruit wine. Let's get to it. Things are happening, we're making it move, let's dance.

"Luca, what happened down in town? You look weird, or *enlightened* or something." (Honest to guts, she used that word *enlightened*.) "And what's these little sweeties, huh?"

"Oh, they'll be dream tablets, them."

"Dream tablets?"

"Yeah. For later."

<smile> <smile back> & I popped and poured the four of us glasses of champagne, some real fancy stuff from the specialist pyramid schlooping door mini-fridge. It seemed the right thing to do, obviously (try obviating, and sluice it free, child).

22

Hi, bonjour, this is JESS. Should I say... DEAR READER? What a gas! Erm, I guess Luca is still a pervert (they told me to write that) and bye-bye. And now hello it's JAIME I am hot! Au revoir!

...she's a poet, did I say that, well, they BOTH are, and quite stunning in their own right, but this Jaime, man, she is a delicious petite smile machine (perhaps the better poet when she finally lets it go) and I understand I haven't done much background on the girls but hell, it just didn't seem right at the time. And it still doesn't.

Harps and wolves, galore now, at the door now, baying... I got Jess to lovewhisper that poem again to us all (teasing Jaime a little about being shy) whilst all this supreme champagne got its barbels into us tight, then slithered slick the whole way down our nobody throats like give-up fish. And then the bubbles jostle their doings and it's cut-to-head-high, whoom. Mean the while, those poet words, her tiny echo words, skipple out and ripple in the air-conditioned unreal nouveau ether here. Sweetly soporific, yeah, there was music too, isn't there always? Even in death. I've heard it. But I can't and couldn't recall whichever tune was playing and now it is way after that moment and I'm all p.m. shower dripdry towel-waisted balcony now, overseeing this nuts builder Gogh-cough world on offer. Still daylight, ornery, timeless, I three-sighed, slow as I could, deep beyond internal chamber deep, and I ran my finger ends over my chest, back and forth, updown, in strange nu-world sensory skin plough. This balcony, all those workmen out there scurrying, grafting, crafting, swearing, being their daily selves, a new-nu planet grows out of the spidery-OLD.

A butterfly appeared. A six-spot burnet it definitely was not. But it's what came to mind. Like that mad lonely crane driver still up there in his little hot box getting madder by the searing ticktock. GOD, his name. Definitely not, but it's what came to mind. You see?

For some reason, I let my towel drop and suddenly waggled my hips and legs about like a lunatic, wild and fired-up hulahula wag, allowing all my goods to free-dance blackpink naked and hairsack and, of course, GOD up in his crane-box spotted me and watched on, face-stuck, he was glued and guessing. My dangle-balls slapped at my thighs and I felt fucking fantastic actually. The crane jigged and jagged and jerked and the groundworkers below bailed out the way into the ditches wondering *whatthefuck*. Jess appeared back in this room, witnessed this, and she just launched fullbore naked and joined right in waggling skirtless topless and shaking like a fitter. It was insane and brutally hilarious, our shrieks of joy catching the other two and reeling those two nutsos now into the all-four JJSL conspiring kooky high GOD show. He was plain dumbed and cracking up now, eyes bulging out his little cab and the groundworkers too in their grime and melancholy garb picked up on the freak-out skin parade and got right down boogie howling out there. BEAUTIFUL INSANITY! someone shouted in 44 languages, we loved it. They all did. Just seconds of all our lives but seriously permanent.

Reckon we are zipping along to a brave new cadence here under this nu-idea regeneration growth roof, where not a soul gives a shit, and everything falls in line. Open up the roof, enjoy the sun. Pac-Men powered up, chasing and eating those ghosts up gone, gobbling down pills – yeah – these little dots, what a-mazing peerless analogy.

"Let's try the dream tablets now."

"It's only 3pm."

"Daydreams...? maybe...?"

"Hmmm... well, it's bedtime somewhere, right?" & I spun the huge suspended art globe into Christie's orbit wallbanger and then, yeah, the skittles got skittling down, those BEER RITZ gifts, and we discussed which colour would mean what, but in the end, we all plumped for who cares? and Pac-Man *schlop!* they slipped on down and we all four strange kids comfy animals wild breaths ssssssmiled huge great big things across our expanding soft-edge faces.

A broken-nosed labourer bustled past the window whistling and smirking and nodded at us, *Bonjour les fous!* and we all giggled, kids-in-class type. Then it was back to the bubbles and flutes. I cheerily searched the music stash and opted for some jazz, peculiar stuff really, totally bang-on. Outside, the darkening heavens and project sorts were all busy planning stuff. Us lot, this plucky bunch, we started to tire and our frames started to slouch and lig and shrink and melt.

Oh boy. Hold on to your knee caps, let your elbows dangle, frame-bending... but wait! I won't do it... I will... I can... I can't... & & & GONE.

23

We all four just woke up independently and spent an hour or so in quiet look-back sensible (considering) head-cleanse. I'll leave it at that. <electricity fizzing in all our early evening systems>

And now it's just us four, back around this table, reborn, it seems, and "Fresh starts...?" someone says and I reckon I'm the only one thinking: *What's wrong with how we've been*? or maybe I *do* ask that out loud; either way, the notion simply disappears and we all then keep very quiet.

Jaime makes some tea. I flick these here pages back a few, catch myself doing it really, not a serious revision, just a *flash*, honest. It reads: *Dreamy. Drunksafe, fearless. Brotherly charmed, I'm sure of it.* I look at Stan. He looks at Jess, who's studying Jaime at the kettle. No music. Just faint tittle-tattle of cutlery and cups. And then back to silent introspection again, sipping and silent, easy as breathing, necessary and fuckdam strange, and in our own time, we all drift off, wooed away to four separate stunning rooms, each to our own.

WHITMAN sings by himself, the song... four solo thrush thrusted together by happenstance and feeling and Stan's cash & the sea.

I ended up in the secret room once again, lying down comfy. One by one, my three beautiful nu-*diff*-friends joined me in that other-world dark, JJSL lying all of us here now, the wall poem in its strident blazing glory on the far wall. We were back connected, but then:

"I want to go home."

"Me too."

...and Stanislas added, "Me also."

I remained quiet. I AM QUITE HAPPY WITH MY CURRENT SITUATION, THANK YOU.

"What about you, Luca?"

We were all staring at the ceiling. Not each other. Not the beacon-frame blazing sense and fire and love-words the other side. They sincerely meant what they said. They were instantly terrifically sad. Such a change. I thought about things quickly, priorities, not the nu-love so much anymore. ME. BACK SOLO. FUNDS? FOLLOW YOUR VITALS...

"I'll leave you money, Luca," said my particular beautiful nu-friend, "if you want to continue your journey, your *enlightenment*."

"Oh no, Stan, I just couldn't..."

Just before noon the next day, Jaime was off to Paris, Jess back to Chester or Cirencester, and Stanislas, looking relieved I'd say, heading away gone to Belgrade. I trotted my bag and me and plenty Stan-family-insurance-bundle-dough straight back to BEER RITZ, maybe an instant-karma surf, some ponder time, maybe that whirling BAR, definitely back solo, Little Old Luca, look at him, perhaps even more happy than yesterday. How is that possible?

GOOD LUCK WITH THIS NOVEL IDEA LUCA written along the side of this page and signed & loveheart sketches – all that – by the JJS triumvirate hopefullers then suddenly non-believers and GONE. Yet I'm freer and freee-er, this seer of things from all angles, new light, nu-light, Little Old Luca, surfing now, nu-RITZing-friends, lost, found, finding... carving up wild and carefree as we could.

"Did you enjoy the dream tablets, Luca?"

"Oh yes, very much," us all between no good sets really, just idling on boards now and chatting. "Not so sure about my amigos, though..." I added.

"Oh no?"

"Hell no. Put the spooks right up them. They've all scarpered back home, all looking rather pale and flustered."

"Oh, they do that to some people... to those people that aren't quite *ready* yet. You must be *ready*. Simple as that."

I nearly asked. But held back.

The remiss right-hand taste-tongues of Biscay had a little lap-lap come-on for us but soon we were out, beach, drink, lounge about, easy as that. I started messing about with patterns in the cool French sands.

My life's been a series of crossroads. Each time I encounter one, the choice is one out of three, as going back the way whence I came is not an option. Well, I suppose that leaves four options: the three roads out, and STAYING STILL. But stagnation = death, research it, it is TRUE. So, I adapt this sand pattern accordingly, I don't mind if nobody else is paying any mind or whether I'm on a damn big screen for the lot of these walkers-on-by <sand finger sketches> – who knows? Maybe it is ALL crooked magic, a *false* enlightenment. It's all nothing too extraordinary, not *ground*breaking, I realise. It's a· very simple idea, quite unrefined. Like me, truly, yeah.

I decide not to take up the offer of joining the BEER RITZ six-berth on account of its already over-occupied situ. But also because it just doesn't seem right. (Phew! Glad I'm still thinking like this even after dream-tablet scare-away of nu-nowGONE-friend status.) Being solo again for a bit does make sense, and I am a sensualist, remember? Now where's the sweetpains patisserie, cola bottle gummery, and vins relatively cheap? (Stanislas only left me €3,000, yeah, *three fooking thousand*, along with a real deepdeep hug realdeep strong.)

Water seeps up playfully, fills all my cool-sands crossroads ideology, drowned-fast, collapses all this *plan*. Flooded! I leave it and look back sniggering, that is in the past now and even this ink right here I write here on this page, well, that's HISTORY now, his story, my story, my oh my, and it's here I think about ALL FRIENDSHIP – how brittle, how floody.

It's getting truly warm now, a little backpack sweat. Along past yesterday's BAR, the same old crags and plumes at the fruit machine, not winning today I see, losing, losing, drinking and coughing, it's what he really wants to do anyway, it's what they ALL want. Want want, desire DESIRE, my motor's all a-cough!

A seahorse sign. Bulging sun revelling in its blue bath. All that. The smell is Biscay, of course, but food and clatter is pure holiday-making, kids on the scatter, a bus stomping on, locals, yes, over there, watching *us* all. Poor sad surf now. Lovely bodies golden and each and every one gym-been and on the make. Coastal littoral peace and tidy attitudes. I grab up and gobble up bright fruit and now beer, it's been so so long and I ponder the post-crossroads path I'm about to tread.

A few more Americana sloganeering nudges and Capital Western pushpush stockpile against my temple one-side... then... the other. More signs. Reckon my gazette past has been riddled with cover version signs and quotes galore... for YEARS. Man, I have to be ORIGINAL, else I'll just wither and die. That's it! Little Old Luca enlightening, and as I write this I spot a girl over yonder (yep, I just wrote *yonder*) sipping and clear, sipping and beautiful now, over there alone together us two immediate here and she mocks my fast-scribble and pen-in-mouth think-scribble more and she holds it up like an artist, comparing perspectives from this angle, that angle, and I smirk and she flicks her hair back behind her ears both sides gently and more beer cold and foam appears jugily, glassily, and it all seems acceptably silly too.

Could I live without sex? without a girl? I suppose *YES* but I don't *have* to. What about music, surf, the buddy-buzz of narcotic surge? *I am no slave!* I am not oppressed, not governed, silenced, trapped, penned in (hear the PEN DIN, hear the *roar*), maybe a bit lost still, but I'm working on that, right? So living and engaging in this existence of *life* without the things I like and enjoy doesn't come into it, does it? And religion? pah! (just seen a Tax-tax cross around her neck.) Forget it. I have rights. *Fuck you*, Godman Buddha Mohammed. I have left. Left and rights. Cross(un-so-angry now)roads, no! else you get taxed by the VATican.

My raving like this, I suppose you think is cathartic. Truly, I don't know, & I wonder if putting two fingers in this new clever girl will help. I'll do it anyway, right here under the table, here in holiday BAR, honestly, here I write, and >>>>>>>>here>>>>>>>>>> insert two fingers in damp sexhole left hand lean under table across slip it down and IN, passers-by know no better but I don't care whatever. Such class, Luca, and this girl is a NURSE, wet and warm and really soft-nice. Sipping away still, wet and beautiful, white teeth, great white *sass*, she comes in my hand now, red face and sundown cute this nurse, fingered through and *done*.

We didn't speak much.

26

I departed the BAR bar, this bar, hopped a bus to nearly the border and walloped down the remainder pills lest a searching unfold me jailcell by job-love smoker epaulette moustache local authority amigo CB-radio alert noise beepbeep sneer sweat uniformio. Spain for Luca, new light, VAAAMMMoooooOOOooosh!

Have I changed any, I wonder on this bus chugging motionary stationless. Dusk lips its licks out there. Crass and daft Old Luca. No! I have moved, I *have*. I have *been* moved. Finally, we all get stamped and allowed on through and the Pyrenees wink and seduce.

Irun, San Sebastián, Basque, real world real people again. There's pain and love and unruly street signs. Not so much

Western sloganism to harass and harangue and feed on the masses here. Small masses, busy and earnest and working, working at the real dirty deal.

I fully disembarked my senses at a B&B-type family place as the rainbow ovals got their serious claws and *boo!*man-handlers into me; my Spanish was fleeting at best, French laughable, and English simply the worst. My face and shoulders melted offa me, I slept quick and did I really do that thing to that sweet sweet NURSE, my unwashed fingers? What would Stanislas say, or the JJ?? Bob the slobGOD? Mum, Dah... ah... forget it again. I drooool and sleep I think nightynight LUCA moonglow are those the famous Pyrenees out there and my knees in here a-creakers nightynight.

(Best-seller NOVEL what a career decision, Luca, you fool... CONSEQUENCES, *trust your vitals.*)

27

Morning whoopdewhoop still questions, moron, what would Tennessee write? Papa... Leo? Martin gun-smith? Worry not and I breakSPAINfast light bread and not huge smile mama welcome coffee and agua cheese.

I've seen this old Spanish woman before. Maybe I fingered her too. I've been in this house before. No I haven't. Neither. I'm whirly-birding hot comedown... gracias, muy bien, all that, shower shave pay another night, just the one more here and saunter-explore gay & free, black & true, doesn't the writing prove it?

Once upon twice fell off three times a lady, four... GET LOST! to the rhythm and beat of my skipstep, 4:4 time, did Newquay actually just-passing happen? remember the recall, thatthat JJSL nu-love room 44?

A kid at a bus stop with his mum in front of a disused factory on a bend, he got a nosebleed and the mother instinctively tissued his leftside tiny beak and got him to raise his right arm straight up in the air. I stopped and watched, trancelike; the blood got pat-patted and stopped. The mother said something like, "See?" to the little boy and he smiled, she didn't. Their bus came and clattered off, over the bridge and gone up a hill. Never seen that before. Left nostril right arm trick. Nor that bus, blue & red, nor its driver, nor any of these other humans. Or perhaps I have.

Justify your flightiness, Luca. Don't shrivel and limp off like an inchworm. Your *snap* judgement words, who puts value on them?

<PAUSE>

<then, pause>

...the world. The other WORLD. No one, not a soul. The soil in the ground. The dead&buried. Ash. TREASURE.

See – you never make sense, man.

Good. It's better off that way, now suck it in, I shall *never* shrivel: I am mountain chest-out-proud, and *WWAAArRRpP!* a blasting biting car horn scares any life whatsoever out the one-man dialogue scene (reality um-bridge overdose). Cognitive dissonance, the fox, the grapes, the nurse, the fix. The Luca, the *dark*. Us, living, that's all.

What are we in it for? The long run, heading off away to better shores? Chasing the horizon instead of taking it on all fours. The West has hit rock-bottom; WE used to fly the flag, valour, pride, and ethos we can only dream we have. I want to be inspired, not burdened by the news of a SLAP-happy gang gone mad, to steal another man's SHOES. Yeah – wow! Maybe I should just become a nu-funky Paul Simon gracing all lands and platinum records, what!

Nah. This is my *novel*. Chuck it, see what sticks. (Is it in the *Sunday Times* bestseller lists yet?) What crucifying tawdry. Jeez, what's next, Little Old Luca? Get off your cross, get the fighter-pilot to wash those hands, man, and tell us, we're dying to know...

Farm-track familiar all around these frill-less outskirts, but yeah, those mountains waggle up there, luring and winding me IN. Another night here, then off again, maybe UP, depends on what's going DOWN in this BAR and locals, different crags to Biarritz, but *crags* all the same, just a little more earthy, dirtsome, a tatty Gauguin print on the wall, that's it.

Ahhh, cold beer, long and golden and a glass a thousand years old, barman too. Smoke, *cough*cough, good beer. Down it all goes, then more.

Just imagine, if you will, all the whizzing imagery that is busting, *busting* thoraxly up carotidly up, up to grey thinkers and out these hands and thank my internal censors for not parlaying the WHOLE, the total words, it is only *THIS*. Thank you, sweet thoughtful Luca, gracias indeed. <Lone ranger rambling alert... rambling alert... whoopwhoop...>

I glugged away, getting gonesome fbtsam, two countries astride me, Pyre Knees in me lap, water on me brain, eyes on the glue, paper doilies on the *suckup* and nada chatter, nillus. Dusty old silence *cough*cough silence drinkup pourdown suckup us ALL, three solo drinkers, one pourer *coughcough* knee tap no music drinkup.

Nothing happened at all. I needed that. I scrawled some awful haiku and thoughtfully left them as tips.

Tomorrow I *will* hike up the hills, round up to those peaks, get real nature-high, check the VISTA, taste the air up there, and I try to find any remnant drug-stash in the backpackery and pocketry but trytry no joy, then B&B woman, tired and had-enough, she pours out some brandy-looking stuff and hints that I stink and points at laundry room and she's a mum-angel dutiful and suddenly beautiful, I wonder which bastard has up and left her or down and got burned & buried or crushed into dust and gone left her alone like this. I insist she has brandy too. And that's it, again, simple virtuous *Vipassana*, just sweet mindfulness and quiet brilliance. I needed *that*.

I lie down. Happy. I wonder about fame and being a famous wealthy writer, a novelist and please, please, Luca, don't *detest* it, as I fear that outcome intensely now... just... *what am I doing?*

A small black comma comma ,, Jewish-looking reggae kid gets in this old Spanish shower and masturbates thinking about the old Spanish B&B woman and if that grey weepy willow pleated purse would squeeze enough to provide enough snug to... to... ach... ooooh... shower scrub now, clean clean even all this afro jangly-headness unthinking normal head protection from ALL that falls, not just scorn but stones, boulders, that dashing OmniGod two-finger zapzappery and cast down fishhook barbel attack. Little Old Luca, still a pervert. *PERVERT!* Stan would write. I miss him. And Jaime. And Jess also, yes, I truly do. I miss a little music now. I miss not England, not Bob, not Maggie's thighs and way down stranglehold DEADdeadlines, man. No way.

28

Negotiate map, OK. Si, si, paid-up, free to go. Two old-skin kisses, stretched out wrinkle smile too, adios, bah-bye. Off I go again, ready for the next novel bit and dust trail and zoom by working man and kids to school and zombies to office blocks, yes! even here has the concrete robotic mashmash time-sheet *YES life*, you know? Thumb my nose to anything that tries RUE my newly hopeful blues and I'm on my way UP I swear (but FAME still sticks in my craw).

Now just bear in open-hearted mind, readers, that if I was PLOT-driven from the BS mould, then spooky relevant daily come-uppances and mentionings and condescensions with other folk would all be lining themselves up for a great Dickensian pull-off. Admit it. And DESorMAIS finally, a publisher has gambled on *actual* originality, now isn't that ORIgInaL.?.?.? My dad would be a very proud black man. And that German bus driver can go to pedal-hell. Thumb my nose – I can see it there at the top of this page – glib mawkish questionably viable spatter. What a gas. And thumbs UP to the gamblers, the layers, the sixth-form players (start young).

29

Campsite empty, two sun-idle MASSIVE dogs chained up, unconcerned. Tents to hire. Tired dusty lives to hire. Water pump, a thousand years old, maybe Moorish. It's hot. Hotter than that. Real hot sweat shower block quick... and si, si, señor, cleanwash and six-pack beer from OVERALLS Spanish nice old face stay here for a bit and food from jars.

Cracking hazy VISTA EXTRAORDINAIRE. I'm at the helm.

Social graces face it have died just thugs on the street pure hate in their eyes honest endeavour will it ever return to a nation's backbone that's crippled that's burned I want to be inspired not burdened by the news of a slap-happy gang gone mad to steal ANOTHER pair of ANOTHER man's shoes prime the oil pressure unfold the map I'm sick of this tattered union clinging to my back I'm off I'm gone join up sign here, no ENVY no real MEANNESS I'm just so sick of the malaise so sick of THE FEAR... & it hurts real bad...

Relax tranquillo sleep if you sundown can with the mountainside your beautiful nightshade bedside comfy insect hum-buzzers. Campsite land owner comes back round in the overalls all scuffed and another steamcold six-pack Gracias Goodnight, nearly a salute, all that grace and flow. Valhalla español Basque tap*tap* Pyrenees on my shoulder and all this THISNESS aqui, right here, is *mine*. I have the con.

Stanislas, are you here too? or are you home by now? How is your cousin? Do not be sad; you too, girls, what did those multi-colour dream pills make you all see and experience and taste? & why you, and not me?

Then it's: "Cerveza is life, salute!" Is this a redemption song, am I a <butterfly>? Destiny>>>>>NO, not destiny, but Destination>>>>>YES. But where to, and what precisely is the .point? Maybe it's all about faith & righteousness & LOVE – Little Old Luca the nu-fool, he's flipping out and maybe sex and beer and drugs will be your ultimate come-on-downfall. No chance, not tonight at least, I'm IN CHARGE, helmsman, I'm *The One*. A tiny spin movie-spin, flickering short-term memories. Still searing out here. The ants all pant.

Wait! how did I get here? Did I seriously trample up this *MOUNTAIN*? Did I chase my clumsy feet one after the other from way down there, beyond the verdant reams and bends and tracks and buses, sweating and grinding, bone on muscle on sinew on path? I can't remember. No pills to blame. This double six-pack can't have rendered me so damn well numb. The trip up here must've concerned a deep-gut fiery urge GO!get-some deep, *Get there, Luca, get up there*, and one, two, three, four, the 4:4 beat a constant little marching drum *ratta tatta batta-bap*! *Ferddop clattah follw-dhat*! on & on up & UP. Blind desire tasty as sin. Little Old Luca, new machine, yeah, I did that and it gets me peaceful within and calm as calm ever propelled itself to be. It is three-sigh meditational kip-time from here to forever stars, me and the world sueño ahora beautiful sleeeep, take me down, we've nearly made it.

...with your asinine pen and Machiavellian wit – don't back me in the corner I'll come at you with fists – *one, two, three, four* – the beat down, it got me ALL the way UP, man...

Holy sueño, I was in chains at the gazette, I was! *Slavus Serious*, can you see it? can you sense them? those urban chains? Without truly realising it, I had taken my place as *bastard* nature had intended, yes. I had. Oh Jeroboams, my intense relief now, even in this sick dream, is palpable, you feel that? It's a pulse and I could wake myself up but I shan't, not just yet, I will remember this... slake & slither at my thirst, I will not HEFT & FIST no more. No, brother, no, children, I will not, now where's next, what is there now for me to feast on, to revel in, tell me! oh Jerry's bones, my feet do not ache, my blood is keen and ready, I am *so* clear-minded and light inside, I FORGIVE, so will I be FORGIVEN also? Still the questions continue, yet the difference is, they now make me deliriously happy...

Dear Stan (I dot-to-dot the starsky) I am happy you are too I know I love you and thanks for the three grand we'll be stars I just know IT

Plaintive cries. What is it that separates any of us? I amyou is he is sheis me etc. yet we ALL have the RIGHT to be LEFT well alone, right? Passivity drift, face your strange new self, it will feel lovely, it's guaranteed, it's in the stars – yessir! But not kismet, your destiny, no, but say it again, I dare you, DESTINATION, that's the transfiguring power, now be you, LUCA, be brave new light.

Tart and ironic, a sexless little voice now murky and spent as steps and pathways littered with smashed-in locks:

Silent intensity an unfailing light morally questionable all-seeing
night it's me at least sweet paradigm peal out tuneless a tolling
kind it's me at least raw tortured hum twisting bedstill swear blind
they will come... and then these heavy moments sway and build
and grow heavier and my head and eyes begin to fail...
sleepGONE.
(Bo Diddley's boots, please no more dream segue plough, *please*.)

30

It's up, cornerless SPAINFRANCE collapsing all its heaviness, reaching, stretching, get-there beauty, it's so obvious, I will obviate and I stoop and grab up some of this earth here, this dirt and bugs and stones. Rub it all right into my hands and arms and chest, rub it in, rub it all in, make it become your skin and become you as a whole, all the while dull-humming a vital de-voice mantra of SOUNDS guttural and machinery.

Overalls suddenly appears and watches me in true loss or wonderment. He has coffee and I *snap* out of it and he looks relieved as hell, I am too! & we sit on border rocks and drink in a bit of this morning. Staccato chat as best we can and a few stars still up there fading away, winking down, no moon, no overseer, only the thumb-smudge sun, amberly announcing, *Yeah, I'm here, I may be slightly late, but I'm here now, so leave me be*. Birds dally, not much to say, this raging beauty below them is theirs every minute of every day, it is the norm. They are the very lucky ones and don't even know it. There's no darting like swifts or tumbling greedy as gulls, it's all long slow cascades of glide, musical, playful, rehearsed patterns like stitchwork holding the skies, and therefore this world, together.

I pay Overalls for the pitch and tent and tip him well and he misunderstands the tip and there's an odd moment of clumsy shapes and gestures. It ends with a handshake and a huge (rare, I'd say) smile, warm as the tardy sun. He scampers off and returns readily and full of spark and hands me a packed lunch of sorts, fresh bread and other sweet-smelling treats, just for me, this strange other-worlder standing in front of him, on his old land, fit for no-man's-land and nowhere else. I pack up my bits, full of hot new (remember *nu*?) joy.

My fresh aspect angles allow me to triple-A see my own forbearance and I tell you, I resemble a beaming queer, full of skip, chainless, godless, at the helm, and *ready*. JUDGE ME NOW. No map, pragma-feet and solo-mindfire and giddy old-nu ideas, yeah, I'm going places.

A friendly hairy old sort stops in an old pick-up and I clamber up into the back and off we rumble at 20mph tops. Undeniable pinnacle of all my views I've ever had rolls on through me, right *through* me. Did I surf? write? dream? wallow? invent? LIVE?

proudly finger under a table? This dirty old pick-me-up feels good.

Grief demands answers, I see that now. I'm going to stop asking questions. My grief is over. These Basque bumps have finally jigged it free. Whoopee.

Lovely find now as this lunchpack reveals some home-made cider and bread, oh yes, boy! I want this forever. Easy.

The driver is full of niceties without words, all tics and nods and thoroughly likeable, all uncle-looking and good-hearted. The sliding window device into the wheelhouse cab gets the occasional grindopen and we *swig*share the cider and one or two other treats. He starts to push the pick-up, it's busting now, busting to get us up another climb. Even the rust and holes back here are acceptable, all part of the moveable feast here open-air a.m. sun-up gulps and diesel fuel. Blue exhaust swirls gulp too, the past back there and rumble-dust frame & fleck the landscape tranquillity. I raise the bottle at some back-bending youngsters working with ancient family tools in a field, they gesture back and holler out all sorts, spritely and dash. This cork struggles to fit back in the top, so best I swig it off.

They must all live off the land here. There is *nothing* else. Now I live *on* this land, for there is *nothing* else. This fecund beauty must feed the WORLD, and I'm sure of it, it is so rich and plentiful yet millions starve, how? and why?

Stop it with the questions, Luca. Trust your vitals, the truth will out, you will save & be saved, rolling and rumbling now, up & round some more, happy as three-sigh itself, unfathomable, yet absolute. Where do harps and wolves fit into all this now? <not a q.>

The noise fades out, even this clunking engine and classical guitar radio in the wheelhouse disappears...

Appropriate anxiety levels of this wily old buxom blue motor slab, this madman happy at the wheel has upped the speed to, wait... wait... 38mph, we'll be in Pamplona for New Year.

Grateful and thanking rumble cease, we stop at a town, well, a *puebla* I suppose, Tolosa, where the driver damn near hauls me physically into a tiny home where a wife and his child (I assume) receive me in as if they were expecting me at that precise moment. It is very special. And we eat and she shows me train or bus times to Pamplona, "Ah, si, si, gracias..." & "Loco?" & "Si, si! Muy loco... hehehee!" and they laugh and I laugh and wine, the immediacy of wine, not so good taste, but then more wine and it improves smartly and cheese and wait... no more questions and glances, something has made them make *me* feel gently unassuming non-important and relaxed beyond horizontal and my ass cheeks sore from that pick-me-up rusty slab and hamstrings strung up; they only pour me a STINKING hot heaven bath and I ease right on into the ecstasy steam.

Talk about Jesus cross tax-tax in this humble crumble stone-built home. All these crosses ornamental and truly mental galore, holding the whole holy place together maybe, mortar belief, GOD only knows what'll happen should they fall. *Religion show & tell operate on the book whoopee.*

Reckon the bath has coated me soaked me pokered me deeply looped. Days without drugs now, I wonder... should I enquire? Hell no! how could I? I'll stick with this *heat-high* for now all clean rubbed down soft family towel up in this stranger's home.

I am warm, inside-out warm, sensualising again, can I say once more...? <HERE and NOW> Little Old Journeyman Luca, what a seer of intimacy and humanness and earthy virtue I have become. Wince.

<pops into my head> CHOICE: I choose to interpret it as DECISION, yeah, that's right. Everything is your own decision. Your desire. Ultimately, your *DESTINATION*. And it certainly is NOT pre-ordained godly starly enterprised scrape*scrape*scratch Atlas boulders see the sparks fly vilify non-believers, oh no. YOU decide. Yep, you too. ALL you. Sure, outside influences affect, bloodlines, cerebral family pulse life, enough meat in your diet, such necessaries, look-back genial build-up data. Personal development. But then it's down to you. CHOICE. I am seeeer. No matter how many e's. Errand boy, no matter how much mail. All answers are light OR dark OR *both*. The ones that truly endure are BOTH. Just wait & see. Flourish together as brothers... die together as fools... CHOICE. I know where I am, and still I grow, still I improve, yes I think of tits and drugs and heathen guttersniping pokeholes and childishness *DESIRE*, what about you? I am here, true-val-value Spain, small goodlove, share home messenger LUCA, mix the light and dark.

31

Hunkered down in this strange warm bed, this spontaneous pensurge bedside antique lamp, all my learning and professional life, writing to formula; becalmed regime round-up shallow disciplined routine surface pragmatic ordinary safe objectify omni-aspect (note well) please Bob (fuck Bob) you must please Bob the man he knows the people what the public want the *caveat emptor* (*ce*) (*finally?*) the real desires and yes Luke run the errand the lukewarm message pay your bills correctly punctuate right OK same again pay more bills hello Mrs Crenshaw feed your fish do NOT think outside the bowl the bulb the gate the pick-up the planet WRITE TYPE FILE EAT SHIT LIVE... What utter slump. I thank my CHOICE valves and my synaptic wake-up. Mum, oh mother, you will be proud. Thank you, Stanislas, Newquay, J&J, and fire. Music and mileage, delicious fearless DESTIN... just where is this headed? Good night, dog bless, where are you now (uncross the road, ask no questions).

(What good is one person's WORD when the very next day an APOLOGY clears their conscience? This wasn't my question, it was my father's, in a dream, whilst arm-wrestling Stan's father on a burn-down boat.)

We all rise like a family here in never-heard-of *heart*land. The child stares young stunning flower eyes at me. Shy head-tilt, androgynous, vulnerable. Fresh juice, all that, coy home, coy tiny town, cobblestone rattle, family fathers trundle off in rattle vans, mothers too, to the shops and offices and schools sound out their call to arms, alms, heads and ears. Life... on it goes.

Pick-up rumble again now, I'd rather sit up here in the back and I hop up, excitement, that woolly *buzz* about me. Contentedness, my new-nu wheelhouse family-frame-friend and I think I'm being dropped off at the bus or train station, but the way he was packed off with flask and me a flask, and lunch bags the pair of us also (this snooping-down prypry sun squints knowingly), he may actually be driving the hundreds of kms to Pamplona himself. My Spanish needs improving; who's in charge here...?

Gumption. Acceptance. Tolerant. Tolerable. (GATT)

32

There are cross words being spoken and solved the world over, languages and conundrums are bang-on analogy for this time of rickety-hot day. It seems to me that it is DURING the workings-out, the *journey*, the route to the DESTINATION – that is where DISCOVERY is found (although it was never actually LOST).

The green-brown agri moo-moo movie reels flicker past. Sweat and toil ditches machinery belch and basketry fruit and vines. In my lunch parcel is homemade delicious yoghurt. Perfect and chilled and smooth, just how, how would you even start to make this at home? I'm not asking or anything, I'm inwardly contemplating so many things that I don't know about, that I have NOT YET learned. Run the numbers. Calculate the calcium, bonework homework hand-me-down family skills, kitchen to bored-room to lecture hall to office block. Break in. Break out. Intendiende, be your true good self and forget the rest. (If you get any, that is.)

Some girls on a bus catch us up (not difficult at these speeds) and wave and cajole at me here in the rust-shaker, yeah, and Little Old Luca gets a hard-on. Yep, it's still me here.

There's some sweet honey in my bundle too and heaven bread – salty, a sandwich on its own. These eats are relief. They're Mum again and Dad at work. They're love and sunlit futures, I can be *anyone*. Know-all sun up high now, it's a changing shimmer, a changing heat and angle, we all grow and learn, you go shine on Mum some, and Morocco, and sinners and kings alike, and all the good fruits (even the bad fruits were good fruits once, remember). Oh honey raw mindfulness, all things must pass.

This rumble-track meanders loop-the-loop on & on. Uncomfy but growing on me, insisting I grow too and understand as each lollop of rust and axle is one more self-image, mirror boy think-tank, rumble grumble on the inside, baking on the out, skin even darker now and oh, that Spanish heart-mum packed some sunglasses for me! Believe it, so thoughtful and the glare recedes. My whole body feels alright. I'm OK. Forge on.

Aah, my novel, *your* novel, how are you, don't answer, don't ask then, I won't, my novel, you are stretching unpeeling into the flesh of bestsellerdom, that doom I know you know.

I balance steady stand and piss off the back of the bed of this pick-up, right out onto the road behind, the past, this piss, surfing this vehicle along, pissing and laughing, helmsman too! howling in his rear-view mirror and jostling me about, the fountain spraying & spewing out. I once used a QC's toilet yet this here, this relieving myself miles from any other soul (except wheelhouse driver mate) anywhere, well, it means more and is more unforgettable than any other passing of waste. Ah, my life up till now, what massive imagery, a novelist's hot wet dream, work on it, milk it, there's redemption in this, think of the lists, think of Middle England, think of Hay-on-Wye. & forget Newspaperland *forever*.

(...I just may be going real deal nutso... but my senses are so so fresh and honest, the sixth one certain, I swear...)

The chariot pushes on. Must be way gone noon. I like noon. Say it. *Noon*, nothing for miles still, and I wonder: is there enough NOON-room here for the novel to expand some more, clarify, answer, and conclude (not a damn question, any of it – do not answer).

I tap out a little beat and try a bit more song-hipster. I am BLACK you know. I am WHITE you know. I'm every shade of every colour imaginable in between – *boom tatta catta boom tat cat*...

Dodge your own very self scared of experience I sing the body electric
you sit yer ass on the fence vir-chew on this and charac-tar the road stick
a thumb in the air and wink at what you chose it's o'clock for
DECISIONS be crazy be blessed borders deep horizons already pumping
in your chest (ba toom ba-toom) be crazy be blessed it's all a game of
CHEST (ba-tum-tumming my chest now like an animal)

So everything I have ever had has always been right here in my chest. What I have seen and learned for years, yeah, that changes large and intense, that's all HEADWORK, the mental stuff, the critical thinkers, seers, listeners, control panel captain. But thorax and in-viscerals, the pumpers, they never change I reckon; sure, adapt and grow some for their growing homes, but the boomboom and hi-ways and bi-ways, we overlook these natural gifts and refer back to the captain up top, who in turn STRONGARMS us into the continuance of disregarding the boomboom box when I reckon we should all sit down a while and really listen to the beat, feel it, move with it, react to it and bounce and smile and thrive. Now I must work with it and I place my hand on my cage for true Luca and then I don't remember too much about the crash, just *thudTHUD* and fairground SKID waltzer then NOTHING. I write *trepidation* and *lovebird squeaks in a cage in the corner* and must be hospital bed trying to think back and this would make sense considering being involved in pick-up crash and all. And *rush* surging pain blur, there's an empty bed next to me and no real noise just a low little buzz and bleach smell. It could be death. But could I scribble arm dangling this book on the floor if this was death or en route or wait! not a question, see, I can't be dead, I recall certain things lucid now, like little black Jewish kid and Newquar I mean Newquay and Argos box van, Australia, Honey Bee Home Little Old Luca, where's your nu-friends now, who are you, what the fuck's going on... answerless, pen tired too, horrible bleach tired as hell no helmsman in here that poor helpful beautiful wheelhouse soul his wife and kid at CROSS-tax heart home... it's so SO dark and this room folds up over me blanket g o ne...

Oh boy, oh brother, oh Fitzwilliam IV, it was all a dream. No, **oh no it wasn't**, children, hell no, it **HUGELY** was not a dream, it is all FULL of heart and unavoidable truth hurt, inescapably **real**.

Yes, it's a weird old Spanish hospital with too-high war-on-film ceilings and one far-end window curtained off, allowing just edge-lines of light in. A beacon. Daytime out there, fighting to get in here, yeah, yes it is. I'm bandaged up, plaster cast on left ankle, yeah the pick-up SMASH. Everything was rumbling along so pleasant and Pamplona and Hemingway surely just round the next bend, those beautiful old white walls and linterns (is that what they're called?) or shutters and red scarves and bulls stupid charging round after Christ-knows-what and Christ is the brave bloodied teenager in the ring, awaiting his final blow. And now this here, must be drugs getting pumped into me making me semi-delirious and pain-free and I remember the lucid (what a coolCOOL writer-word) head rush of narc-pallery in-out bull-rush hyphen-hell stabstabbing but nice and fuck Hemingway and Stein and those bully old gangs (don't know why I say that, I love their words – I *do* – I *did* – Little Old Luca, I can remember, you know).

So would you care to invest in my treasure chest of hope and fear and love and dreams and chance 'cause the days are over of fortitude working all year long you know it's true saving month to month for that week in the south of France Côte d'Azur are you sure so come with me on a merry-go-there we'll dance and drink the days into the nights who cares if the sun will rise if the clocks all work no matter what the time just toss your watch come on kick-start your life Côte d'Azur sling it on it's money well spent on your new coat d'Azur feel the lure... BONJOUR...

33

I must get out of this cuckoo place. The doctors and nurses are pretend, I'm sure. All these drugs, man, and gawping hallway drifters. Check bedside backpack, sewn-in safe passport and cash and I'm blasting out the blinding sun side-door FREE again, crutches yeah, but FREE and I fast-hobble off to a parked-up bus revving and smoking, ready to go. Balls to Pamplona. New light Luca with whooming pot-leg and boxes of painkiller supra is heading south, is it south? not sure, just got to get me some surf, soonest closest wherever...

My head spins but it is back vital and new, ready, out of breath, DID ALL THIS HAPPEN, still no questions, there are so damn many and not enough sluicing time, I'll tell you till I'm blue in the ears. I quick three-sigh, test all my senses and thinkers – I'm alright. I wonder about pick-up wheelman, maybe perished in the crash, his family back in that lovely little home. I cry a bit, leg up on the back seat of this clatter bus. (I write BESTSELLER and consider what that actually means now and my heart nearly gives in, I don't give a hoot about it, I just want something which blatantly screams out at you: ARE YOU THE SAME HAVING READ THIS? And don't answer, you pricks, because I ain't even asking (ouch).)

I demand the sea. Pop up a real winder. Ride it out. Holler at the world. I wantit needit want it need it DESIRE, the surf of life. I'M SORRY, SWEET SPANISH FAMILY, I HAVE KILLED YOU...

The bus trugs along. I flip-flop stagger crutch off bus, shuttle train, back bus, fast train SOUTH gotta get there, eat up this hot land, gobble up the sun *pound pound pound* painkiller dumb slumber, pulses of sharp life in my system and blood runners and sinew and these cuts and bruises make other passengers SWooN on their way past, but hey, conversation is minimal, thank you, it's HYPNO *ZOOM* TIME on non-prescribed serio-power narc-pallery, ah my pals! now hand fist over tongue over dub boom cuckoo cuckoo, all that *FIZZ & TONK*.

Eat me up, dear south, DEAR east, any which today, and forever. I'm coming, je viens, get there get there, fix bones, head's on the quick mend. Still sorry, was it... should I... oh shit.

34

(Dear Stanislas, I am down, way weigh down, but not OUT. Back on my way UP, heading to the SEA. Make sense? Fine. Love Luca.)

35

Even asleep now, fast & deep, there's a whirring old donkey engine generator like the ones that run temporary traffic lights and temporary power lines for temporary digger drivers and cranes (part time in their GODliness) whistling and whirring & whizzing away even on these smooth zip*zip* trains some of them up & over double-deck spacers and rocket affairs.

Stan's good money is still well over two grand, these purloined cuckoo tranquilliser pellets are not quite Pac-Man beauties but still suspensory kind and head-over-a-heel considerate. Agua, every stop, agua, more agua, hobble to piss, hop to seat, days now, vast sprawling SPAINFRANCE clicking on by, tapas, sweetpains, gummy bears to suck-try to forget, zigzag skip rope, I'm on the fix. Smiles and giddy faces out there are growing thicker and faster with every station lull & surge, lull & surge, mile on mile, searing hot mechanical boomboom, diesel, electric, kinetic coin-toss, shall we deliver these passive slugs to their DESTINATIONS, I dunno, maybe, are they good, are they seers, is he Little Old Luca, yeah, that black kid there in plaster cast gloop...(?)

Yabberla bood Yabberla bood

1, 2, 3, 4

4:4:4:4

Bauhaus Steptoe

JJSL

Yabberla bood Yabberla bood

36

4:4 what a discovery room, what a capsule of kick-start watch-toss journey. O that surf too, that wet kiss and stretched-out stillness riding the WORLD & Biarritz, BEER RITZ, the secret room, that mad crane GOD about to *snap*, where are you beach and sea and DON'T EVEN ANSWER... I see you all looming up over there grinning wild and blue and hazy got-it, "I GOT YOU!"

37

Man, look at yourself, Luca. Check it out, Luke. Cuts and bust-up and shunting lip-chin. Leg, well, done-in, hip all bent and ribcage tender as a virgin's groom. Things have changed. You *have* been moved. It is NOT YOUR FAULT.

Eloquent unique diverse Mr Publisher I promise to do my best just remember my propensity to curse and to rave like Cheswick from The Cuckoo's Nest

38

And here I am. And yeah, stolen me a wheelchair, a scorching opportunity outside a fruit shop I couldn't pass up and off I go, crutches splayed out like tank guns, backpack life safe on my lap, 100-metre free-wheel down to that golden sweet beach, ahh, the smells (this damn pen just about running out, we're both tired but we are here come on keep going...) royal blue heaven look-down gulls on their hungry din-play, I'm here, my NOVEL & ME, free-wheeling and dirty busted hot. You got me, I know it and I'm here for you and you alone...

39

(Dear Stan, I made it! I don't know what it is, but I've made it.)

40

Picasso-legged women in shops I've seen before and melting *clack*clack of sidewalks and roundabouts, mopeds and taxi-cabs. Schcooching this parade endless bright tomfoolery and YES! YES! finally, ahhhh the girls and beachfront tans, yes it is tootoo fashionista, but I don't care...

41

"You are lucky, friend, there is rarely surf here in ANTIBES, but only in the wake of a big storm, and last night we have bigBIG storm, so surf is coming but WAIT! you are bigBIG disabled, non? Look, your leg, you can NOT surf, no, non, my friend..."

I absorb the Antibes Cap out the coat-hang there, and yeah a touch of *break* and it is building, the back-end gesture of storm whip, scuttering off as it waves toodaloo and heads to Africa and the rest of the greedy winking world. Then it's *hack* at my plaster cast and ask my new friend to help, por favor, s'il vous plait, no, please please, and this kid, a surf kid for sure, gets his grubbies on some scissors somehow – some scissors! – ah, the florist friend, he looks on, smiling, he knows, and I cut away, it's the ONLY thing I need, everything else is just a GIANT NOTHING (stems and petal lips flying about and smelling good).

The surf kicks up into a thin little triangle of rolling, licking sweetsweet-child popping-options. Impossible to ignore. Yeah, I've got a board. I feel no pain. The sun is up. I am up, CHRIST, I can taste the world, let me BE IT, allow me to wallow and savour every soul's pain, let me suck it all up, I'll be *the one*, whip me into a frenzy, thrash me about in bone*crack* euphoria, fling me along, that's ME, I'm LUCA, *HERE I AM*! Hurt me, give me it all, I say, and my holler unforgettable now I AM SORRY... TRULY SORRY... FORGIVE MEEEeeeeeeee!!>>>>>>...>>>

Boats and yachts and loopy old money, lapping it all up, man, I'm here alright, sore as old hell, but I got it. Seriously, I just might have it made. There's forgiveness everywhere. I'm thanking everything.

42

Some new nu surf buds and pallery locals reckon it's more than First Aid Sam required now and one of these beautiful ones gets me and my gear, wheels and all, up and in the back of his ute – a fucking UTE! beaut! – and it's local hospital and insurance forms and not so meaningful smiles off busy busy medicine types scurrying the triage corridors, three or four worlds different from that other backwater mend-up place (did that happen, was I there?), a newer smell, brash and clean, way clean and much more light, yeah, it is wholly acceptable. And people galore, younger faces the lot of them and visitors existing with Lacoste sweaters tied around necks, oh my what a *louche noose* – ahhhhhaahhaa! – whadda crackpot! – I'm back up, taking somewhat of a serious word from senior doctor now having curtly finished the patch-up work and re-caster-perlaster and all that. "Do not worry," I told them all, **"for I am LUCA."**

> *the riddle of the Surf the battle of the sands*
> *searching since birth for the one to truly hold my hand*

Sure, I think about Jess and Jaime, Stanislas the most. Bob & Maggie, that scolded scalded dog, crushed to bloody dust Dad, Morocco Mum. Pick-me-up wheelhouse family man. What does it all mean? Someone once said to me:

EVERYTHING IS MENTAL or else it wouldn't be worth thinking about

...and he's got a point but I'm through quoting every prick else and reading all those old heroes and listening to all the old classics. They are ALL cover versions anyway, right? & now it is time for my very own. I'll leave my own marks, carving for real. It's NOVEL-time (what a hoot).

43

There's weeping and howling and angel sounds, harps and wolves
the new world we are bound.

Everything is a matter of *light & dark*, children, understanding
vitals, catching *breaks*, ahaa – the hubris of being *hip*! (Don't ever
look too far back, you'll get a cricked neck – let's cut down on all
the *ouch*.)

Ride it out, COON! (my how even *more* novel) Plus tard,
retards, write on, dream on, repletely break it all down... I shall...

44. 44. 44

Today

Dear Mother,

I hope, *truly* hope, you are happy. I love you very much.
Even more so now. I suppose it's because of my little
journey I've just been on; well, let me say it's the start of
many journeys. Destination? Who knows? But I don't think
it'll be too far from any SURF, which is still so very dear to
me. (I find many answers in the sea, you see.)

I feel truly free now, I do not write for the newspapers
any more, I am trying to write a few novels. Yeah, I know,
Mum, a novelist, me, Little Old Luca.

Everyone calls me Luca now. Even all the French folk
around here. There are rich Americans and dirt-poor
Africans here too. Everybody, and I mean *every single soul*, is
lovely and I am in great frolicking spirits. I am finding
EVERYTHING, Mum, even forgiveness.

I will write again soon. Please do write back, I would love that. And the postal service here is excellent (except when they go on strike and bash pots and pans all the damn night).

What do you get up to in Morocco, Mum? How is your new husband? *So many damn questions, not enough sluicing time* – one of Dad's sayings you taught me, remember?

Ah well, I write with a true love in my entire system now, which you instilled in me... and I love you for that. I had forgotten or misplaced the whole *Notion*, but now it is back... thank YOU.

Your son, Luca. *I am new light.*

I enclose a very special type of shell which reminded me of your beauty. If it is missing, start asking questions.

P.S. I have met quite simply the perfect girl. She is alive with life and French and is easily a dream. She is moved by me too, somehow! Her name is Élodie Faurlain and yes, when you pronounce it... it says L.O.D. as in *Light Or Dark.* Insane, right? We are to visit her place in Paris soon. You have been there before, I think? Is it beautiful?

Oh, yeah... is there any reggae in Morocco? What about harps... or wolves? And have you seen my novel in the shops yet? Write soon. Bah-bye. X

...

<fin?>

...

MODERATELY
NOT
RUSHED

1.

MUSIC

Let's all judge a man by the shirt that's on his back
Or the ideas he has built on the face
Of what's fact is truly fact

Even maybe the skin he wears or the way he rides the bus
Or what about his sisters and brothers
Or what he merrily sings while he readily cooks?

Now look...

2

This is a strange NOW. Here, I mean... HERE? & Now. I write this
and I look around at where and who and all that. Me. I know I've
been *out* for some time, but yes, I do remember the BUG, you
know, that spindly haunted dragonfly bug, and now here I am, in
this bed, in this room. Paris. Oui, yep, yes it is. And there is that
terrific writer: Luca. *Light & Dark*, I realise we are all in the know
about it now, I sure do. Well, let's face it; his book struck
something in me so strong and meaningful that it made me write
like this and act like this, BE like this (my NU-me, he would say,
right?). And there is Celine, undoubtedly glorious, and this sister
of hers, Élodie, yes, and the doctor, too, he has gone now in that
strange little hat he wears but he feels so strongly involved and
yeah, just WOW really. Christ, Queequeg, I musta been out for
weeks, man. It's September the 14th! Can that seriously be true?

We chatter and meet and dig all the queer randomness vibe
and, really, the girls are quite *au fait* with all the madness and

223

happenstance and I'm slowly regaining my strength and mental awareness and heart pumpability of blood and feeling and, well... what the true fuck is going on?

There's a real endlessness to this classical music, it is perfect. I recall all the good-good gigs and tours and my gone-joy-piece in the manky hands of that manky boy in scurrilous Trieste with nothing but shorts on. Wait! Quee-*lamperelli*... that IS Celine. Utterly beautiful and just look at her! Is that mine? I have had beauty before, but not like this. She keeps looking at me and looking away and whoop! yes, one of those non-winks, like a slant of suggestive bang-on kook-time RIGHT. Wow. I got it. I'm back *zhoom*ing and I feel just fine.

Writer-boy Luca keeps on about the fates and words and music, *THE BLOOOOZE* he calls it, hell, I've a suspicion we may already love each other, all us vivid dreamy souls here.

It's tonight now, we are all preparing for a delivery-dinner of sorts, pretty high-faluting kinda deal really, which goes against any of my fast-food aspirations immediately and it's all *YOU SURE YOU'RE OK TO COME DOWN? SHALL WE ASK THE DOCTOR OVER FOR DINNER JUST IN CASE?* etc.... and I just say yeah, I'm fine, I'M OK, I'm Oscar, I'm Katrina... and everyone disappears like dust to get blown and skinn'd up into their no. 1s or something.

I look around this sickbedroom with all its wires and machinery and miraculous contraptions which have kept me alive during coma-time. Oh, it's weird alright. And my wrist is now just slightly bulbous, yes, but not ripe, not ready to lunge its killer blow, it's a has-been, a tried-that, failed-there, just rather ugly now and tired-looking hanger-on. Queest! Have I mentioned my stump dreams? Must have. Ah, come on, forget it, let's go...

My tiny case is here. All my old clothes, sure, and they smell, wait... they smell brand new! They are mine, but everything so fresh and abundantly vital. There's France out there and Paris, *o Paris*, there you are; rangy, elliptical, loose and all things sparkle. Mystifying sun-dog, splitting the sky into dozens of daytime searchlights, prowling around, looking for Christ knows what.

I move and jiggle first my fingers, the lazy thumbs, arms. Shoulders, neck, shed the sick clothes and announce my new-me NU-me arrival back in this nu-Francelife and here's that magic *lift* coming to wallop me up... WAMMO... up I go, BLAMMmmm!

3

The Faurlain girls get busy doing whatever they kitchen fancy. It's me and the writer. The writer and me.

I tell him just how much his novel means to me. Its effect on me. Seriously, I confirm, I mean it. He's just all: Well, you know, your music has done the same for me, for years now, released me, made me believe, shit, I'd be back in Local Newspaperland with Maggie & Bob if it weren't for you, and isn't every little piece of capricious art just a damn cover version anyway, where is true originality, is it in the improvisation of form? and it all flows out this fast and everything feels just right. We smile, we even break out in this little sing-song which reminds me of the time with the big Greek fella back in Barça. See, I *am* OK. A tremendous fraternal ether binds the two of us almost immediately and isn't it peculiar how that just *happens* at times?

Pine bouquet wine. The girls, the pair of them jostle and joke and feed and pry and suggest all in their classy Frenchness and it is love... ly.

I fancied asking Luca about his pals Stanislas and the J's from his novel. Whether they were real or not or what... but I refrained.

225

Instead he launched full-bore into asking *me* about *my* writing. Not my music, nah, my writing. Hah, unbelievable. & *Why wouldn't it be successful* and all general niceties come out of him. *Let's have a look at it, we could work together perhaps, my lying slimeball agent's dumped me for some other hero, and my publishing contract is currently worth about* <tears napkin to shreds>, *so timing is swell*, and I just go: OH GOODIE.

These secret life-speakers, *satori* speakers, burst into action and us four we all lean in and listen and feed and slake and really get busy on the actual NU-life meet.

I have lifted a lot of your sayings and ideology from your *Restlessness*, you know? You HAVE? Oh yes. Well, isn't that simply beautiful? and there's zero sarcasm or mawkish sleights, none of that awkward business, he really means it and is quite proud, chest out, chin up, alive. Thank you, he adds. And I say the same. Perspectives and perceptions get mentioned and ripe and rife and teeth and cleave. Learning fresh, a nu way to breathe. On y va... and both the girls join in now... ON Y VA! And there's a gentle little rap-rap at the front door and then a louder bangbang and some audible excitement chatter out there and we all consider & tic-tac-toe who's the delightful chosen one with enough *Caña Brava* to go see to it.

4.

PANOS

This may be remarkable. Or maybe it ain't. Either way, here's my remarks...

Call me Panos. I am a proud Greek man. Here I have lived, Paris, the most beautiful city in the world, for over three decades now, I realise, yet a proud Greek man I remain.

My English language, I suppose, is acceptable. Please forgive my *wrongthings* (the good doctor told me to use that word) as my think-translate-work goes Greek–French–English, so do afford me some EU slack if you will (maybe huge commercial metaphor here lies within... suck it & see perhaps?).

I'm remarking to fetch this whole she-bang a little closer together it seems. To near a conclusion for this writer artist TRIPTYCH ensemble or something. Here to clarify and to put any worries and concerns in to their respective hammocks to swing away, nice and easy. Respect perspective. And MY perception of all this, now this is what matters most I have been re-assured, so here goes...

5

There exists an old Greek saying which roughly suggests: I will not spoon-feed you, I shall provide the spoon, the rest is up to you... the usage, the scraping and shovelling of foodstuffs, the inserting into mouth and then taste/savour/digest if you can/want, well, that's up to you and now I think about it, I better tell you we're all here, at the stunning Faurlain Residence, Paris, France.

Me, I am gardener. I have Benzema, my dog, a Labra-stiff cross I rescued from a Pyrenees campsite I visited a few years ago, way up in the clouds on the end of a chain.

I work here for 33 years now for Monsieur Faurlain who is now himself gone even beyond chains and clouds where no rescue exists.

Benzema, me, all this garden, the three-circle pool, flora & fauna I understand, you see. Human forms, not as much, and hence, I provide spoon, the rest is up to you. (Understand so far? I hope so.)

Celine Faurlain. The beautiful eldest daughter who now owns this whole estate. She is here and beautiful, yes. The sick black Music Man who now gets his health better. Celine loves and cares dearly for this famous man. I believe them to have a gorgeous future together, for many years.

The sister Élodie Faurlain. They are different indeed, these siblings, yet alarmingly similar too, at the same time. She is here. As is Luca the great writer fellow. Already successful here in his half-brown skin and long dirty bundles of hair and wonderful general outlook on things. Now Élodie loves and cares dearly for this man. Their futures together? Hmmm, not sure, but at least for now, they are happy. Incredibly young all these characters, the good doctor also, whom I have mentioned already, Dr Sagan. He comes every few days for check-ups with Music. So that is six human forms us here. Plus Benzema the dog form. And NOW wait for it... these two arrive. Another damn writer and his blonde child-like girlfriend just sauntering around getting to know the place and all of us seem to understand or at least lean towards the reckoning of how we have all ended up here, at this time. But please tell me... why so many writers of a sudden? And are they any good, will they stand the test of...

TIME ISN'T YOURS TO LOSE
POSSESS YOUR **LIFE**
IT'S THE ONLY THING YOU'LL EVER TRULY OWN

7

But we can't all sincerely question why and where4 too much or else we shall just overthink and wither and die. No, we must continue from here on in, here we go... (I am seriously trying to remain in control of this pen but I am not a man of the word, you must realise this by now, well, WHO THE HELL IS? Maybe these so-called best-seller chaps, I'll ask them...)

They appear to have formed an alliance of some sort, these dreamy characters here. Near enough strangers not so long ago, yet now, their collective reasoning/metaphysical acceptance of coincidences and fates and desires and this undeniable spirit of a tantalisingly wet-ONENESS, the type of which I have never witnessed before. Even before my work-life, when I was a studying type, all over the world.

The overriding sense which I gather (indeed they have elicited this intention to me quite clearly, so *I* am not a genius) is that they are all now embarking on a literary adventure together, to best sell I suppose even though Luca is the only one already recognised as such. And all their energies seem to have stemmed from his success with *Light & Dark Restlessness* novel (yes, I have been introduced, it's here in my pocket).

Sure, the Music Man is already a famous artist, a horn-blower, in fact, an art form I truly admire. This other, new writer fellow, still very mysterious and free-spirited and full of genuine ease &

flow. And all their respective female partners. It is a strange going-on, I'll grant you that, and I am trying my damnedest to explain but remember I still have my job to do, Benzema and me, we are gardeners, for the sake of *cieux*.

One of my sons, Dimi, he must be involved here somehow. This is all right up his avenue. *Craziness art beauty adventure philosophy life-changing happenings.* Yes, it truly is.

He is also with a Faurlain girl, a cousin, and together they live in Barcelona. Celine mentioned that she and Music visited them on their way here and they passed on their regards to me. How nice. And then that bug got into Music and it knocked him real sick. Yeah, you are surely aware of all that, non?

So, yes, Dimi may well visit here soon, so, what is it, yeah... *hold your horses...* but do hold on and read on & persevere because brevity is the soul of wit and I am short-winded in this world and this writing caper and ENDS SHALL MEET, I swear. (Back to garden work and pool dredge... they pay me handsomely, the Faurlain estate, always have, and Benzema eats well.) I do wonder what it all really means and where these beautiful kids-in-the-heads are going with it all, but hell, mind I little.

8

(The fantastic Dr Sagan is quite clearly helping me with translate work. Yet they all insist on me saying whatever pops into my head and through my core and out my *proxy*; incite and encourage *VIPASSANA*, it has to be your immediate thought-work, Panos, just let it out, be water... it all makes me laugh inside and this experiment of these boy-men seems absurd from every angle. Best-sellers, pre-conceived fame, associated wealth and lucid tenets and understandings and love-lives indulgence and *qui la baise* le Queequeg anyway?)

9

M. Faurlain was very decent man to work for. After he died, not so much. (I kind of lost the fire.)

He liked to keep his distance from me, socially versus professionally, you understand, even though we were very similar in age. He was constantly a week younger than me, all his life, and maintained a rank system between himself and the staff quite firmly. One day he just un-employed the entire house staff + two drivers. Simple as that. A day or so later, he died. I wondered if he just plain forgot about me and Benzema and his beautiful plot of garden land. But then, after the reading of the will, it directed the estate to continue my employ, my flat in the city, my motorbike maintenance, healthcare for Benzema. The lot. It was astonishing. But real and heart-warming.

I once made him really laugh with another old Greek hand-me-down from my great father:

If you are on the throne
And it is approaching wipe-time
And you feel a sneeze coming on...
Well, sneeze first

O yes, he laughed at that and chuckled his whole body away into the house most likely mentally discussing with himself all the possible meanings (ALLEGORIES the good doctor reassures me, that is what he was considering, NOT the crass overtones).

Another time, the cars + drivers were away winning medals at a country fair somewhere and he absolutely required to get into the city with immediacy and roused me from my outdoor toil reverie (it was raining all sorts of domesticated fauna at the time) and I got him on the back of my TRIUMPH with Benzema left in charge of the house and garden, and no helmets off we roared, my racing experience serving us well on the slimy roads.

We got there. M. Faurlain was clamped onto my back like a crab-shell. And he was the odd colour of midnight snow and speechless. He needed a good drink and a short massage before he remembered exactly where he had to be with such urgency. He got a taxi back. Never rode with me again. He did put my wages up after that incident, which I was very grateful for, and I treated the TRIUMPH to an oil change and Benzema to steak.

"Sneeze first," he'd whisper at me in passing and sort of wink. "Heehehehee..."

We liked and respected him very much. We never ask about Mme Faurlain. She was never here, and that was that.

10

Has anybody mentioned my heart operation yet? Or what about all the writings on the walls inside? I think you know of this already, although I have yet to read all this dynamite triptych starting with Luca's novel here in my tap-tap pocket. Well, M. Faurlain started the words on the walls business, years ago, and these kiddy characters now add to it all and carry on like circus freaks with their dancing and music and all-round decent, freely-intentioned living that seems to be hot and bouncing nowadays (right this second I can hear 'Wear You to the Ball' in all its pure reggae vagaries blaring out from inside there and foot stomps and celebratory whoops. How do they do it? Paracetamol? And how long will it continue?). I love this new action, it has been frightfully dull the last few years, understand, but I realise it must end soon, and this peaceful VIPASSANA (further update from new writer & Luca again) does sound attractive and damned if it isn't 'Shaving Cream' by the Fabulous Five in its parody FIZZ & TONK (guess who) all brave and crackly reminds me of my dear old friend Purvis from Bridgetown. Lots of towns are bridges, right? Lots of people are bridges, too. Are bridges just bridges? Christ, I am as bad as these over-thinking fruits.

I worry about this writing charade, I do, and I wish the good doctor's father from Morocco would help and all this best-seller chatter from this lot... "It'll be fine, we swear," and I think to myself: I know you swear, I hear you all damn day and night, you mother-fuckers. Always half-naked japery and handstands and water games, cavorting and tireless.

Luca says he must go to find some surf soon. He comes and chats to me the most, not just at random meal times, but most afternoons, and we drink and talk about dogs and history and death. He is one-of-a-kind this man-boy and what a presence he has, an aura golden and definite. He laughs a lot. Lovely and loud, and his skin is caramel, lighter than Purvis once was but very similar faces and he reminds me of pure youth and hopefulness and he helps me garden sometimes, strong and patient. He and Benzema play and chase about. Then the remaining cast come join in and days melt away, a few weeks now have gone by, months? Who knows? Senseless time rules this ship now and it is quite decent especially since "There's nothing wrong in being a dreamer, just don't ever wake up," someone keeps reminding us and it certainly reminds me of yet another great father hand-me-down which I can't fully remember right now.

Enough, I will write more soon, my wine and garden and dog await me outside, and I still have to write to Dimi also, ask when he comes visit. My other son Kostas is a drummer with a band, a not very good band, but I rarely hear from him. Maybe he will visit also, I do hope so, who knows. Peace and unity and everything, Panos.

11.

SAXON

& call me Saxon. Or Vivian. Quentin Crisp or Amundsen's teeth. The divine Edgar, Cain. I care little for straps and tags. Yet love, real love, hope-full love, oozes and squirms around me like sweet protection wherewithal snakes, calm and coping.

You celestial simpletons, you. Of course you all understand this situation. Of course we are here at the sumptuous chez Faurlain. And of course the Musician and the girls, Panos the gardener, big boy Benzema and Dr Patrice Sagan are real. This beautiful discourse has crests, ons, offs, sure, but what shall remain is the truth. Hearty giddy-up brow-sweat truth. Light, dark & every shade imaginable, charted or not, in between. Phew. That particular sluice felt good, feels good, we've been caught right up, introduced and rip-tide drunk.

September, October, not one of us here seems too concerned. Maybe Benzema, who longs for cooler days, no doubt, shedding and panting and sun-dodging like a soldier.

Déjàs vu occur, mainly for me, which reminds me of one more Irish granddadness: *déjà vu? Well, you are on the right path, my boy.* & this seems to tickle Luca the Great into tremendous reminiscences about Jaime and Jess, Stanislas and surf. Yes, we are all quite familiar, perhaps not Panos just yet, but that knowledge will happen soon, I am sure.

Candi Staton comes on, the music so constant and necessary. Like blood flow, pump pump, lizardless, but the hearty snakes still appear to me, serpents at door jambs, stairwells, inside cupboard space, secret back-room hullaballoo areas, the lot.

Adele and the French near-royal girls get along just fine. They whisper and giggle and shop together having reinstated some driver staff formerly employed here by M. Faurlain (now dearly departed, yet impossible to portraitly forget) via telephone. "It's only right," one of them qualifies and *phhwwoppps* yet another wine cork to go spiralling up amongst dusty chandeliers.

The Musician is convalescing wonderfully, Dr Sagan confirming that with each visit, & yeah, he can take alcohol on board now, but go gentle, like a child. "Aren't we all?" chuckle time. And over-the-road hyphen-Rob? Well, he's still back over wet homeward roads no doubt, but quite absurd, isn't it, how he knew about all this panning out before the story had begun its very own ink-path? The story came from him! Now just remember... WHERE THE FUCK IS THE DESTINATION? And what's that blood-curdling Dan bastard Kemp up to? Oh, that guy.

WHO CARES? And it's hot meal day and the delivery service in their town cars are bang on time, whatever in the hell time that is.

This is bliss. Sincerely. Some literary BIOPIC bliss, I swear. Right up there with, well, nothing else. Wow. At last, ORIGINALITY in all its blatant dressings. Success. Tastes and smells like it ought to and the hot food sails down and youthful exuberance prevails (Music is almost 40 years of age, it transpires) & this will prove a smashing triptych, I just know it. Maybe overwhelmingly so. (Reckon Panos the gardener is about 60-some, Benzema just fearsome, but sweet also, and ready to go giddy-insane at chin-scratch.)

Have our characters developed any? Our styles? Our art of capriciousness? Has that lik(e)able rogue PLOT peeked its curious peepers over the dam yet? I would love to have a thrash on that TRIUMPH. (Can you fully comprehend the excitement and recent fantastical ambition of Adele? Dan fucking Kemp's sweet former underling. Can you? After the initial BOOM of realisation and acceptance, including the announcement of *I just got his damn autograph at Charles de Gaulle airport the other week!* she simply folded her own persona and understandings within these luxurious ingredients and bakingly funny hideousness took a hold, tasty as risen sin itself. Desire. There she is. It didn't take long.)

12

"Well... haven't you just cheated, though?"

"What?"

"You know, the story, *this* story of the Musician, ahh, *Leisurely Moving Without Hate...*"

"Without *HASTE...*"

"Yeah, yeah, well, it has actually happened, hasn't it? It ain't fiction. It ain't original. I mean, come on..."

<pause>

"Yes, sweetling. But I didn't know, did I?"

"Well, who did, then?"

& all relevant parties gently raised their paws in the air one after the other, here at the big main table, pretend shy-looking, and someone even suggested over-the-road Rob may have his slick paw in the air also, maybe at the Golden Galleon, or maybe on hold with TOSHIBA customer care, but oh yes, it was a coolcool laugh alright, magic throughout and an ancient live recording of some madmad poetry by silly William Burroughs came pouring forth from speakers cornerly strung. We all quite tritely tore into some post-prandial paper acid strip-down squares and toasts to ponconby-tri Bloomsbury & whacked-out discussions fluid and real got borne were born, we all screamed *LUCID*! like loons &

considered notion after KeY-SeE-notion mainly about these novels best-selling, big deals, helter-skelters with hippos in tanks.

Music just sort of shrugged and smiled, then roared with delight. Deep down helpless laughter. Contagion, all of us gone then. Now. Maybe forever. "LIFERS?" Luca suggested & we all slipped off into a dream.

13

I awoke to some news whispering about mal-this and mal-that. Fleurs and temps, perdus and defenestrations. I only made out about 15 words in all, mostly badness, worldwide havoc. What can be done?

Considered some cheer-up tonics like "Chin up, Buster" and gorgeous young old Rip, now cavorting with elm roots and wormage back in Sussex firma. My gone folks, Tabasco. Brighton marina wall & Jesse James. Then: am I really here? Has all this actually taken place? "Do not ye worry," I am reassured. Outside I can hear magnificent church bells and the unmistakeable clutch of a Citroën. (Today I may just jump aboard that glorious TRIUMPH and ride like the wind.)

Defiance. Loop. Immortal. Coin.
Fear. Fly. Internal. Boom.

14

You know on awakening after a decent night's snooze when you half-absorb the real-time morning and simply incorporate it into a continuance of dream world? Yeah? Good. Because I know this feeling ridiculously well. As does Emin the great. I just asked her.

I look up. At least 15 suns winking down at me, dancing, leading the way, ah, the right path, pirrow-sillloow-ettes, I think, & leave the property walls behind me, the Triumph beneath me throttled, gargling, dying to unleash in tights, in mirrors oblique and sweet.

Providence, that ultimate show-off, had allowed for this, my solo adventure, as Panos had dreamily agreed the bike-loan under the hot afternoon duress of siesta. Benzema? Out cold. Hot as hell. Paws twitching like Rip in a storm. And the rest of the party? Lost in their own familiar chatter now, rampantly wide-eyed and happy.

I opened her up and *whooshed* off on stones, gravel, semi-grass, then crispy tarmac. Oh as I was young and at the mercy of T's means sang Dylan or Jimmy or something of that chainful painful order. I knew my rights and lefts, thank the cages and their wages because fellow traffic here all seemed unmanned and melting.

I reined her back in on approaching the whistle and fugue of Paris for real. Funny how I felt so much better at low speed now, utterly at peace with all the TRIUMPH power at my beck & call, knowing damn well I could explode and soar at any time I wished.

Lights and bends and horns and footfall desperate to die. I slung her into a tiny space plumb outside a Joycean café, between a beaten-in old Mini Clubman and a gleaming Rolls. HA! Yes, this is Paris, I confirmed with a *Metro*.

Once inside, alone except for the rest of France getting served before me, I started riffing on existences and fortitudes, pre-lives who had been in here before me, real, de-real, people and their means, each and every cadence and swirl on Earth had visited every square inch of this venue and I had met them ALL, surely and why oh why in the name of sweet sattva did I order vermouth?

Meaning and analogue emotion are escalating inside me like rudimentary black & white flicker-ticker-footage tape morphing into digital space-age and crystal. My head remains free-form, sure, engaged in the *everything*, yet has such a sensible veneer that my core and fronds rest deliciously, patently clear, full of forever kindness.

Oui, monsieur, I say and water, just bottled water turns up on my table. It is sensational. There's a swan on the bottle. Here I write these words and off we go again on the yawning morning stoop of the planet declaring: "I am here, sweet milk, watery loot, hello, do you hear me? HELLO?? I say hello, cielo, of course you hear me, sure you do... I say greetings, o terrifying world... I LOVE YOU!" and right then and there I promise myself and the ghostly waiter that I shall continue to grow and search right to the VERY END>>>>>>. The Duke comes out these cracklers here and pours about these heavenly airwaves and yeah, it is 'Sophisticated Lady/Solitude', course it is, I know it is and I catch myself in a mirror and I become 15 people, blurry, moon-faced, idealised, at serious peace, even with this grumpy vermouth.

15

THE BEST PEOPLE POSSESS A FEELING FOR BEAUTY, THE COURAGE TO TAKE RISKS, THE DISCIPLINE TO TELL THE TRUTH, THE CAPACITY FOR SACRIFICE. IRONICALLY, THEIR VIRTUES MAKE THEM VULNERABLE; THEY ARE OFTEN WOUNDED, SOMETIMES DESTROYED.

HEM

WHERE IS THE SUNRISE? WHERE IS THE FROST? WHERE ARE MY SEAGULLS? WHERE IS MY COFFEE? WHERE IS LOVE?

MALC

The writing certainly is on the wall here. And the mirrors multiply angles, perceptions, meaning.

16

I dialled the number.

"Kemp?"

"Yeah..."

"Hey."

"Oh... hey, kid, what's up?" & all the rest of it.

"You what! Paris? *MY* fucking Adele? What the fuck, man?" & even more of it.

I told him (à la Luca) it seemed like the right thing to do at the time and hung up. Then asked myself what and how I immediately felt. And I answered NOTHING. Sincerely, not a thing. No envy. No fear. No meanness, what-so-Leonard-ever. Just nothing. Levelled that heavy vermouth with more water, green bottle, empty bottle, swan-like, triumphant.

17

Rumbled through some hectic narrow streets with all that potential humming beneath me like a seething volcano. As slow as mud. Growling, slovenly mud, creeping and confident. It felt good. Eyes followed me, not heads, just the eyes in straight-forward heads, follow follow. Unravel Debussy, I thought and this place sure does feel fantastic and I could hold her back no more

bbbBBBrrrrraaaaaaahhhhhhhhahhhhhhhhhhhhhHHHHHHHHHHH

& I balled on out to the freeway now, shot from a gun, laser-eyed snakes leading the way.

The most natural, simple thing in this universe is a miracle. As passive individuals, we have no say in the matter whatsoever. We get born. Then these plumed serpents start their splurge and grow and lead us through this life BESET by miracles that go flashing by our very eyes attracting ZERO recognition on the hour, the half-hour, by the bloody week.

How do we get by? We ignorant drones, dumb as lamps, tell me... how do we get by? How can we honestly shed light on this ceaseless circle when we don't even fully comprehend our own damn selves? Stop & think. Then you may as well just have a long drink. Because everywhere you look there's a dog-damn miracle going down. Deny it. I dare you. Then finish the drink and start again.

Yep, I reckon it's the back-end of the latest acid-banger creating this miracle jabber and a sudden *Whizzer and Chips* moment in my mind's 30 eyes. Even at these speeds with the arrondissements flashing by and the spindly trees peacocking their indifference and the threat of a serious downpour and what's that noise, that high-pitched faraway squeal, and bugs squish on the goggles of Panos on the head of my frame still rollicking along at 99 and not far from Faurlain now, shit, SHIT, it's a siren whining, and lights now, SHHIIIT speed kill speed 80... 65... shit no licence, nothing, I'm going to fucking jail... 50 to 20, stationary heart in gob and legs a-rattle and GENDARMERIE car siren out he gets talking fucking furious French into his CB radio. Glad I kicked the gears down fast. & glad that bastard siren's stopped.

He immediately speaks broken English. Now that's not right, is it?

I oblige and kill the TRIUMPH fully and de-goggle and bug blood and guts on my shaky fingers now. Christ. Breath test? Drug test? Jail//..,,,,<<<>./>>>///.,,mmmmm/.<.?.,..................

18

"How do you know my name?" I instinctively ask.

"Now please, remain calm."

<pause>

"Calm? I am calm," I lie.

"OK, good. Ah, well... you must understand *implosion*."

"What... *implosion*?"

"EXPLOSION, yes. Explosion."

"*Explosion?*"

"Yes, chez Faurlain, the house, it has gone" <hands gesture blow-up> "*boom.*" He points into the distance too and yeah, there's a fucking plume, a stream of thick, black smoke spiralling skywards on the horizon like a victory monster. A leviathan, an untamed sick nasty A-bomb nimbus-whore, slithering, proud, ghastly.

"They all dead."

WHAT? ALL? DEAD? and I can't really, well, I go a bit numb and chokey. I don't think about jail then. I think about human forms blackened like coal and Japanese mushrooms and I strangely think about Panos and his REMARKABILITY and my head turns into an acrylic smudge swirling the WORLD in its swaddling colours and only time, real FRENCH time will tell if I am dead or *alive*, stoned and rolling to hell and that cop looks just like Proust, are you fucking shitting me? He gives me a half-arsed hug, a consolatory act. I wipe the bug blood and guts off my fingers onto his shoulders.

It rains now. Not real heavy, but sheety and very wet. The cop says, "That is good for the fire," and leaves.

19

Anti-novel uncle book
Who truly cares
Whose fuck's been fucked?

Wane the wax the Beats the Creeps
Who truly cares
Whose luck's been fleeced?

Load the dice crying's real nice
Who truly cares
Three times or thrice?

Anti-novel a writer's whim
Who truly cares
If the hero wins?   **WHO?**

20

(Newspaper A-frame headline translations: Asylum-seeker slays local man over half a chocolate Pop-Tart. Two men argue in McDonald's queue, agree to a shoot-out in neighbouring street. Promising young poet dies after falling down a chimney at a

Marxist roof party. I can see it over the road there. All that suffering and loss.)

21

I'm still here in this lay-by. Hot visions are all vertiginous and sickly. Just thinking about that word *sickly* makes me heave. I heave. That comic-death monster cloud forms and curves and licks into an eyeless quasi-animal face, wait, it's fucking pre-bug Gregor Samsa, now half-bug mouth loosing off with ravenous guilty .22 bullet teeth and *bangbang* tongue: *There's a true difference, child, between disruptiveness... and REAL problems.* (I can smell extreme ugly, more vomit, bile, vermouth and captain slop yet can NOT drag my eyes away from the cloud face.) *Once you understand that seemingly unfair developments in your own ENLIGHTENMENT are all part of a broader and ultimately ESSENTIAL cycle of change, these un-Earthly twists and sickly* <heave> *turns you are encountering will become acceptable. You will see. Things will turn out. Trust your vitals, tonight's new moon ushers in momentous breakthroughs, and you will grow and benefit from them, only if you believe in them, you simply MUST! Now get up! Be a man, get up and GO!*

(I *am* going insane.)

22

That beastly marauder Kafka cloud, that gobshite plot-house cinder plume, that up-there smoky death cunt, well, thankfully it starts breaking up now, fragmenting into tiny diamonds and Pollocks. I'm on my knees looking up still. Desire this man's art, that man's scope. LIFE is all before me. Providence is tickling my

245

balls with an unused paintbrush. Squirms and pinches up there now, and yes, it is, it's gathering back into itself, a mass of unctuous ugly deepdeep purply-black nightmare stuff. Refolding, rethinking, replanning. And yep, here it comes, unreeling vast and fully towards me, slowly and building and pumpy hypnotic, tie-dye shit. Dark, real dark, crimson gunshot, liver SmUdGe. Bruise and dried bloody knots, chimera river flow, the lot. And it's gonna get me, here I am, still empty, powerless, vomity, gone. And in it all comes, as easy as that, painless, acceptable, in it all comes now, I can't stop this natural selection, can I? Fuck no. *SSCCHHHHLLLLOOOooooooppppppPPPP* in it comes, in my eyes, ears, mouth, under fingernails, squirting and jetting in through leg wounds and tiny half-mended seams in shin and ankle bones, plug-hole spiral into navel, into cock-hole. I'm groaning and moaning like a happy pig. I can't stop it. I can't choose to do anything. Not a thing. There's no point anyway, in it all seeps, fast as bats, as stoned and spooky as flying monkey bats of Torrid Oz. O what substance, what ceremony. And I want it all now, I DO! Gimme it all... AAAAaaaLLLL of it. You hear me?? ALL, damn you, and my squawks are good-God awful alright, and passers-by where are you now, where are you all, my audience, I'm supplicant, tormented, yet actually, I'm quickly semi-content, I AM! in a morbid death paralysis happening... yet... well, perfectly in balance now, I'm fully up, back upright, tall as an elm, yesyes my stock's been rebooted, I'm UP! I'll get back on board this TRIUMPH, yeah damn straight I will, and off we will roar, OK? ça va? OuiSiJa... it's Murakami, it's Kubla Khan, MC5, Hawley's mam. All that death and loss, that !LIFELOSS! Fuck it. **I AM *on course, my pen will not die,*** these little white lines in the middle of this freeway go *flim-flamming* by as I 4:4 figure-8 try to slalom the damn lot and if only there was a fresh gallant sunset for me to write about and this steed silhouette would ingrain and remain forever.

Moderately, not rushed.

What the screaming fuck have I gone and done? Just, oh my... Stark and haunting. I ain't right.

23

(Some bits of that Malaysian flight MH370 have turned up at Réunion Island.

That legless murdering runner is about to be freed from prison.

Tesla remains yet to be truly recognised. Now that IS genius. Whichever way you look at it.)

24

Now what do I want? What do you want? What do you honestly DESIRE?

Because now I am ready, busting to go. Somewhere, something incredible is waiting to be known... limitless possibilities perpetuated by a single man's actions... "You are ENGLISH...? Oh, you boogaloo dude!" and I meet this man at the bar. Where else? He's all: "A writer, you should go to Shakespeare & Co." and I haven't the grown-up thread to tell him I've just about failed at the writer bit and pretty much lost all touch with reality, and just... it is peaky-troughy blinded paradox up down updown madness. Snake-back, broke-bat, fuck that coaster.

Hippolyte Belle, his name. I got him to write it down because: **Hippolyte**. **Belle**. Seriously.

"Ambivalence turns to rigid perfectionism in all successful writers."

Bullshit, I advise.

"Are you a successful writer?"

No.

I get more drink. More mirrors in here. Things begin to tremble. *Rigid perfectionism, pah!* How can that be art? Where's the magic of spontaneity... all the good stuff I rattle on about endlessly, huh? The snakes, the grapes, the path, the passion. WATER. All that shite. Where?

26

"I think I have fucked it all up," I say to Hippolyte. "Honestly, I reckon I have."

"Well, fix it, then," he suggests. "Quit your whining."

And I think, yeah, I'll fix it. That's exactly what I'll do. RIGHT NOW. He goes for a piss. I take a slug of this smooth glass of swan-ruby and *crash* goes a bottle somewhere and I get out my pen and notepad and begin:

I watched as he came back from the gents' all nonchalant, trenchcoat all detectively flung about him and a hat and a bag under his arm, this Hippolyte character all boogaloo dude what-have-you. Where'd he get all that clobber from, the toilet? And he just breezes on by, zero eye contact, speechless, bag drop on the seat next to me, his old seat, and gone, simple, rapido like that, out the door this place, this Joycean café, and I screw my brow and take another slug, it is somehow endless Bloody Mary, FUEGO! FUEGO! SANTE!SANTE! and look at the calico hessian bag thing with blood seeping through or beetroot juice or tomato flesh and think wow, here we fucking go again. SEARING HOT CHAOS. Fairly heavy whatever it is inside there bulging and weeping like this and yeah, goddamn reeking the place out. Opt to finish the drink and just take the thing outside, get outta there, all these bastard images through windows and mirrors and glass*crash*, people and waiters gawping, spitting feathers and stressing and all this batshit crazy unfurling of timely events actually seems OK to me. I swear it does, it's just *meant* to happen I suppose, so out on to the street I go again, and prepare for TRIUMPH and look in the bag, and sweet Jesus fuck, that mothercunting *CHIN UP, BUSTER* herring gull is in there, dead, stinking, the Sussex chimney-top cackler, its head by its side where it doesn't belong and blood and stink, yeah, man, yeah, boy, freaking *Hippolyte and the Plot-Bags*, sincerely *hoooooooww*... shit. It's all going off.

I rip the body of the gull apart. Savage, desperate, dreadful. Blood and guts and veins and strings, and yep, here it is, the motherfucking fob. The USB best-seller gunge in all its glory. I raise it up, the covenant, the shroud, the receiving, the grail. *Ahhhhahahaahahhhhaaaaaaaaaa* <...and a royal fade-out...>

27

I look up. Smokeless, scarlet, cool. I head back to chez Faurlain, terrapin speeds, snakes all gone. TRIUMPH sad.

I need some calm, to have a look around, am I still writing the decent truth?

Christ, I need me some Bourbon, some Bulleit. Alright. Three-sigh meditation time, shop for booze, it ain't the bloody USB fob I've retrieved, it's a goddamn bottle in my hands, return saddle-borne sans panting and sans fear anymore and nearly back now, the whole estate and house and garden are fine. No fire, no explosion, oh my, *what a fucking trip*. That copper Proust, Hippolyte, monster plume, what a wheeze, what a hoot. Is it really necessary?

"Ah, you're back!" and truly I could kiss them all, Panos and Benzema, Luca the catalyst, the lot.

We're all straightened up, I get pouring some Bulleits. "Now I have something to tell you all," I announce quite grandly. "Gather round." Here we are, at comfy timely peace, round the big main table, and off I wheel (fragmented, stubborn, determined and tidied up a little afterwards):

Now hear me out. Interrupt me not.

I have just made a sensational discovery: I, and I alone, must clean up the rest of this thing on my own. This end-of-triptych destination. If I don't, you will probably all perish in this place, in the guise of an explosion. And I don't want blood on my hands or knees or soft-sole espadrilles. So listen in... IT IS ALL ABOUT THE DESIRE. For one of us men here, it is desire for a *woman*. For another it is desire for a *book*. And for the third, it is desire for *freedom*. We must understand this, and move on with our lives. I have been brought to you all to make this clear, to put you all back in charge of yourselves, back in control of your pens, your detailers, your machines... each of you to be the seer, the chaser, the feeder, the ONE. You follow? Do you?

<SILENCE gawping stations at my strength of delivery. Girls too.>

Well, I mean it, and here I am, doing it, for you, hell, for ALL of you. So get back, brothers, to the might of the ink, and forge on with your stories. Stay powerful, burn to the edge of every page, for Chrissakes, just LIVE!

<Head swings at one another. Even Panos is stunned.>

So there you have it. We continue.

<I get up and end this charged particular discourse with a well-earned chair scrape and slip out the door to the kitchen. To the fridge. Time to celebrate the announcement of all this wily virtue.>

28

Yeah, they're all a-chatter back in there, considering if I have truly gone and flipped this time, flipped for good. But I feel fine. I get some more rampant fluids in me. Head-levellers, you know. System soothers. Now, whatever next...

29

Panos appears, here in the kitchen, just the two of us and he's at the father-figure moment in his real-time juicy-père schnapps station. "OK, now you hear me out..." <he takes a good drink on board and *ssstthhhhhhhkkk* intake happy> "...I just got a call from my friend down at Le Même Sang café. Hippolyte, Hippolyte Belle, well, he just explains what just happened down there, my boy." <He has most my attention now.> "You wrestled one of their stuffed birds to the ground, an artwork, understand, ripped its head off and spilled bloody drinks everywhere and rolled around in the place and out the door like a lunatic. Serpents et échelles!

All you Mammothrepti, whooo, you have it so so easy and don't even know it, ahahaa... Now," <pause... pause... another *ssstthhhhhhhhkkk* intake kind of eruditely this time...> "listen, my boy, my good new friend, are you losing your mind, are you completely losing the plot?"

Well, what else is there to answer? It is a very easy solution to all this:

"Panos, my new, dear friend... how can you lose something which you have never EVER had?"

There's some gentle music rolling around, isn't there always? and we just lean our bodies against the granite top in this kitchen, speechless, accepting, head-sway the pair of us and the chatter continues in the next room amongst the rest of these daft fruits involved here.

30

"So Hippolyte Belle is your pal?"

"Yes. For years. We call him 'Pencil'."

"Pencil?"

"Yeah, HB, you know, and he draws and writes. He had relative commercial success years ago with a magical book about bicycle spokes."

"Bicycle spokes?"

"Yes, you know, the thin sticks inside the wheels...?"

"Yes, I know what spokes are."

"Good."

We finish a couple more helpers apiece and my head is feeling rather grand by now, his too, I reckon, and he confirms his TRIUMPH has passed a rudimentary inspection after my trip out and we are all at a new gathering understanding moment here at this glorious stage in life, in proceedings. We get back to dining area where Benzema is mopping up leftovers as giddy as 15 fish and the human sorts seem well. Very well. Extraordinarily well. Luca and me exchange leg injury updates. Musician says he's feeling <hand shake, head shake> just about perfect now. The girls sip like wonderful seventies glamour pics. Funny how even Adele seems continental now, full of glee and gusto. Then we be discussing this (that's how someone put it):

Let's grow some new NU fruit. And vegetables. And meats.

Plantain cocaine, XTC celery, absinthe apples, melon mescal! et al.

One of us even draws out some radical plans on the tablecloth and some skilful soul transcribes generalities directly onto the wall and music gathers and builds, course it does, and blows wild and free, yeah, off we go, and Hippolyte gets mentioned more and my, how we are all determined to be our true damn selves and these words rattle out, Panos back to the garden, shuffling about out there, and, well, what a life. The ride goes on. Updown UPUP down, clown faces, dodgems, elephants' trunks, swan wrestling, plume chutes, rapid rabid development of – what? Wait! No, Luca, don't leave yet, we are finally getting somewhere... and he and Élodie just up and start packing, discussing surf and how it belongs to his insides and off they must trot right this afternoon, so best I pen-down and try make them stay.

"Please remember," he says, "all the waves belong to the shore, the shore to the Earth and moon, the sun ultimately to the father."

"Well, who is the father? Where is your father?"

"He is right here..." soft press against his chest, eyes half-closed, Élodie perfectly in sync at his shoulder and all things make immediate clear clear SYZYGY seer sense. (One of his many stolen terms, remember, best-buy reader guy?)

"Even if the world would end tomorrow, I'd still plant an apple tree today... MLK," he says, and I am assuaged, fully, and I immediately rethink about the geniusness of biting into an absinthe apple. (Fickle. Fast. Learning. Perhaps.)

?

31

It seems to me that we'll all be fine. Over-the-road Rob even, in his illicit creation life, he'll be sound. Hippolyte Belle, sound. Benzema, big and furry and sound. Panos and the doctor... hell, everyone involved. But what's most intriguing is just what has come of it all. You know, the Morocco connection, the outplay of potty circumstance, all that. Hell... I just kinda wish the Musician would have another full-on wrap-up chapter, but he says nah, he's *good*.

Adele is cute. The world turns. We are every single person similar in a ton of internal ways, sitting on docks of bays, looking out, and Herman's way out there somewhere, humming like a poor boy, but definitely happy. Yep, I can guarantee that.

The bestselling idea is charged to the gills still, that's for sure. But Dan bastard Kemp like Luca's editor Bob and whosoever else decision-makers at their own little helms can go to hell. In fact, I'd rather set fire to this whole MS than be controlled by one of those stretchy urban thorns. Balls to them. Compromise would mar this portrait. And balls to me too. And we discuss this situation a little more, and we eat and share continued ideas of growth and piss-take discovery.

Seemingly so, that's that. Us here. Them souls there. Every prick else in between, and ALL things move. At great speeds and under severe duress, sure, but least we move. Christ, I'm parched.

Reckon there's more to come. There always is, right? And what makes us run? Or fly? Or lunge and break?

I dunno. I'll ask Tracey, she's lying right next to me. Constantly agile, permanently full of grace.

There is a new moon way up there, proud and raging. The sell-out stars all gathered, sparkly, anticipatory, yeah, awaiting a certain what was it... **SYZYGY**, that's it. Three celestial bodies lined up like magic. Please let it happen to us lot down here, sometime in the next few light years preferably, some *thing* to get all us fruits and bells and horns lined up at the perfect moment, to really burn, ahaa, THE PAYOFF.

But the truth is, and that is what matters, right, the truth and the passion and the desire, right? Well, it is all just child-art up there, smudgy and smeary, and therefore perfect.

32

I poured some drinks. Some food turned up.

I thought I'd write this on the wall, so I did just that.

The devil fetch ye, ye ragamuffin rapscallions; ye are all asleep.
Stop snoring, ye sleepers, and pull. HM. MD.
I shouldn't publish that if I were you, Tennyson.
Tennyson replied: If it comes to that, Master, the sherry you gave
us at lunch was downright filthy. PL. PR.

There is something inherently noble and virtuous about taking a walk, I then told my crazy face in the mirror. And so I also did just that. I took a walk. Thinking about providence and mystery and art and Bunuel's balls. Hippocampus and wax. For Chrissakes, you still holding on?

<fin>
<?>

Then I discovered my very first response:

Dear Mr Pepperdine/Weepinghawk/whoever the hell you are...

I have indeed read some slack-waisted slop in my time, but sweet Jheezus, your submission really takes the biscuit, and it wants to, so starved of clarity it is, and reason, plot, talent, structure, fbw, craft, skill, intrigue, development, decent evolution of a sensible outcome, you know, conclusion... well, all of it, really, I am truly shocked it survived its limp-dick journey through the post. I feel bilious, suicidal, cheated. Like I have been shat on from a great height.

Do not send anything else. Ever.

I cannot even bring myself to return your 'manuscript' and therefore, ergo and all that, I shall do the honourable thing, and also do the world at large a huge favour, by simply allowing my recent bitch's litter to housetrain amongst its shreds.

Sincerely,
London

P.S. No doubt we shall meet in the summer at Hay, in some conceptualist tent or other. What a circus! I'll be the one with the grin and the eyes like prunes and the paunch of Geneva and the lacklustre hair of a visionary.

Goodbye good luck good fuck forever.
(heard that before? Good-looking reviews, I do not foresee...
Break a leg!)

PL Travers giving Rockwell head is all I can think.

And that Triumph has a No. 44 painted beautifully on its fuel tank.

36

Sure, there's Chekhov over there, ambling along, juggling commas, balancing himself with cross-stitch pocket ideologies, puffing on a Viceroy, sucking on a Bulleit, hammering his overnight fiction to telegraph poles, nowhere to flick spent ash... 'Try the street,' I suggest, but he's gone, *whoosh*, gone, just like that, like Cooper in Fez, like DBC in a Jimi haze, like mother-humping Paine slaughtering a Samuel.

Yep, there's pangs of angry recovery deep and shallow ting-ting portside limb-pinball-galore.

Yes, there's art and adventure and philosophical bullshit in every single tangible breath.

And, yup, you guessed it, all the bestsellers continue their swell and surge the world over, I mean, CHRIST, how will that ever cease?

(shall we just let the dead guy sleep, mister?)

Waves go bah-bye, bye-bye, buy buy, bi-bi.

And here is the Seine, in and out, oozing and bruising along, and believe it, you must, a damn shop called NOWHERE and I think I am now here and feeling about as fine as frogs' hair.

I kick a stone, it tumbles off.

Jules et Jim scuttle by, giggling.

The sky, well, all that fucker does is it just skies along, weird and broad and incapable of making a decision, a conclusion, a final salute.

A stuffed swan's leg, I notice, is poking out my buttonhole.

<laughter, more children, perfect>

And at spotting this trite cute little beast, right here, hobbling along, left leg all screwed and bent, I just have to ask: *what you done, little bird?*

Of course it's a bird, a gull, a herring, hop-skipping in the key of sea, whatever the hell hideous truth that actually goddamn means... ahahahaAAAaaa.

I swear, it is right here, now, and that response from London is here, spat and slapped up on the front door of *Nowhere* – this shop attempting to best-sell shit, well, I've found it, and I seriously just hyphen-wonder if any of us fine old souls will ever truly make it.

<where you from, bird...who are you, bird?>

Here! have this spare limb, it's yours! And he just casually hops up to it, beaks it up and swaggers off like a hero. No look-back kinda hero, you know.

Desire. What a gas. I'm just gonna keep moving along, I suppose, but what about LUCA, MUSIC, PANOS, any other CAPITAL-soul? The beautiful ones, the girls, what about those sweetsweet souls, hay?

Well, let's just see about that, lemme pull it all together in order to make this thing a realreal BESTSELLER, see? Gots to quit the stymied stop-and-start scribbledown, right? Gots to get on with some TRUEtrue fiction, right?

37

OK, wait. Just wait a goddamn second here. Something very moist and very warm and extremely soft is suddenly dragging my whole being in, right the fuck in, deeper down & deeper still, head first, feet tucked in. Oh, never a journey was ever so sweet and weird and dark. Just what the hell is this? What is this strange tangy SUCCUBUS? And when will it all end?

38 - 44

So sigh with me, absently. Our reward? The perfect ending.

Ah, I get it. Each of these legs contributes crucially to the contemporary understanding of brokenness. Wow. What closure. What a fix. Re-born! You GENIUS!

Now piss off. And press release.

[some other hunt may now begin...]

Lightning Source UK Ltd.
Milton Keynes UK
UKOW06f0613010616

275379UK00007B/162/P